**"BEAU DOESN'T UNDERSTAND HOW TINY HE IS," ELLIE SAID. "HE THINKS HE'S AS BIG AND TOUGH AS ANY DOG AROUND."**

"Thanks for saving him. But that looks like a nasty cat scratch on your hand."

The girl glanced down. "It's not too bad. The sergeant didn't mean to hurt me. He was just upset."

"Maybe so. But cat scratches can become infected. I'd feel better if you had it checked and cleaned at the emergency clinic. Please tell your dad—"

"Tell him what?" The gravelly baritone voice came from behind Ellie. "I've been waiting for you on the porch, Gracie. What's the holdup?"

Slowly Ellie turned. A man stood with his back to the open doorway. Morning sunlight silhouetted a tall figure, ruggedly lean with broad shoulders and an unruly thatch of chestnut hair that wanted cutting. Only when he shifted did his face come into focus—the square jaw, the stubbornly set mouth. And the eyes—a deep, startling blue like his daughter's.

Ellie's breath caught in a gasp.

She was staring up at her teenage love, Jubal McFarland.

## More Christmas romance from Janet Dailey

# JANET DAILEY

# *Just a Little Christmas*

ZEBRA BOOKS
KENSINGTON PUBLISHING CORP.
http://www.kensingtonbooks.com

First Kensington Books Hardcover Printing: June 2017
First Zebra Books Mass-Market Paperback Printing: October 2017
ISBN-13: 978-1-4201-4008-8
ISBN-10: 1-4201-4008-6

eISBN-13: 978-1-4201-4009-5
eISBN-10: 1-4201-4009-4

10 9 8 7 6 5 4 3 2 1

Printed in the United States of America

*This novel could not have been written without the friendship and contributions of my fellow writer Elizabeth Lane.*

# Chapter 1

Late on a chilly November day, Ellie Marsden came home to Branding Iron, Texas.

Driving her black BMW sedan along the two-lane road, she gazed across stubbled fields, dotted here and there with grazing cattle. Under a soot gray sky, scattered houses, barns, and silos rose out of a landscape that matched Ellie's bleak mood.

San Francisco was behind her, most likely for good. For the foreseeable future, she was right back where she'd started—smack-dab in the middle of Nowhere, U.S.A.

When she'd left Branding Iron after high school, she'd vowed never to return except for brief visits to her mother. But now, ten years later, the small town had become her refuge. She had no place else to go.

A stray snowflake spattered the window as she neared the city limits sign. Just ahead, a worn dirt lane cut away from the asphalt. Ellie's memory traced its path through fields and stands of cottonwood, to the swimming hole where, one moonlit summer night, she'd almost surrendered her virginity to Jubal McFarland.

They'd been crazy in love back then. But when he'd asked her to marry him, she hadn't loved Jubal enough to spend the rest of her life herding cows on his family ranch. She'd turned him down and never looked back.

The last she'd heard of Jubal, he'd wed another local girl. By now he'd probably sired a brood of little blue-eyed McFarlands as handsome as he was.

And Ellie had gone off to law school and married cheating, lying Brent. End of story.

A plaintive *yip* broke into her musings. Harnessed into his booster basket, Beau, her white teacup poodle, was due for a potty stop. Ellie blew him an air kiss. "Hang on, boy," she said. "We'll be there in a few minutes. Then you can do your business on my mother's nice, clean lawn."

Beau yipped again, dancing in place as if to let her know he was getting anxious. Ellie pressed the gas pedal, pushing the speed limit. Beau was well trained, but his tiny bladder could only hold out for so long.

Lately, it seemed, she'd been experiencing a similar problem herself.

Feeling a solid thump, she glanced down at the rounded belly that barely cleared the steering wheel. Her unborn daughter was kicking up a storm. It wouldn't have surprised Ellie to learn that she was carrying a future Olympic soccer star—as if anything could surprise her after discovering that she was not only divorced but pregnant.

Brent had never been keen on having children. He'd always used protection. But during their disastrous trial reconciliation last spring, the unimaginable had happened. Now Brent was married to one of his wealthy law clients, and blissfully unaware that he was about to become a father.

Forcing the memory aside, Ellie drove down Main Street, where, on this, the day after Thanksgiving, the traditional Christmas lights were already being strung between the lampposts. Christmas in Branding Iron would be a far cry from the holidays in San Francisco—the glittering shops, the glamorous gowns, the cocktail parties and charity galas, which Ellie had always enjoyed. But that life was behind her now. It was time she adjusted to her new reality.

For better or for worse, the prodigal daughter was home.

Not that she planned to stay forever. She had an unfinished education and ambitions for a law career of her own. But right now there was this baby. She wanted to give birth in a safe place, surrounded by her caring family. In a few months, maybe a year, when her daughter was old enough to be left with a good nanny, she could start planning the rest of her life.

Minutes later she pulled up to a stately, two-story frame house and stopped in the driveway.

By now it was dusk. The porch light was on, as well as the lights in the kitchen and living room. Clara, her mother, would be on pins and needles, waiting for her to arrive.

After freeing Beau from the basket, she scooped him under one arm and eased herself out of the car. Her spine and knees were stiff from long hours of driving. She set her dog on the ground. Then, keeping her eyes on him, she reached under her loose-fitting jacket and massaged her lower back. A few snowflakes drifted down from the darkening sky.

Beau sniffed the grass, his little body quivering. Catching a scent trail, he made a beeline for the giant sycamore that grew in the front yard. After checking out the canine calling cards around the base, he lifted a leg and added his own. He might weigh in at barely four pounds, but he was all dog.

The front door opened, and Clara burst onto the porch. Once tall, slim, and dark, she'd resembled Ellie as a young woman. But she'd been forty when Ellie was born, and now she was showing her age. She'd shrunk in height and looked as if a strong wind could topple her to the ground.

Clasping the side rail for support, she hurried down the steps. "Thank goodness you made it!" she exclaimed. "With a storm coming, I was afraid you might get caught on the road, and with you being pregnant . . ." She let the words trail off, imagining, no doubt, a blizzard scenario with Ellie sliding off the shoulder and going into premature labor.

Ellie took a moment to snatch up Beau and tuck him under her warm jacket before turning back toward her mother. "I knew you'd be worried," she said. "But I was fine driving. The baby isn't due till the third of January. That's more than a month away. Let me get my suitcases inside, and I'll have some of that chili I can smell."

"No, you don't!" Clara moved to block Ellie's way to the trunk of her BMW. "You're not carrying those heavy bags in. Your brother's home from work. I'll ask him to come over."

"Great. I'll be happy to see him." Ellie's older brother, Ben, just reelected county sheriff, lived in the house next door with Jess, his wife, and Ethan, his son from a previous marriage. Ellie would have been fine unloading the car herself, but seeing Ben would lift her spirits. And having him here would ease the tension between her and her overprotective mother.

"I'll call him right now." Clara hurried back toward the steps.

"No need. His lights are on. I'll just go next door and surprise him." Ellie strode down the sidewalk to the modest, one-story house next door and rang the bell.

Ben answered at once. Dark, husky, and handsome, he was just putting on his coat. "I was about to come out and welcome you." He gave her a quick hug, then thrust her away for a better look. "I'll be damned, sis, you really *are* pregnant!"

"You noticed!" Ellie joked. "Where's your family?"

"Jess is at the B and B, getting ready for the Saturday buffet. And Ethan's at a sleepover. So it's just me. Come on, we can visit after I haul your stuff upstairs."

"Great. Mom's made chili."

"Here, take my arm." Ben stepped outside and closed the door. "That sidewalk's uneven. We can't risk having you stumble."

"You sound like Mom," Ellie said. "She's already treating me like an invalid."

"Well, it doesn't hurt to be careful." Ben slipped a hand behind Ellie's arm. As his fingers clasped her elbow, Beau's head popped out from under Ellie's jacket. With a protective growl, he glared at the stranger.

"Good Lord!" Ben pulled his hand away, then chuckled. "What've you got there, a fuzzy white rat?"

"Don't you dare insult my dog!" Ellie eased Beau out from under her coat and cradled him in her arms. "Beau's got grand champion bloodlines. You'd faint if I told you how much I paid for him."

"I still say he looks like a fuzzy white rat. Does he bite?" Ben offered a finger for the tiny dog to sniff. Beau growled again.

"He hasn't bitten anybody yet," Ellie said. "But he takes his job of guarding me very seriously, especially when it comes to men. Beau may be little, but he's got the heart of a Rottweiler."

"I'll keep that in mind." Ben walked her back to her car and took her keys to open the trunk. "Nice wheels, sis. You won't see any vehicles like this in Branding Iron."

"It got me here. Flying would've been easier, but I wanted to keep the car and load it up. The backseat's full of boxes. They'll all need to go inside."

"That's what I'm here for." Ben hefted a suitcase out of the trunk. "You must be planning to stay a while."

"I never wanted to come back here. But with the baby . . ." Ellie shrugged. "Maybe a few months. But not forever."

"No chance you'll go back to Brent?"

"Brent remarried as soon as the divorce was final—not that I'd have him if he hadn't. He doesn't even know about the baby."

"What about child support? Aren't you going to need it?"

"I'll manage with the settlement I got. That should do me until I'm ready to get a job. I don't want Brent in my life—or in my daughter's."

"If you ever want to talk—" Ben reached for another suitcase.

"Don't wait for it. My divorce is a closed book. But thanks for the offer. I'll see you inside."

Ellie carried Beau into the house and gave him some water and kibble. She'd already cleared her pet with Clara, who liked dogs and didn't mind having a little one in the house.

After turning him loose to explore, she helped her mother set the table for three.

By the time Ben had finished carrying her things upstairs to her old bedroom, supper was ready. Ellie joined her mother and brother at the table, with Beau at her feet. She was hungry, and Clara's chili, with fresh homemade bread and salad, was as good as she remembered. But Ellie wasn't kidding herself. Moving back home was going to be a huge adjustment.

Ben gazed around the table. "This is kind of like the old days, isn't it? The three of us eating supper together."

Ellie nodded, thinking how wrong he was. This was nothing like the old days. Not for her.

"Say, I've got an idea!" Ben grinned. "Jess and her mother are planning the first breakfast buffet of the Christmas season tomorrow morning. It'll be extra special with the tree up and Christmas music—just the thing to get everybody in the spirit. We can take Ethan and all go together."

Ellie stifled a groan. Her brother had always been like a kid when it came to Christmas. But the last thing she felt like was celebrating.

"Why, that's a wonderful idea!" Clara exclaimed. "Let's plan on it!"

Ellie shook her head. "Count me out. I'm not in any condition to socialize—especially if it involves stares and gossip."

"Really, Ellie!" Clara punctuated her words with a motherly click of her tongue. "You can't expect to hide in the house like a hermit until the baby comes. And nobody's going to point a finger at you. Heaven knows, you're not the first woman in this town to be single and pregnant. You need to get out there and show people you've nothing to be ashamed of!"

"Mom's right," Ben said. "The longer you stay home, the harder it'll be to get out and make friends. You need to come with us tomorrow. Hey, it'll be fun. And Jess's mother makes a great breakfast."

Ellie sighed. "I can see I'm outgunned. All right, I'll go. But don't expect much. I'm never at my best in the morning, especially now."

It felt strange that night, lying awake in her old room, with her cheerleading photo still on the dresser. For all she knew, her pom-poms could still be tucked away in the back of the closet. The last time she'd been in Branding Iron was for Ben's wedding this past summer, when he'd married spunky, redheaded little Jess. Ellie had been almost three months pregnant at the time, but her loose-fitting matron of honor gown had hidden any sign of it. Not wanting to dampen the day's happiness, she'd said nothing about her situation. But come tomorrow morning, the whole town would know that Ellie Rae Marsden, daughter of perfect parents, high school honor student, cheerleader, homecoming queen, and big-city sophisticate, had fallen off her pedestal and landed hard on her butt.

Gazing up into the darkness, she felt the featherlight pressure of tiny paws on the quilt. A damp button of a nose touched her face. A wet tongue licked her cheek. She snuggled her little poodle close. At least somebody seemed to know she was hurting and needed comfort.

Ellie kissed the top of Beau's fluffy head. At last, with her small friend curled against her side, she drifted into exhausted sleep.

The next morning, as promised, Ellie was ready when Ben came by to take her and Clara to breakfast. Last year, Ben's wife, Jess, and her mother, Francine, had opened the Branding Iron Bed and Breakfast—known as the B and B for short—in an old house off Main Street. Their Saturday morning breakfast buffet had become a popular tradition, with scores of townspeople lining up to socialize and feast on Francine's delicious cooking.

Ellie and Clara were waiting on the porch when Ben pulled his club cab pickup into the driveway and climbed out to help his mother. His gaze fell on Ellie's Gucci bag and the small, fluffy head peeking out of the top.

"I see you're bringing your pet rat along." Ben was not above some brotherly teasing.

"For now at least, where I go, my dog goes." Ellie ignored the good-natured jab. Leaving Beau by himself in a strange house, or in the car, had been out of the question. As she'd often done before, she tucked the little dog into a section of her roomy leather handbag, with a doll-sized quilt folded on the bottom for comfort and enough of an opening left at the top for Beau to stick his head out and look around.

While Ben helped Clara into the passenger seat, Ellie climbed into the back. "Where's Ethan?" she asked.

Ben laughed. "Evidently the sleepover didn't involve much sleeping. He came home this morning and went to bed. When I checked on him, he was out like a light."

The drive to the bed and breakfast took only a few minutes. Cars and trucks were already lined up along the one-way side street. It was barely 9:00, but the Saturday buffet, which opened at 8:00, was doing an overflow business.

"We'll never find a parking place!" Ellie said, thinking of Clara and the distance her mother might have to walk.

"Not to worry. Being married to the owner has its perks." Ben swung the truck around the PRIVATE DRIVEWAY sign and parked next to the house. "Jess has even saved a table for us."

Dread congealed in the pit of Ellie's stomach as Ben helped her out of the truck. Why had she agreed to come here this morning? She would choose a den of man-eating tigers over what she was about to face—people she'd left behind ten years ago, people who would stare at her and snicker behind her back. What a comedown for the girl who'd thought she was too good for Branding Iron.

"Come on, dear, it'll be fine." Clara took her

arm as they mounted the steps. "It's not as if you've done anything wrong."

*As if that would make any difference,* Ellie thought as Ben held the door for them. Sucking in a last breath of wintry air, she stepped across the threshold, into the crowded, noisy space of the breakfast buffet.

Aromas of bacon and fresh coffee assailed her senses. Some of the townsfolk eating at the tables or lined up at the buffet looked familiar, but everyone had aged. The place was decorated for Christmas with an old-fashioned tree by the window, lights strung from the ceiling, and Christmas music drifting on the air. The atmosphere was warm and festive in a tacky sort of way, but if Ellie could've gotten away with it, she'd have turned around and fled out the door.

Ben pointed toward an empty table with a RE-SERVED sign on it. To Ellie's dismay, it was on the far side of the room. To get there, they would have to weave their way between the tables. Lifting her chin, she followed her mother and brother. As she clutched her bag, she could feel Beau quivering, as if he sensed her anxiety.

Jess, wearing a cute ruffled apron over her sweater and jeans, bustled out of the kitchen, headed for the buffet table with a platter of flapjacks. She flashed her family a smile, as if to say, *Catch you later.* Ellie had met Ben's wife only once, on the day of the wedding. There'd been little time for them to get acquainted, but now that she was back in Branding Iron, Ellie knew she was going to need a friend. Dare she hope that Jess might become that friend?

Reaching the table, which was covered with a red-checked oilcloth, Ellie chose the chair that faced the corner, then set her bag underneath and draped her jacket behind her. Ben seated his mother. "Let me fill your plates, ladies," he said. "I'll get you a little of everything. It's all good. Somebody will bring you coffee."

He vanished toward the buffet tables. Moments later, hands reached past Ellie to fill her coffee cup from a steaming carafe. "Nice to see you again, honey," said a chatty voice at her ear. "Goodness, you do look ready to pop! How soon are you due?"

Ellie looked up to see Jess's mother, Francine, smiling down at her. At the wedding, Francine had been dressed from head to toe in red. Even today, with her overdone makeup, bleached curls, and long fake nails, she looked like the town floozy. But Ben had insisted that the woman had a heart of pure gold, so Ellie resolved to give her the benefit of the doubt.

"Not until January," she replied, reminding herself that in Branding Iron, personal questions were to be expected. "So, no popping yet."

"Ben and Jess told me about your bad luck. But don't you worry, honey. When that little baby gets here, she'll have lots of folks to love her!"

"Thanks—and it's nice to see you again, too." As Francine moved to another table, Ellie turned her attention to the heaping plate Ben had set in front of her. The scrambled eggs, bacon, hash browns, and flapjacks looked and smelled delicious. But nerves had dulled her hunger. Every bite would be an act of will.

Determined to try, she speared a slice of crisp bacon. It crumbled on the plate. Picking up a lean sliver, she thought of Beau, safely tucked into her bag under the chair. She rarely gave treats to her dog, but she knew he loved bacon. Surely one little piece wouldn't hurt him.

Bending, she caught the handle of her bag and pulled it out within reach. The bag felt curiously light. Ellie's heart dropped as she realized why.

Beau was gone.

"What is it, sis?" Ben was staring at her face, which must've gone dead white.

"It's Beau!" she whispered, not wanting to create a scene. "He's not—"

From the far corner, a dreadful sound erupted— a hellish cacophony of hisses, yowls, barks, and high-pitched yelps.

"Oh, Lord!" Ben was on his feet, upending his chair. "Your dog's found Francine's cat!"

He lunged between the tables with Ellie on his heels. Beau would stand up to anything, but even a fair-sized cat would be capable of killing him. This one sounded like it had murder on its mind.

Even with people clambering out of the way, they made nightmarishly slow progress across the crowded dining room. Ben and Ellie were

JUST A LITTLE CHRISTMAS

little more than halfway when the noise abruptly stopped.

The silence that fell over the room was broken only by the tinkling strains of "Silver Bells" from the speakers. Ellie plunged past her brother, heart in her throat as she braced to scoop up her bloodied little dog and rush him to a vet—if he was even alive.

Abruptly she stopped. Facing her was a small, pigtailed girl, about eight years old, dressed in jeans and a plaid jacket. Beau was huddled in her arms. He was shaking but didn't appear hurt.

A scruffy-looking ginger cat, three times Beau's size, crouched on the floor, glaring up at the dog. Fur bristling, it hissed and showed its fangs.

"Sergeant Pepper, you rascal!" Francine rushed out of the kitchen with a broom, which she used to scoot the cat away and send it scurrying off toward the rear of the house. "Sorry, honey," she said to Ellie. "The sergeant doesn't have much use for dogs, especially little mites like that one."

She hurried back to the kitchen as her customers settled back into eating and visiting. Ben returned to his mother at their table. For now, at least, the drama was over.

The girl looked up at Ellie with a shy smile. "Is this your dog? He's really cute. What's his name?"

Ellie's legs were threatening to give way. She sank onto a nearby chair, putting her gaze on a level with the girl's. She was a pretty little thing, her braided hair a rich brown. Her eyes, framed by a sun-freckled face, were the striking hue of Texas bluebonnets.

"His name's Beau," Ellie said. "I'm thinking you must've saved him from that cat."

"I was following my dad outside when your dog went after the cat," she said. "They'd just started to fight when I grabbed him." She snuggled Beau close. One small hand bore an ugly-looking red scratch. "Can I hold him just a little longer?" she asked.

"You can hold him as long as you want. Did you say Beau went for the cat?"

"Uh-huh." The girl nodded. "Sergeant Pepper was eating a scrap of bacon off the floor. Maybe Beau just wanted the bacon. He was brave, but he wasn't very smart."

"Beau doesn't understand how tiny he is," Ellie said. "He thinks he's as big and tough as any dog around. Thanks for saving him. But that looks like a nasty cat scratch on your hand."

The girl glanced down. "It's not too bad. The sergeant didn't mean to hurt me. He was just upset."

"Maybe so. But cat scratches can become infected. I'd feel better if you had it checked and cleaned at the emergency clinic. Please tell your dad—"

"Tell him what?" The gravelly baritone voice came from behind Ellie. "I've been waiting for you on the porch, Gracie. What's the holdup?"

Slowly Ellie turned. A man stood with his back to the open doorway. Morning sunlight silhouetted a tall figure, ruggedly lean with broad shoulders and an unruly thatch of chestnut hair that wanted cutting. Only when he shifted did his face come into focus—the square jaw, the stubbornly set mouth. And the eyes—a deep, startling blue like his daughter's.

Ellie's breath caught in a gasp.

She was staring up at her teenage love, Jubal McFarland.

# Chapter 2

Jubal's breath caught. He hadn't recognized the woman talking to his daughter with her back toward him. But as she turned, he'd felt the same slammed-in-the-gut sensation as he had on the day when Ellie Marsden had loaded her beat-up Chevy and put Branding Iron—and him—in her rearview mirror.

Now, ten years later, here she was in the flesh—a little older but as beautiful as ever, her dark eyes skillfully made up, her ebony hair anchored in a sophisticated twist. It was really Ellie Marsden, or whatever her name was now. Elegant, citified, and—Jubal's stomach lurched as his gaze moved downward—*pregnant.* Lord help him, she was as round and ripe as an October pumpkin!

"Hello, Jubal." Her throaty voice had taken on a huskier, richer tone with the years. "I was just thanking your daughter for saving my dog."

"That's a *dog?*" He scowled at the little white fluffball in Gracie's arms. He should have come up with something clever, Jubal thought. But nothing had come to mind. He was still the same country bumpkin she'd left behind ten years ago—and damned proud of it.

"He's a miniature poodle—a teacup." Gracie loved dogs and had read a lot about them. She'd begged him for a small dog, but Jubal didn't have much use for anything that didn't earn its keep. The two mutts that helped herd cattle on the ranch were friendly enough. If she wanted a pet, the girl could make do with them. He didn't need the complications of another animal.

*Especially now, when it seemed he was about to lose everything.*

"His name's Beau. I saved him from a fight with Francine's cat," Gracie added. Knowing she'd want him to be proud, Jubal patted her shoulder. The tiny dog sniffed his fingers with its button nose.

"She grabbed him away just in time," Ellie said. "But I'm concerned about that scratch on her hand. It really should be checked and disinfected. Is the emergency clinic open on Saturdays?"

"Just in the mornings." Jubal frowned at the scratch on his daughter's hand. On the ranch, Gracie always seemed to be getting stuck by barbed wire, pecked by chickens, or stung by bees. This scratch didn't look any worse than the usual. He had salve and Band-Aids in the truck. And Gracie had gotten a tetanus shot last year so that wasn't a worry. But seeing Ellie's concern put a new light on things. Maybe it wouldn't hurt to get his daughter checked out at the clinic.

"So it would be open right now," Ellie said. "Please let me pay for her visit. I was about to offer when you showed up."

"I can pay," he said. "Go finish your breakfast, Ellie."

With his hand still on Gracie's shoulder, he pressed his daughter toward the exit. Still clasping that useless fluff of a dog, Gracie resisted as if her boots were glued to the floor. "I want Ellie to come with us," she said.

"Ellie's got other things to do," Jubal told her.

"No, it's fine. I was planning to come along, since Gracie got scratched saving my dog." Ellie stood, giving him a full view of her belly bump, which was covered by a loose black cashmere sweater that had probably cost more than new tires on his truck would. "Just let me get my bag and my jacket, and I'll be right behind you."

"You're sure your . . . husband won't mind?" Jubal had noticed her bare finger; but if her hands were swollen from her pregnancy, she could have removed her wedding ring.

"No husband," she said. "I'm—uh—recently divorced."

Whatever *recently* meant. It was hard to believe any kind of man would leave a wife in Ellie's condition. Maybe she'd had an affair and the baby was somebody else's.

Jubal swore silently. Ellie's life was none of his

damned business. Speculating about her now would only distract him from his real problems. But if the way his daughter was clinging to that ridiculous bit of a dog was any sign, he hadn't heard the last of Ellie Marsden.

Ellie made her way back to the table to get her things and let her mother and Ben know where she was going. Ben gave her a teasing grin. "See, I told you it was a good idea to come with us this morning. Now everybody knows you're back in town and that you're pregnant. No more hiding. Where's the rat?"

Ellie resolved not to be baited. "Gracie has Beau. We're taking her to the clinic to get the scratch on her hand looked at."

"We? You and Jubal?" Ben's grin broadened. "That didn't take long."

Ellie shot him a warning glare. "Don't start any rumors, Ben. I'm not one bit interested in Jubal McFarland—especially since I know he's married."

"Oh, but he isn't married," Ben said. "Not anymore. Jubal lost his wife four years ago. It's just him and that little girl, all alone on their ranch."

Stunned into momentary silence, Ellie forced herself to speak and move. "That doesn't make any difference. I came home to have this baby, not to troll for men. So give me a break, big brother!" She shrugged into her jacket and snatched up her purse. "Don't wait for me. If you're not here when I get back, I'll walk home. I could use the exercise."

"What about your breakfast, dear?" Clara asked. "You need to eat."

"I'll be fine. Why don't you box it and take it home to Ethan? He'll be hungry when he wakes up."

Before Ben could needle her again, she turned and made her way to the door. The strains of "Let It Snow" muffled the buzz of conversation as she passed each table. She'd probably triggered some juicy gossip this morning, but that couldn't be helped. Before long she'd be old news, Ellie told herself. And it couldn't happen soon enough.

Jubal and his daughter were waiting on the porch. Gracie had tucked Beau under her jacket to keep him warm. "Can I hold him in the truck?" she asked.

Ellie studied her dog. Beau seemed to have taken to his young rescuer. Peeking out from under Gracie's jacket, he yawned, a sign he was relaxed and contented. "Okay, you can hold him a little longer," she said. "But when we get to the clinic, he goes back into my bag."

"Come on." Jubal led the way down the walk to where his pickup was parked. The breeze was cold, the air specked with lightly falling snow.

Ellie stifled a gasp as she recognized the red '82 Ford Ranger they'd dated in. The truck had been old at the time. By now it was practically an antique. But it was freshly washed and appeared to be in good repair. Jubal, she remembered, had always believed in taking care of things and making them last.

"Up you go." He opened the passenger door and gave Gracie a boost to the jump seat in the rear of the cab. Then he offered Ellie a careful arm-up to sit beside him. Memories swept over her as he closed the door and went around to the driver's side. How many nights had their teenage lust steamed up the windows in this truck? Just thinking about it brought a flush to Ellie's face. But the past was a closed door, and she knew better than to open it, especially with Gracie here. As far as Jubal's daughter was concerned, she was just a friendly lady who'd shown up with her little dog.

As Jubal drove to the clinic, Ellie cast glances at father and daughter. Today she'd barely glimpsed the Jubal she remembered. Time and hardship had weathered him like a dry Texas wind. Creases framed the corners of his azure eyes, and his mouth had settled into a grim line. Did he ever smile? Did he ever laugh the way she remembered—laughter so deep and warm that she could feel it when he held her in his arms?

And there was Gracie. Anyone could see that Jubal loved his daughter. But she had the look of a little girl who'd grown up without a mother—the boyish clothes, the pigtails, which she'd likely braided herself, the ragged fingernails on her small, chapped hands. Ellie sensed an absence of soft, pretty things in her young life—

things a man like Jubal was bound to overlook. Maybe that was one reason his daughter was so drawn to Beau.

Warm beneath Gracie's coat, the tiny poodle had fallen asleep with his head resting on her sleeve. Gracie lifted her gaze and gave Ellie a smile. Her blue eyes sparkled with tenderness.

Ellie felt something soften in the region of her heart. This young girl, so appealing and so needy, would rouse all her motherly instincts if she allowed it. But Ellie couldn't let that happen. She was here to have her baby, regain her bearings, and get on with her life—and that life didn't include settling down in a place like Branding Iron. Bonding with this vulnerable child would only hurt her when the time came to leave.

And Jubal . . . Ellie studied his profile, her gaze lingering on the strands of gray that silvered his temples. He was barely thirty-one—she even remembered his birth date. But he looked older. Hard work and loss had taken their toll on the boy she'd left behind. Once he'd been her world. But there could be no going back. He was someone else now. So was she. All they could do was bury the past and move on with their separate lives.

The low brick building that housed the Branding Iron Clinic stood at the far end of Main Street. Staffed by a rotating doctor and nurse, the facility had saved many town residents the forty-mile drive to the hospital in Cottonwood Springs for treatment of cuts, sprains, fevers, and other minor ailments, as well as immunizations, prescriptions, and checkups. For life-threatening emergencies, the local fire engine, driven by volunteers with paramedic training, doubled as an ambulance. But some things couldn't wait. Over the years, a surprising number of babies had been born in the clinic's treatment rooms.

Jubal pulled the pickup into the empty parking lot. After coming around to the passenger door, he offered a hand to help Ellie to the ground. Her skin was baby soft, the contact brief against his work-roughened palm. As her boots touched the asphalt, the poodle, who'd been handed back to Ellie when they parked, poked its white head out of her purse to look around and sniff the air.

Gracie hopped out of the truck, closed the door, and followed them into the clinic. This was silly, Jubal thought. With a little antibiotic salve, her hand would be fine. Was he going through the motions just to impress Ellie?

Damn fool waste of time and money on both counts. Ellie was a spoiled princess. She'd always been a princess, even back in high school. She was never cut out for Branding Iron. He should've realized that before he humiliated himself by asking her to marry him.

A young Latina woman in a white lab coat greeted them at the front desk. Jubal had assumed she was the nurse until he read her name badge—DR. PAULA RAMIREZ.

Her gaze fell on Ellie's bulging middle. "Sorry, I'm new here and on my own today," she said. "Have you been in before? Is everything all right with your baby?"

Ellie looked flustered for a moment. "Oh, we're not here for me. It's her." She nudged Gracie forward. "She got a bad cat scratch. We just want to make sure it won't get infected."

"Oh." The doctor held out her hand to Gracie. "Come on into the exam room and we'll take a look. Your parents can come too if they want."

"Oh, we're not—" Ellie protested, but Gracie and the doctor had already vanished down the hall.

"You go on," Ellie said. "I'll wait out here. Maybe you can explain that we're not—"

"Why bother? This is about Gracie, not us." Jubal walked away, leaving Ellie in the empty reception room with her dog.


Stung, Ellie sank onto a worn vinyl chair. If Jubal had wanted to make her feel like a fool, he'd succeeded. After a put-down like that it would serve him right if she left now and walked the six blocks back to the bed and breakfast.

But Gracie would be disappointed to find her—and Beau—gone. And she was still determined to pay for the treatment. If Jubal was still driving that old truck, he couldn't have much spare money.

And she could pay. She was doing all right with the cash settlement from the divorce. Despite the limiting prenuptial she'd signed, she'd gotten enough in a lump sum to set aside a fund for her daughter's education and get by until the time came to leave and find a job. She could certainly afford a few dollars for the clinic fee.

*Was it that, or did she just want to show Jubal that she was her own woman?*

Just to be ready, she found her credit card and placed it on the counter. Beau was squirming in her bag, wanting to get out and investigate. She let him loose on the floor, where he went into a joyful frenzy of checking out new smells. He was sniffing a chewing gum wrapper next to the vending machine when Ellie heard the door of the exam room open and the sound of footsteps coming down the hall. She picked up Beau and tucked him back in the bag as Jubal, Gracie, and the doctor came into the reception room. Gracie's hand had a Band-Aid decorated with superheroes.

Ellie stepped to the reception counter and pushed her credit card toward the doctor. "This is on me," she said.

Jubal had his wallet out. He grabbed a fistful of bills. "No, it isn't," he said. "The girl's my daughter. I'm paying."

The doctor glanced from one to the other. Even if Jubal hadn't told her, she'd probably figured out the two weren't a couple. "I'll tell you what," she said. "Since the nurse called in sick, and I don't even know how to run a card or make out a receipt, it's on the house. No charge."

Ellie saw fit to protest. "Oh, but we can't just—"

"It was only a disinfectant wipe, a little salve, and a Band-Aid. She'll be fine. Don't worry about it." Her dark eyes met Ellie's. "Please know that we're here if you have any concerns about your pregnancy."

"Thank you," Ellie said, feeling Jubal's gaze on her. "Since I just got into town, that's good to know."

"Have you made arrangements for your delivery?" the doctor asked. "We work with the hospital in Cottonwood Springs. We can find you an obstetrician and do most of the paperwork from here if you like."

"That sounds like a good idea. I'll be in touch later this week." Ellie turned to go.

"Don't forget this." Jubal picked up her credit card and thrust it toward her. His look reminded Ellie of a thunderstorm lurking just out of sight on a blue sky day.

"Oh—thanks." She took the card and put it in her bag. After making sure Beau was comfortable, she led the way outside to the truck. Gracie stuck close to her side, reaching down to tickle Beau's fluffy ears where they stuck out of the bag. The little girl still deserved a nice reward for saving the dog.

"You can take me back to the bed and breakfast," Ellie told Jubal as he opened the door of the truck and let Gracie climb onto the seat.

"Ben said he and my mother would wait. But before I get in, I want to ask a favor."

Jubal's eyes narrowed. He waited in silence, clearly not trusting her as she stepped out of the girl's earshot.

"I'd like to do something nice for Gracie," she said. "I was thinking I could pick her up after school on Monday, maybe take her for pizza or an early movie. Then I could take her home. Would that be all right?"

He frowned and rubbed the bridge of his nose—a gesture Ellie remembered from the old days. The wind had taken on a biting chill. Snowflakes peppered Jubal's face as he spoke.

"I don't know if that would be a good idea, Ellie. I can see that my girl's taken to you and that little mutt of yours. But Gracie's got a tender heart. It would damn near kill me to see it broken."

*Like I broke yours,* Ellie thought. But she wasn't about to give up.

"I hope you won't deny your daughter a little bit of fun and attention. She deserves it for what she did. And don't worry, I'll make sure she understands that I'm not here to stay or to be her regular girlfriend. Please, Jubal. I know she'd enjoy it. I'll even give you my cell number in case you need to track us down."

He released a long sigh. "All right. I guess I owe her that. She doesn't have much fun living out there on the ranch, helping me with the chores. And she doesn't seem to have many friends at school. At least she doesn't bring them home or go to their houses. That's why I'm asking you to be careful."

"I understand. I can tell you really love her."

His mouth tightened. "Gracie's all I've got—and all that's left of her mother."

Ellie nodded. She knew better than to ask Jubal for details. Even if she'd chosen to speak, the lump in her throat would have choked off the words. With the wind blowing through her jacket and Beau shivering in her bag, she accepted his hand and climbed into the truck.

A few minutes later, Jubal dropped Ellie off at the bed and breakfast. On the way, he'd listened as she'd told Gracie about her plan for Monday. Gracie had clapped her hands with excitement. It had been a long time since Jubal had seen her so happy. Still, he couldn't help wondering if he'd made a mistake. People didn't change, and the Ellie he remembered could blow hot one minute and cold the next. If she hurt his daughter, he would never forgive her.

"Can we turn on the radio?" Gracie asked as they took the road out of town. "I want to hear some Christmas music."

"Sure. Go ahead." He let her punch the buttons and select the station—not that there were that many to choose from. The strains of "Silent Night," sung by a children's choir, drifted from the aging radio in the dash.

"Listen, Dad. Doesn't that song make you feel like Christmas?" Gracie asked.

"Uh-huh," Jubal lied. Thanksgiving had barely passed, but Gracie was already getting excited about the holidays. She'd even been badgering him to get a tree and put it up. But Jubal had never felt less like celebrating Christmas. The best he could do was try to get through the season before he had to tell his daughter the truth—that the ranch his family had owned for four generations, along with the sturdy rock house that had sheltered them, was no longer theirs.

"So how did it go with Jubal?" Ben swung the pickup onto Main Street and headed for home.

Ellie sighed. "It didn't *go* anywhere. Grow up and stop teasing me, Ben. I'm not sixteen anymore."

"But teasing you is so much fun."

Clara shook her head. "She's right, Ben. You're old enough to know better. Stop it."

Ben's only response was a chuckle, but he didn't say more. Light snow peppered the windows as they drove. Windshield wipers swished and thumped in the silence. Ellie's hand stole into her bag to rest on Beau, who'd fallen asleep.

"There are a few things I didn't see fit to ask him," she said to Ben. "Who was Jubal's wife? What happened to her?"

"Remember Laura Gustavson? Jubal married her about a year after you left town."

"I do remember her." Laura had been in Ellie's class. She was pretty and smart but so quiet that nobody paid her much attention. A farm girl, she'd worn hand-me-downs and done chores every morning before riding the bus to school. Jubal had made a wise choice.

"I was on duty the night she was killed," Ben said. "Awful accident on a rain-slicked road. Her car hit a bad spot and hydroplaned into a big truck. She didn't have a chance."

"Was she alone?" Ellie thought of Jubal and how he must have taken the news.

"Jubal and their little girl were waiting at home. But she wasn't really alone. She was six months pregnant. The baby died, too."

"Oh, no. I'm sorry." Heartsick, Ellie mouthed the empty words. She thought of Jubal, the worry lines etched into his face and the gray hair at his temples. All this while she'd been living the good life, blissfully unaware, in San Francisco.

"What about Jubal's father?" Ellie remembered an irascible, middle-aged man who'd barely spoken two words to her when she came out to the ranch to ride horses with his son.

"He died three years ago. A stroke, if I remember right." Ben pulled into the driveway of his mother's home. "Jubal's had a hard time of it. But the man's tough and proud. Smart, too. I hear he's got some big plans for the ranch. If I were a betting man, he's one I'd put my money on."

He came around to open the door for Ellie and help his mother down from the truck. "The two of you are invited to Sunday dinner at our place tomorrow. Jess says she's looking forward to some girl talk."

"Tell her I am, too. And thanks." Ellie squeezed her brother's arm, then turned away to let Beau do his business by the big sycamore. It meant a lot that Jess wanted to be friends. Maybe tomorrow she could enjoy a peaceful day with her family—a day free from concerns about Jubal, his tragic past, and his heart-stealing little girl.

Jubal tucked Gracie into bed, kissed her forehead, and turned off the light. His daughter was growing up fast. Before long she'd be too big for a nightly tuck-in. But he would enjoy the sweet ritual for as long as it lasted.

Moving as if under a heavy weight, he walked back down the hall and stood looking out the front window. The wind had picked up, blasting the house with snow as fine as sand. So far, the storm didn't look that bad. The few head of cattle he'd kept to winter over were safe under the cover of the open shed, with plenty of hay and water. The horses and the two dogs were snug in the barn, the chickens locked in their sturdy coop. This would be a good night to light a fire, make some coffee, and settle down with a book. But Jubal knew it wasn't going to happen. He had too much on his mind.

An alcove off the living room served as the ranch office. Jubal sat down at the massive desk that had been his great-grandfather's and switched on the computer he'd bought the day after his father's funeral. A staunch traditionalist, Seth McFarland had refused to have a computer in the

house—didn't trust the contraptions, he'd said.
He had kept the ranch accounts in an old-fashioned ledger. Only after he was gone, and Jubal
was transferring the records online, had he realized what a godawful mess the old man had
made of the ranch's finances.

Jubal had been hoping to raise certified organic, grass-fed beef that would command pre-
mium prices. It was a risky business, but if done
right, it was one way a modest-sized spread, too
small to support a big herd, could earn good
money. But making the needed changes—buying new equipment, replanting the pastures,
buying a prime bull and some top-grade cows
and calves, and contracting with a processor that
handled organic beef—would require plenty of
ready cash. For that he would need spotless
credit.

Putting his plans aside, Jubal had spent almost three years paying for his father's mismanagement. Little by little, by working hard and
squeezing every penny, he'd made good on the
old debts. A few weeks ago, he had paid off what
he'd thought was the last of his father's credi-
tors.

With high hopes and a detailed business plan,
he had gone to the local bank and applied for a
loan. The day after Thanksgiving, after hearing
nothing for more than a week, he'd gone in to
check the status of his application.

Clive Huish, the bank's loan officer, had lived
in Branding Iron for the past six years. A friendly,
easygoing type, he had ushered Jubal into his

private office, shown him to a seat, and closed the door.

"Is something wrong, Clive?" Jubal had asked. "I submitted everything you asked for."

Huish sat down. A bead of sweat gleamed on his balding head. The file folder containing Jubal's application lay open on his desk. "Your plan looks good and your credit is clean," he'd said. "But we did some due diligence—looking into the legal background, the usual stuff—and something came up. I'm sorry, but we can't give you an unsecured loan."

"That's not what I'm asking for," Jubal had argued. "The loan would be secured by the ranch."

The bank officer had shifted in his chair and cleared his throat. "You don't own the land your ranch sits on," he'd said. "It was transferred four years ago, before your father passed away."

That was when the bottom had dropped out of Jubal's world.

Now, after checking his e-mail, Jubal spent a few minutes updating the ranch account with the feed and other supplies he'd purchased over the past week.

On the desktop screen, the cursor hovered over the file he'd created for the proposed changes to the ranch—his dream file, as he'd jokingly called it. A couple of mouse clicks and it would no longer be there to torment him. Just like his real-life plans for the future, the dream file would be gone.

His finger quivered over the mouse button, then hesitated as he thought of Gracie and all that he wanted for her—security, nice things, the college education he never had. With a ragged sigh, he moved the cursor off the file. Call him a mule-headed fool, but he couldn't give up on the one chance to give his daughter a better life.

He'd been in a state of shock since getting the news from the bank. But now that he'd had time to think about it, he had plenty of questions. What had compelled his father to transfer the land? Who really owned it now, and why had he been allowed to keep running the ranch as if nothing had happened?

And the most puzzling question of all—why in hell's name hadn't his father told him about the sale?

He needed answers. If there was any way to salvage this mess—so help him, if it meant selling his own soul—he would find it.

# Chapter 3

By the next morning the storm had passed, dusting the landscape with a glittering patina of light snow. The sky was clear, the air cold and still.

Ellie had spent most of the morning organizing her room. The cheerleading photo, the stuffed animals, and the ruffled pillows were gone, shoved into the back of the closet. The high school fashions had been bagged for donation to the next church rummage sale. In their place, Ellie had hung her few maternity outfits—mostly basic black knits—and some comfortable clothes to wear after the baby came. The high-fashion party outfits and shoes she'd worn in San Francisco had been given to friends or donated to charity before Ellie left the city. Nobody dressed up in Branding Iron—except maybe Jess's mother, Francine.

In the bottom dresser drawer, she laid the

things she'd bought for the baby—tiny ruffled dresses with matching tights, dainty shoes, hats and headbands, a pink angora sweater set, and a designer christening dress trimmed with hand-made Belgian lace. True, she was short on prac-tical wear, like diapers, sleepers, and onesies. But she could buy those at Shop Mart, or maybe at one of the better stores in Cottonwood Springs. There was plenty of time.

*Wasn't there?*

A solid thump from her unborn daughter jarred her back to reality. In less than six weeks, whether she was ready or not, she was due to give birth. Heaven help her, how was she going to manage? She'd known from the beginning that she wanted her baby, but she didn't have a clue about being a mother. She'd never taken care of an infant. Now this tiny human life was about to be placed in her incompetent hands. She was scared spitless.

She gazed down at her blossoming belly. "You poor little thing," she murmured. "Do you have any idea what you're getting into?"

As if the question had been meant for him, Beau raised his head and yipped. Earlier he'd found a cozy spot between the pillows on the bed and settled down for a nap. Now he was ready for some attention.

Picking him up, Ellie carried him downstairs, took him outside to his favorite tree, and stood shivering while he sniffed around for recent callers then finally lifted his leg. Back in the house, she found a chocolate cake mix in the cupboard and whipped up a dessert to take next door for Sunday dinner.

Clara was at the church service she attended every Sunday. She'd invited Ellie to come with her, but she'd asked out of politeness, as if knowing what the answer would be. Ellie hadn't been to church in years, and she was in no mood to put herself on display this morning. She'd already made a spectacle of herself at the B and B.

As she washed the cake bowl and wiped the counter, Ellie found herself wondering if Jubal still went to church. He'd gone in the old days. She'd gone too back then, just to look at him. She'd had a crush on Jubal for a couple of years before he even noticed her. When the magic had finally happened, Ellie had been over the moon with happiness.

Strange, how a single decision could have so many consequences. Because she'd chosen not to marry Jubal, he'd wed Laura, who'd suffered a tragic death on her way home to him. Ellie's own life had changed when she'd met Brent and dropped out of law school to marry him. Their glamorous lifestyle had been nothing but a shell, hiding the hollowness of an empty relationship. For a long time she was in denial about Brent's cheating and his explosive temper. She'd fought to save her marriage, telling herself that with time and patience she could change him. But she should have known better. With the divorce almost final, he'd begged her to give him one more chance. Like a fool, she'd agreed to try. Their trial reconciliation had lasted only a couple of weeks before things got bad again. When she'd caught him cheating with a wealthy client, she'd left him for good.

Yet from the shambles of failure had come this innocent little baby—never planned, but loved all the same.

What if she'd said yes to Jubal when he'd proposed? How many lives would have been changed, for better or worse, by a single word?

At 4:00 that afternoon, Ellie and Clara walked next door to the smaller home where Ben, Jess, and Ethan lived. Ellie carried a covered sheet cake pan. Her bag, with Beau tucked inside, was slung over one shoulder. Clara clutched her arm for balance on the uneven sidewalk.

They mounted the porch to an open door, held by Ethan. Ben's son, a young charmer at this past summer's wedding, had grown taller in the past six months, but his grin was the same. "Hi, Aunt Ellie. Dad told me you carry your little dog around in your purse. Is he in there now?"

"He is. I knew you'd want to meet him. Help your grandma to a chair, and I'll get him out for you."

Ellie stepped into the living room. The décor was plain, and most of the furniture looked secondhand. But there was an aura of welcoming warmth about the little home. The dining room table was set for five. From the kitchen, the aromas of roast beef and fresh-baked rolls drifted tantalizingly. Ellie glanced at Ben, who'd just taken their coats. She'd never seen her brother look more contented.

Once Clara was seated, Ellie lifted Beau out of her bag.

"Wow! He's so little! Can I hold him?" Ethan loved animals. Ellie had no worries about trusting him with her dog.

"Let him sniff the back of your hand first," she said. "When his tail starts to wag, I'll hand him over."

Getting acquainted didn't take long. Beau was licking Ethan's chin when Jess popped her head around the kitchen door. "Dinner's almost ready," she said. "Give me about ten minutes and it'll be on the table."

"It sounds like you could use some help." Leaving Beau with his new friend, Ellie rose and hurried into the kitchen.

Jess, in a red sweater and tight jeans that outlined her tiny waist, was stirring gravy in a pan on the stove. "Oh, thanks!" she said. "You're just in time. How would you like to drain and mash the potatoes?"

"Sure." Maneuvering her belly into a corner next to the sink, Ellie set to work. "Thanks for making me feel useful."

Jess flashed a grin. "You *are* useful, and you're looking good."

"Thanks. I feel like a big, clumsy elephant— especially next to you."

"I'm the one who should be envious," Jess said. "Ben and I have been hoping for a little one. So far, no luck—just a lot of fun trying."

"Maybe you're trying too hard. Give it time. You've only been married six months."

"That's what the doctor says. Everything's in the right place. And Ben's already a father, so he's fine. Maybe I need to stop working so much."

"Just relax. It'll happen when it happens."

*Like it did with me. What a shock.*

Jess skimmed the fat off the gravy. "I've been thinking I'd like to give you a baby shower," she said. "I know you're going to need a lot of things for your little girl. And it would be a fun way for the ladies in the town to get to know you."

Ellie's grip froze on the potato masher. "But why on earth would anybody come? After ten years away, I'm a stranger here. I have no friends at all—unless I can count you."

Jess squeezed Ellie's arm as she turned away from the stove to get the gravy boat. "You can. You can count on my mother, too. And don't you worry about who'll show up—hey, it's a baby shower! In Branding Iron, that's a big social event! Everybody will want to come. We can have it at the B and B. All I need from you is to agree on a date. I'll do the rest."

Ellie sighed in surrender as she scooped the mashed potatoes into a bowl and added a dollop of butter. "That's really sweet of you. I'll need to—uh—check my very busy social calendar."

"Seriously, let me know. We'll want to do it soon, before Christmas. Okay?"

"Okay. I'll give you some dates. Since you know what else is going on in town, you can narrow them down. And thanks, Jess. Really." Ellie picked up the bowl of mashed potatoes and carried it to the table.

In the living room, Ethan and Beau were playing fetch with a rolled-up sock. The little poodle was having the time of his life, chasing the thrown sock and dragging it back to Ethan for a gentle, growling tug-of-war.

An ironic smile tugged at Ellie's lips. She'd fled San Francisco with the idea of becoming invisible—lying low in her mother's house until she could have her baby, get back on her feet, and leave as quietly as possible. But she should have known better. Little by little, whether she liked it or not, she was being pulled back into Branding Iron and the small-town life she'd vowed to leave behind.

On Monday morning Ellie stopped by the clinic to have a routine checkup and start the registration process for her delivery in the Cottonwood Springs Hospital. Somebody had put up a shabby artificial Christmas tree in the reception area. The lights were burned out and the ornaments looked left over from the seventies, but at least they had enough holiday spirit to make the effort.

It was more than Ellie could say for herself. She'd had a restless night, with the baby kickboxing her bladder and Beau starting awake at every unfamiliar sound in the old house. At 7:30 she'd hauled herself out of bed to escort Beau to his favorite tree, then made coffee for herself and her mother. Clara had been glad to watch the little rascal while Ellie reported to the clinic.

The nurse, a young man in scrubs who looked like he belonged in middle school, took the form she'd filled out, jotted down her weight and blood pressure, and ushered her back to an exam room to change and wait for the doctor. The room was chilly, and Ellie had left her coat outside. By the time the doctor walked in a few minutes later, she was seated on the edge of the exam table, shivering beneath the thin cotton gown.

"Oh, I'm so sorry! This place takes forever to warm up in the morning." Dr. Ramirez looked fresh and pretty. One hand carried Ellie's chart on a clipboard. The other hand held a plaid flannel blanket, which she draped around Ellie's shoulders. Ellie closed her eyes. The blanket was *warm.*

"Thank you!" Ellie breathed the words. "This feels heavenly!"

"We have a warmer in the back. Nice on mornings like this. Now, let's see how you're doing." She studied the chart a moment. "You say you're due in January?"

"January third—more or less."

"Your weight looks about right. But your blood pressure's a little high. Is that usual for you?"

"Not really. But I've been under some stress. Moving here from San Francisco took a lot out of me."

"You're divorced?" Ellie had checked the box on the form.

"Yes. Recently. It's a long story." Ellie hoped she wouldn't be asked to tell it.

"Having a baby alone is tough," the doctor said. "Believe me, I know. I'm raising a ten-year-old daughter. While I'm on rotation here, I drive back and forth between the clinic and Cottonwood Springs five days a week."

"I'm luckier than some." Ellie realized it was true. "I have family in Branding Iron—a mother and a married brother. That's why I came here to have my baby."

"You *are* lucky." After checking for the baby's heartbeat, Dr. Ramirez slipped on latex gloves and swung the stirrups into position on the table. "I'm sure you know the drill by now. We'll just take a quick look to make sure everything's all right. Not fun, I know. But I promise you, the speculum will be warm." She laughed. "Only a male doctor would use a cold one."

"Thanks, that helps." Ellie willed herself to relax.

"Oh—how's the little girl with the cat scratch?" The doctor was chatting, probably to put her at ease while she did the delicate exam.

"I haven't seen her since Saturday. But I'm sure she's fine."

"Her father, the man you came here with. He's your brother?"

"No, he's just . . . an old friend."

"Oh—a *friend*. I had the feeling you weren't

related. And those blue eyes! He's a *mango,* that one!"

"A mango? Like you eat?" Ellie was confused.

"Sorry." The doctor laughed. "In Cuba, that's what we call a really good-looking man."

"You're Cuban?"

"I was born in Miami. But I did my medical training in Cuba. My grandfather still lives there. He pulled a few strings for me."

"But you didn't want to stay?"

"No . . ." Her pause spoke untold volumes. "I didn't. I couldn't." Her tone changed. "All done. Everything looks just fine. So you can get dressed. Ryan, outside, will help you register with the hospital."

"Thanks." Ellie sat up and swung her legs off the table.

"We'll want to keep an eye on your blood pressure. Getting more rest may bring it down. But you should come back in a week to have it checked—sooner if you don't feel well for any reason." She picked up her clipboard and headed for the door. "See you next week. Say hello to the *mango* for me."

By the time Ellie had dressed and finished with the hospital registration, the clinic was filling up with people. Making a mental note to come early again next time, she put on her coat and went outside.

A couple of elderly men were standing by her BMW, looking at the car and commenting. "Ain't never seen a car like that for real," one of them said. "Bet it'll go like a bat out of hell."

"Maybe." The other man spat a stream of to-bacco onto the asphalt. "But I wouldn't have one here. If it breaks down, there won't be no parts for it in a hundred miles."

As Ellie walked toward the car, the men smiled, tipped their hats, and moved away. She wouldn't have expected that kind of politeness in the city. At least folks in Branding Iron still had manners.

She started the car and drove down Main Street under strings of glowing Christmas lights. She needed to pick up some groceries and a pre-scription for Clara, who didn't drive. Then she'd have some time to rest at home before picking up Gracie after school.

*Say hello to the* mango *for me.*

The doctor's parting words replayed in Ellie's memory. The pretty Latina had probably just been making small talk. But Jubal was a com-pellingly handsome man—like Harrison Ford in his prime, but with Paul Newman's eyes. If any-thing, the maturity of ten hard years had only added to his appeal. A decent, responsible man with his looks could likely get any woman he wanted.

So, Ellie wondered, with his wife gone four years and his little girl needing a mother, why hadn't Jubal married again?

But what did it matter? She'd turned her back on Jubal ten years ago. His life was no longer any of her business.

Jubal would doubtless feel the same way about her, especially given that she was pregnant with another man's baby and looked about as attractive as a cow.

The cavernous Shop Mart store was crowded. The list Clara had given Ellie was a short one, but it took her a long time to locate each item. By the time she'd waited in the lengthy checkout line, with "Grandma Got Run Over by a Reindeer" blasting her ears and the baby flip-flopping like a little gymnast, all she wanted was to collapse somewhere and rest.

The grocery items—eggs, oranges, bacon, potatoes, a half gallon of milk—filled the large paper bag Ellie had chosen instead of plastic. By the time she'd paid for everything, another shopper had wheeled off her empty cart. Never mind. There was no reason she couldn't carry the bag to the car.

Concerned that the paper handles might break, she slung her purse over her shoulder and hefted the bag in her arms. It was heavier than she'd expected. As she made her way out to the parking lot, she could feel it slipping.

Which way was her car? Heaven help her, she couldn't see over the top of the bag! Ellie could imagine her blood pressure rising as she twisted sideways, trying to look around the bag and spot her BMW. No luck. Wherever it was, the low sedan was lost amid a forest of tall SUVs and pickups. And her grip was weakening. The heavy bag was sliding downward, onto her belly. If she didn't find her car soon, her arms would give out, and the bag would go crashing to the pavement.

"Could you use a hand?" The deep voice came from behind her.

Turning, Ellie looked up into Jubal's mocking eyes. She could feel her knees start to give way. "I could use *two* hands," she muttered.

As if it weighed nothing, he lifted the bag out of her arms. "Now, where's your car?" he asked.

"I . . . don't know. I can't find it."

He shook his head. *Same old scatterbrained Ellie,* he was probably thinking. "Okay, I'll help you look. Do I need to guess what kind of car you have?"

She remembered then that he hadn't seen her car. "It's a BMW."

"Of course it is. And I won't need to ask you the color because it'll be the only one in the parking lot." He scanned the sea of vehicles. "There it is, two rows down. Come on."

He led the way, Ellie struggling to keep pace with his long strides. She used her remote key to open the trunk. He lowered the bag inside and closed the lid.

"Thank you, Jubal." She stood looking up at him, her eyes on a level with his stern jaw. "I owe you."

"You don't owe me anything, Ellie. I'd do the same for anybody who needed help." His expression was guarded, almost cold. "Will you be all right?"

"Yes. Fine." She let him open the driver's side door. Maybe if they had a chance to sit and talk they could settle things between them and at least be polite, if distant, friends. But that wasn't going to happen now. She lowered herself to the seat and eased her belly into the space beneath the steering wheel. "Thanks again," she said, thrusting the key into the ignition.

He took a step back, then paused, with her door still open. "Gracie hasn't stopped talking about your plans for after school today. I hope you didn't forget. Not that it would make much difference to me, but she'd be mighty disappointed if you let her down."

*Like I let you down?*

"I haven't forgotten," Ellie said. "In fact I'm looking forward to it."

"I called the school office and told them you'd be picking her up, so they won't be expecting her to get on the bus."

It would be like Jubal to think of that. In his quiet way, he'd always taken care of whatever needed to be done. "Good idea," she said. "I'll be there early, so she'll see me when she comes outside. And of course, I'll drive her home afterward."

"Don't keep her too late. She'll need time to do her homework before bed. Gracie can show you the way to the ranch."

"I know the way, Jubal."

"So you do." Something flashed in his eyes and was gone—as if a memory had come to light and been forcefully blotted out. "Here's a card with my cell number on it," he said, reaching into his jacket's inner pocket to remove it. "Keep it in case anything comes up." He handed her the card, closed the car door, turned, and walked away.

Jubal willed himself not to look back as he crossed the parking lot to his truck. He had come into town to check the property deeds in the county recorder's office. On the way home, as an afterthought, he'd stopped at Shop Mart for a few basics. He'd loaded the groceries into his truck and was about to pull out of his parking space when he saw Ellie staggering out of the store with her heavy bag. Without a second thought, he'd leaped out of the truck and raced over to help her. Somehow he'd managed to stop behind her, catch his breath, and calm his nerves before speaking.

Lord, why Ellie? Why now? Even after ten years—even pregnant—she still had the power to make him feel like a hormone-crazed six-teen-year-old. But letting Ellie distract him was the last thing he needed—or wanted. She'd walked out on him once. Given the chance, she'd do it again without a flicker of regret.

Not that she was going to get that chance. Whatever her story was, he didn't need her, didn't want her. Besides, he had far more urgent things on his mind.

At the recorder's office, he'd found the deed to the ranch. Updated four years ago, the owner was listed as Shumway and Sons Property Management, Inc., an outfit Jubal had never heard of.

It had been all Jubal could do to keep from ripping the recorded deed to shreds and stomping on the pieces. This was crazy. Who were these people? How could his father have let them get their hands on the family ranch? And why hadn't they tried to boot him off and take possession of the place?

As he drove home, Jubal forced his memory back four years, looking for answers. It wasn't an easy time to revisit. Laura had recently died, taking their unborn baby with her and leaving him a grieving wreck with a small daughter to care for. Little wonder that his father, who was still running the ranch, didn't want to bother his son with financial matters.

The old man, his mental powers already failing, must have made a deal with some shysters who'd taken advantage of him. Since he didn't gamble or drink to excess, that was the only explanation that made sense.

But what could he do about it now? Jubal's hands tightened on the steering wheel till the knuckles ached. If a crime had been committed, where could he look for proof, especially when the one person who might tell him what had happened—his father—was gone?

In the years they'd run the ranch together, Seth McFarland, as the legal owner, had insisted on handling the finances himself, while Jubal shouldered more and more of the physical work. Toward the end of his life, the old man had become secretive, even keeping his ledgers, bills, and receipts under lock and key. Jubal, weighed down by his own burdens, hadn't realized how far his father's mind had slipped until it was too late.

And now the ranch his family had owned for generations was gone. Really gone.

Jubal took a deep breath, willing himself not to panic. There had to be a way to fight this. But first he needed to know who and what he'd be fighting. This afternoon, while Gracie was off with Ellie, he would begin the search by going through every line of his father's ledger. If the answer wasn't there, he would keep looking until he'd inspected every piece of paper stuffed into the drawers, files, and boxes the old man had squirreled away.

It might take days or even weeks to look at everything. But one way or another, Jubal swore, he would find some answers.

# Chapter 4

Ellie was parked at the curb in front of the school when the bell rang. She watched the boys and girls spill out of the low brick building, laughing, talking, fastening their coats, and shouldering their backpacks. As she stepped out of the car, her eyes scanned the crowded sidewalk, searching for one small girl in pigtails and a faded plaid jacket.

Only after minutes of looking did Ellie find her. Gracie was standing alone in the shelter of the entryway, clutching her backpack and looking worried.

Waving, Ellie hurried toward her. Gracie's face brightened. She scampered down the steps and came racing along the sidewalk. "I was afraid you'd forget," she said.

"I'd never do that." Ellie squeezed her shoulder and guided her to the BMW. "Come on, let's get something to eat."

Remembering safety rules, she let Gracie into the back and made sure her seat belt was buckled. "Where's Beau?" Gracie asked.

"He's home with my mother. We're going to Buckaroo's. They have a NO DOGS ALLOWED sign by their door."

"That's not very nice. I wouldn't mind having dogs around."

"Not even if some big old farm hound came over and tried to gobble your food?"

Gracie giggled. "That would be funny."

"To you, maybe. But not to some people. If you want to play with Beau, we can do it later."

"This is really a nice car," Gracie said. "I've never been in a car with real leather seats."

"The seats even get warm," Ellie said. "Can you feel the heat?"

There was a moment of silence before Gracie exclaimed, "Wow! That's amazing! Wait till I tell my dad!"

Ellie sighed. Something told her Jubal wouldn't be impressed by heated leather car seats. That morning in the parking lot, his manner toward her had been almost contemptuous, as if having an expensive car in Branding Iron were some kind of sin.

But Jubal's world didn't revolve around her, Ellie reminded herself. Jubal had looked preoccupied before he'd even seen her car. Odds were, his gruff behavior had nothing to do with her.

Whatever was bothering him, she knew better than to get involved. She would have a good

time with his daughter today, then gently extri-
cate herself from their lives. That might sound
cold, but she had her own issues to deal with.

Buckaroo's, the only regular restaurant in
Branding Iron, hadn't changed since Ellie was
in high school. The menu—burgers, pizza, ice
cream, shakes, sodas, and beer with an I.D.—was
the same. Slim, the owner, in his greasy white
apron, looked as if he'd been frozen in time. Even
the Christmas decorations—a string of lights and
tinsel that hung above the counter—were the
ones she remembered.

At their table in a corner booth, she ordered
a large pepperoni pizza along with two root
beers, which the teenage waitress brought to
their table. The way Gracie's eyes sparkled made
Ellie suspect this was a rare treat for the little
girl. Maybe Jubal was struggling to keep his
ranch afloat. That could explain his careworn
look.

"Can I ask you something?" Gracie asked.
"And will you promise you won't get mad?"

"Of course I won't get mad. Go ahead and
ask me."

"If you're going to have a baby . . . where's the
dad?"

At least the question wasn't unexpected. Gracie was a ranch girl. She probably had some idea
of what it took to make a baby.

"We're not together now," Ellie said. "We're
divorced."

"Why?"

That was a tougher question. "He wasn't happy.

I wasn't happy. We didn't even like each other anymore."

"But you made a baby. My Sunday school teacher says you have to love each other to do that."

The conversation was getting too deep for Ellie. "That's certainly the best way. But sometimes things just happen. Hey, guess what. I'm having a little girl."

Gracie's blue eyes widened. "How do you know?"

"My doctor in San Francisco used a machine that takes pictures."

"Wow! Does she look like you?"

"She looks like . . . a baby." The murky sonogram hadn't shown Ellie much. But the technician had seemed pleased with it. *Everything looks good,* the woman had said. *Since I don't see any outdoor plumbing, I think we can safely say you've got a healthy little girl.*

"When will she be here?" Gracie asked.

"Pretty soon. The third of January, my doctor said."

Gracie sucked her straw, savoring the sweet, cold root beer. "My mom was going to have a baby, too. But she got in a wreck and went to heaven. I guess she took the baby with her."

"Oh, honey—" Ellie blinked back a rush of tears. Impulsively she reached across the table and clasped the small, chapped hand. "I know about that. My brother told me. I'll bet you still miss her."

"I miss her all the time. So does my dad."

"I went to school with your mother. I remember how pretty she was, and how smart. She was nice, too."

"That's what my dad says. I keep her picture by my bed, so I won't forget what she looked like. But it's getting hard to remember how it was being with her. That makes me sad." She slurped the last few drops of root beer. Ellie caught the waitress's eye and signaled for a refill.

"Did you know my dad, too?" Gracie asked.

Ellie glanced down at the table. "He was a few years older, so he wasn't in my class, but we were friends," she said. "You know, the high school isn't very big. Back then it was even smaller. All the kids knew each other."

Just then, to Ellie's relief, the pizza arrived. Too hungry to ask more questions, Gracie dived in, wolfing down three hot, cheesy slices before announcing that she was full. Ellie, who'd barely been able to eat one slice, ordered a box for the rest. "You can take it home and warm it up later," she said.

"Dad likes pizza. I'll save the rest for him," Gracie said.

"So what would you like to do next?" Ellie asked as she paid the check. "There's a movie about dinosaurs playing at the Main Street Theater."

Gracie shook her head. "That's a little kid movie. I'd rather go to your house and play with Beau. Is that all right?"

"Sure." Ellie hadn't been looking forward to the dinosaur movie either. "Let's go."

Outside, the sun had sunk below the horizon, streaking the thready clouds with crimson and violet. A chilly wind had sprung up. With Gracie clutching the pizza box, they hurried to the car, buckled up, and headed for Clara's house. Ellie knew her mother, who'd been the city librarian for years, enjoyed children. Having Gracie there would be a treat for her.

When they opened the front door, Beau jumped off the couch and came bounding to meet them. Wriggling and yapping, he seemed as happy to see Gracie as he was to see Ellie.

"Do you think he remembers that I saved him?" Gracie picked up the little poodle, giggling as he licked her face.

"Maybe," Ellie said. "Or maybe he just likes you. Or just maybe . . . you taste like pizza."

Clara stepped out of the kitchen. "Hello there, Gracie. Ellie told me you might be coming, so I made a batch of brownies, just in case. Come on in the kitchen and we'll have some, with milk."

"That sounds great," Ellie said. "But first I'll need to take Beau out for a minute."

"I can take him," Gracie said.

"Thanks, but it's getting dark. I think I'd better do it." Ellie took her dog from Gracie and carried him out to his favorite spot by the tree. It would be a good idea to buy some puppy pads like the ones she'd used in the San Francisco condo, she thought. Beau loved his tree, but if the weather got any colder she wouldn't want to take him outside. Surely Shop Mart would have the pads in stock.

Beau was sniffing his way around the base of the big sycamore. Ellie shivered, wishing he'd hurry with his doggy business. By now it was so dark that the poodle was nothing but a small, white blur against the grass. He started to lift his leg, then lowered it and disappeared behind the tree. Seconds passed and he didn't reappear.

Wondering if he'd found a new spot or something special to sniff, Ellie walked around the tree to check.

Beau was gone.

Choking on panic, she wheeled this way and that, her frantic gaze searching the shadows. Why hadn't she brought a flashlight with her? Now there wasn't time to run and get one.

"Beau! Come here!" Heart pounding, she called and whistled. No response. Where had he gone? There were coyotes on the farms and ranches around Branding Iron. What if one had stolen into town and made off with her precious dog in its jaws?

The distant but chilling cry of a barn owl quivered through the darkness. Ellie's pulse slammed. An owl could snatch Beau up and be gone in a flash. Just like that, her beloved pet could be lost forever.

Still calling and whistling, she peered into the shrubbery, then up and down the sidewalk.

Beau almost always came when he was called. Something had to be wrong.

Then she saw him—a dot of white, partway down the block. And he wasn't alone. On the sidewalk, bathed in the glow of a porch light, a huge wolfish-looking mutt was sniffing Beau as if he were a well-seasoned lamb chop. Beau stood as if frozen in place while the big dog investigated him. Was the scruffy creature just curious, or sizing him up for a meal? Ellie didn't wait to find out.

"Shoo!" She charged the big dog, one hand poised to throw an imaginary rock. Probably more startled than scared, it slunk backward, giving her the chance to dart in and scoop up Beau. The little poodle was shaking, but safety gave him courage. From the height of Ellie's arms, he gave his rival what-for, barking, growling, and yapping up a storm. Unimpressed, the shaggy mutt trotted off down the street.

Ellie's knees were shaking. Tears welled in her eyes as she clasped her little poodle close. She'd only lost sight of him for a few seconds, but that was all it had taken for him to walk right into danger.

How many stories had she heard about children drowning or running into traffic or being kidnapped because a parent looked away for the flicker of a second? How could she manage to be responsible for a child? She could barely keep her dog safe!

Heaven help her, she didn't know the first

thing about being a mother. Most of her friends in San Francisco had live-in nannies for their little ones. But she couldn't hire one here, or impose on Clara's fragile health. For nurturing and protection, this poor little baby would be totally dependent on *her*. What if she were to do something wrong? Even the thought of it terrified her.

But the last thing she wanted now was to upset Clara and Gracie. Standing on the porch, she took a moment to breathe and collect herself. By the time she'd closed the front door behind her and walked into the kitchen, she'd managed to paste a smile on her face.

Gracie and Clara were already at the kitchen table, with glasses of milk, saucers, napkins, and the pan of brownies between them. "Sit down," Clara said. "Gracie and I were just talking about the Cowboy Christmas Ball."

Ellie put Beau on the floor next to his water bowl, then took a seat. In Branding Iron, the ball was the biggest event of the year. The whole town came, dressed for an Old West party with traditional food and a live big-name country band for dancing the night away.

Ellie dished out the warm brownies, one on each saucer, and passed around some forks. "Don't plan on me for the ball. I'll be even bigger than I am now. Jess can keep my old ball gown, which you lent her last year. She must've looked stunning in it with that red hair and tiny waist. Anyway, after this baby, I'll never be able to fit into it again."

"I don't recall seeing you there last year, Gracie," Clara said.

Gracie looked downcast. "My dad says that he and Mom used to go. But now, being there just makes him feel sad."

"I remember seeing your parents there. They were a lovely couple. Such a tragedy, that accident." Clara shook her head, then smiled. "But you could go with our family, Gracie. I know Ben and Jess would be happy to have you along."

"That would be nice," Gracie said. "But I'd have to go looking like this. I don't have anything to wear."

Clara's face brightened. "I can fix that! I have a length of calico in my sewing cabinet that would do nicely for your ball dress. Let me bring it out so you can take a look."

She rose out of her chair and, with surprising energy, hurried down the hall to her sewing room. Gracie gave Ellie a hesitant look.

"Does your mother want to *make* me a dress?"

"It looks that way."

"But that would be a lot of work. I don't think my dad has enough money to pay her."

"Oh, she wouldn't take money, Gracie. My mother loves to sew, and she has shelves and boxes full of fabric. She would do this just for fun." Ellie gave her a reassuring smile. "It'll be fine, you'll see. Now finish your brownie and milk, and afterward you can play with Beau."

A few minutes later, Clara returned with a bolt end of blue calico, dotted with tiny yellow flowers. "I think this will do if there's enough of it," she said. "Stand up, Gracie, and let's see."

Gracie stood still while Clara doubled the length of cloth and held it up in front of her. "Oh, there'll be plenty," she said. "And that blue, with her eyes—what do you think, Ellie?"

"I think it's perfect. How about you, Gracie?"

"It's . . . beautiful. Nobody ever made me a dress before. Thank you!" She flung her arms around Clara's waist.

Clara dabbed at her eyes. "I'll just get my tape and take your measurements," she said, easing gently away before she hurried back down the hallway with the calico in her arms.

Gracie sipped her milk, frowning. "I hope my dad will be okay with this. He won't take anything for free. He calls it charity. He'll probably want to pay for the dress."

"Tell him it's not charity, it's a gift." Ellie studied Jubal's daughter, thinking how wise she was for her years. With no mother to take care of her, she'd probably had to grow up fast—just as Ellie and Ben had after their father was killed crashing his small plane.

"Is your father all right?" she asked. "I've only talked to him for a few minutes, but he did seem troubled about something. We were friends once. I care enough to wonder about him." All true, Ellie reminded herself.

"I wonder, too," Gracie said. "He seems kind of sad and quiet. But he hasn't told me why. I think there might be something he doesn't want me to worry about."

Just then Clara returned with her dress-maker's tape. Ellie had already decided not to ask Gracie anything more. It would be too much like prying and might upset the girl.

Gracie stood still while Clara measured her, but her eyes were on the dog, who was chewing one of his squeaky toys on the rug. Knowing that Beau was the real reason she'd wanted to come here, Ellie brought her Beau's basket of dog toys and invited her to play.

While Ellie cleaned up the kitchen, Clara settled in her rocker to watch the fun as Gracie and Beau played fetch, tug-of-war, and hide-and-seek. Beau loved the games, but after half an hour running back and forth on his short little legs, he began to flag. Finally he curled up in Gracie's lap and went to sleep.

Seated on the low ottoman, Gracie gazed down at him. Then she looked up at Ellie and grinned. "Well, it looks like I'm stuck here for a while," she said.

Ellie returned her smile. She couldn't blame Gracie for wanting to be here, where it was warm and cheerful, with two women to fuss over her, treats to snack on, and a cute little dog to play with and cuddle. But Jubal would be wanting his daughter home soon. And much as she enjoyed Gracie, Ellie had no desire to anger her father.

Clara was sitting behind Gracie in her rocker. "What lovely hair you have, Gracie," she said. "So thick and such a pretty chestnut brown. Do you braid those pigtails yourself?"

"Uh-huh. I do it every morning before school," Gracie said. "My dad doesn't know how to fix hair."

"When Ellie was about your age, I used to French-braid her hair. I'll bet yours would look pretty that way. Would you like me to try it?"

Gracie looked uncertain. "I guess. Can I hold Beau while you braid my hair?"

"Of course. Just stay right where you are. Ellie, would you get a brush and a comb out of the bathroom?"

Ellie hurried down the hall and came back with the things her mother needed. Gracie sat still while Clara unwrapped the elastic hair bands and unraveled the braids into a wavy cascade of hair that fell to the middle of the girl's back. Taking the brush, she began smoothing away the last tangles. Gracie really did have pretty hair. In years to come, with those blue eyes and delicate features, she would be a lovely young woman.

Reaching forward, Clara sectioned the hair at the crown of Gracie's head and began braiding the first locks. Gracie sat straight and still, one fingertip stroking Beau's head.

"When are you going to get your Christmas tree?" she asked.

"Why, I don't know," Clara said. "I haven't even thought about it yet."

"Your tree always looks so pretty through that big window. At Christmastime, I make my dad drive by your house so I can look at it. Every year, you have the most beautiful tree in town."

Ellie glanced down at her hands. The thought of Jubal driving past her old home because his daughter wanted to see the tree stirred emotions she'd long since vowed to forget. She had loved Jubal with all the passion of her young heart. She just hadn't loved him enough to spend the rest of her life in Branding Iron. She'd made that decision once. Given a second chance, she would make the same choice again.

But what was she thinking? Jubal wasn't the kind of man to offer second chances. As it was, he was barely speaking to her.

"For the past few years, Ben has been the one to get the tree up and decorated." Clara lifted more strands of hair into the thick braid she was making. "He liked having it ready when Ethan got here for the holidays. But this year he has his own house. And Ethan is going to Boston to spend Christmas with his mother. I can't get a big tree up myself, and Ellie is certainly in no condition to do it. So who knows? We might not even have a tree this year."

Gracie sighed.

"How about you, Gracie?" Ellie asked. "When are you getting a tree?"

The look on Gracie's face told Ellie she'd asked the wrong question. "I don't know," the girl said. "I've asked my dad but he says it's too early. He says that if we get a tree now, the needles will fall off. I just hope he remembers. Last year we bought the only one left on the tree lot. It was little and crooked and most of the needles were gone. Hank said we could just have it, but Dad made him take the money. We took it home and put Mom's decorations on it."

Beau woke up and yawned. Gracie scratched his ears. "It was a really good Christmas," she said. "Dad gave me a new saddle for my horse. It must've cost a lot, but he said it didn't matter."

"You've got your own horse?" Ellie asked.

"Uh-huh. His name's Jocko. I ride him when Dad and I go out to check the cows. Dad says that when I'm older I can go riding by myself. We have dogs, too. But they're too big and dirty to live in the house like Beau. They sleep in the barn and help with the herding."

Clara had finished Gracie's hair. The weaving in started at the crown of her head and ended in a gleaming braid that hung down her back. The flattering style made her look chic, like the young girls featured in ads and on magazine covers. When Gracie saw the full effect in the angled bathroom mirrors, she gasped with delight. "Wow! That's so cool! I didn't know my hair could look like that!"

"Your hair is beautiful and so are you," Ellie said. "But we need to get you home now."

Gracie sighed. "All right. Maybe sometime I can come back and play with Beau some more."

"Maybe. We'll see." This could become a problem, Ellie realized. She enjoyed Gracie, but something told her Jubal wouldn't be too pleased with his daughter's choice of new friends. "Get your coat and say good-bye to

Beau," she said. "Then I'll run you home to the ranch."

"Can Beau come with us? I can hold him in the car."

"It's cold and dark. Beau will be better off here."

"Oh—okay." Gracie put on her jacket. Picking up Beau, she kissed the top of his head and set him on the ottoman. Then she followed Ellie outside.

The BMW was chilly inside but it was warm by the time they passed the city limits. "Did you get your backpack?" Ellie asked, suddenly remembering.

"I've got it. I left it right here in the backseat."

"Your father said you had homework."

"Not tonight. I usually get my work done in class."

No homework. Jubal must have wanted an excuse to get his daughter home at a reasonable hour. But she could hardly fault him for that white lie. He was just being a protective father.

"Is it okay if we turn on the radio?" Gracie asked. "I like to listen to Christmas music."

"Sure." Ellie recalled the oldies station that played holiday music in December. When she found it on the dial, the familiar notes of "The Little Drummer Boy" boomed from the speakers.

"Sing with me, Ellie." Gracie's small, clear voice joined the song. Ellie had never been a singer but, wanting to keep things light and cheerful, she turned up the radio to hide her off-key notes and sang along.

The ranch was several miles out of town. By the time they turned off the highway and onto the narrow side road that skirted other, smaller farms, they'd sung their way through "Frosty the Snowman" and "Rudolph the Red-Nosed Reindeer." Needing a break, Ellie lowered the volume.

"Does your dad sing with you?" she asked.

"Sometimes. Not so much lately."

"Why is that, you think?"

"I don't know. Maybe he's remembering Mom and how we all used to sing together in the truck. Or maybe he's just getting old."

"Your dad isn't old, Gracie. He's not much more than thirty-one." Ellie steered the car around a pothole in the road. "Do you like it, living out here on the ranch with your dad?"

"Mostly. It's fun when he's got workers here to help with the cattle. And I love riding Jocko. But in the winter, when it's dark and cold, I get lonesome out here. I wish he'd get married again. It would be nice to have a mom, like other kids do."

"Do you think he might?"

"A bunch of ladies have liked him. Some even brought us cookies and meat loaf and stuff like that. But after a while they stopped coming around. Maybe he just didn't like them back. But I think he likes you."

Gracie dropped that bombshell just as Ellie drove through the gate and pulled up to the house. There would be no time to respond because the porch light was on, and standing in its glow, huddled into his sheepskin coat, was Jubal.

# Chapter 5

As the BMW's headlights swung through the front gate, Jubal forced himself to take a deep breath. There was no reason facing Ellie should set him on edge. The past was over. They'd both moved on. But even after ten years—seeing her alone, pregnant, and vulnerable—the old wounds still burned.

He'd have been better off if she'd never come back to Branding Iron. But here she was. And in this small town, there were bound to be encounters—especially since Gracie was so keen on that useless little fluff of a dog. It was time he and Ellie had a talk. If they could come to some kind of understanding, maybe things would be less awkward between them.

After she pulled the car up to the porch and switched off the engine, he came down the steps and opened her door.

"I hope we're not too late," she said before he

could speak. "Gracie told me her homework is already done."

"No problem," he said. "It's barely eight. Come on in. I've got hot chocolate on the stove. It's okay if you want to bring your dog in."

"Beau's at home with my mother. And I hadn't planned on staying. I just came to drop Gracie off."

*Whatever. He'd shown himself willing, and that was that. It was probably just as well if she didn't come in.*

Jubal was about to wish her a safe drive home when Gracie opened her side of the car and came around with her backpack slung over her shoulder and a pizza box in her hands. Somebody had changed her hair. She looked pretty, but more grown-up somehow. He already missed her little-girl pigtails.

Jubal took the pizza box. "If this is for me, thanks," he said. "I'll warm it up later."

"Please come in, Ellie," Gracie begged. "Just for a little while."

Jubal sensed Ellie's hesitation. Was he the one she wanted to get away from, or was it her memories of his place? "I really don't think—" she began.

"Please, Ellie! Please come in!" In the glow of the porch light, Gracie's eyes would have softened any heart.

Ellie sighed, took the key out of the ignition, and slung her purse strap over her shoulder before she climbed out of the car. Taking an extra moment, she locked the door with the remote button. Jubal could have reminded her that out here, with nobody around to steal things, she could have left her keys and purse in the unlocked car. But she'd been away from Branding Iron long enough to develop city habits. Trying to change them wouldn't be worth his time.

Ellie took the arm Jubal offered as she mounted the steep porch steps. She could tell he was trying not to look at her belly, which stuck out so far that she could no longer see her feet. But he had to be curious about her situation. Was that the reason he'd invited her in, or was he just being polite? At least, given her appearance, she could rule out any desire to rekindle the old flame.

Gracie put her backpack down by the door, took the pizza box from Jubal, and carried it into the kitchen. Ellie released Jubal's arm as they walked in from the porch. Without asking, he stepped behind her, slipped off her jacket, and hung it on a handy coatrack.

Looking around, she couldn't help comparing what she saw to the place she remembered from ten years ago, when Jubal's widowed father was still alive. Seth McFarland had been something of a pack rat. When he'd lived here, ruling the house and ranch like a despot, every surface had been stacked with newspapers, old ranching magazines, bills, and catalogs, which no one except him was allowed to move. Only Jubal's room had been orderly. Now it was as if everything had been stripped bare and put in order. Coals glowed in the fireplace. Laura's senior yearbook photo in a simple silver frame was the sole adornment on the mantel. Even the book-shelves, which covered one entire wall, looked organized. Only the refrigerator, seen through the kitchen door, showed signs of clutter. It was covered with drawings, most of them on yellow notebook paper.

When Jubal shed his coat and walked into the kitchen to heat the pan of cocoa on the stove, Ellie followed him. Standing in front of the fridge, she studied the sketches, which could only be Gracie's. Most of the pictures were of animals—horses, cats, and dogs, along with a few unicorns and dragons. The figures, though imperfectly drawn, had a playful charm about them, as if they were dancing on the paper. Jubal's daughter had the makings of a talented artist.

Gracie was setting the table with cups and saucers, clearly pretending not to notice that Ellie was looking at her artwork. She glanced up as Ellie spoke her name.

"Gracie, these pictures are really good. I didn't know you liked to draw."

"I guess you never asked me," Gracie said.

"She draws a lot." Jubal poured the hot cocoa into the cups. "Not much else to do out here on cold winter nights." He pulled out a wooden chair for Ellie. "Have a seat. Sorry, no marsh-mallows."

"That's fine. I've outgrown marshmallows." Ellie sat, fitting her middle against the edge of the table. The chocolate was hot and good. The taste of it brought back the old days, when he'd made it for her in this very kitchen—with marshmallows. She almost mentioned it, but caught herself in time. The past was a closed book, better left that way.

"Oh—I just remembered something!" Gracie bounded from her chair and raced out of the kitchen. Moments later she was back with a sheet of white paper, which she handed to Ellie. "I made this for you," she said.

"Oh, my goodness!" Ellie gazed at the life-sized drawing of a little white poodle. "It looks exactly like Beau!" She spoke sincerely. Gracie had done an excellent job of capturing her dog's personality on paper. "He almost looks as if he could bark!"

"Do you like it?" Gracie asked.

"I love it. I'm going to take this home and put it somewhere special." She reached out and gave the little girl an impulsive hug. As Gracie's arms slipped around her neck, Ellie glimpsed Jubal's face. The pain and concern in his eyes cut into her like a laser. Knowing she'd crossed the line, she eased Gracie away and slipped the drawing into a side compartment of her purse. "Thank you, Gracie," she murmured.

"Finish your chocolate, Gracie." Jubal spoke in a flat voice. "Then it's time you were in bed. You've got school tomorrow."

She glanced at Ellie. "Can't I stay up just a little longer? Please?"

"Bedtime. Now. I'll come and tuck you in when you're ready." Jubal glanced at Ellie as if to say, *See what you've set in motion?*

Ellie emptied her cup and rose from her chair. "I really should be going," she said.

"No, stay. This won't take long." *We need to talk*, his expression told her. Strange, after all these years, how easily they read each other.

Gracie finished her chocolate. "Good night, Ellie," she said. "Thanks for a wonderful time."

"You're welcome," Ellie said. "I had a good time, too."

Gracie gave her a hopeful smile. "Maybe we can do it again soon."

Ellie glanced at Jubal and saw his eyes narrow. "We'll see," she said.

Jubal rose. "Brush your teeth, Gracie. I'll be there in a few minutes."

As she scurried back toward the hall, Jubal began clearing away the cups and saucers from the table. With his back to Ellie he rinsed them in the sink, along with the empty pan, and placed them in the dishwasher before turning back to face her. "I'll be right back," he said. "Don't go."

With that he strode down the hall toward Gracie's room. Ellie imagined him tucking her in, hearing her prayers. The Jubal she remembered could be sweet and tender. Was there enough of that tenderness left to spare for his daughter, or had time and grief worn it away, leaving only a hard shell of the man he'd been?

Rising, she walked back into the living room and sank into a corner of the worn leather sofa, which faced the fireplace. She felt exhausted, but her frayed nerves kept her on edge. Whatever she and Jubal had to say to each other was bound to be painful.

A few minutes later she heard the light creak of his footsteps on the hardwood floor. He came around the sofa and sat down at a comfortable distance—close enough to talk but far enough to give her space. The coals in the fireplace cast a glow over his rugged features.

"Are you cold?" he asked. "I can put another log on the fire."

She shook her head, pointing to her belly with a feeble laugh. "Don't bother. I've got a furnace in here. The house looks nice, by the way."

"Not much different. Just cleared out some." He leaned forward, hands resting on his knees as he gazed into the fireplace. "How've you been, Ellie?"

"How've I been?" The irony of his question struck her. She shook her head. "Since you're probably wondering, I might as well tell you the whole story. I married a man I met in law school—didn't finish myself because he had a great offer from a firm in San Francisco. Lived the good life for a few years—fancy condo, cars, clothes, high society. Then I found out he was cheating. I went through counseling with him, trying to make it work. Even after I'd filed for divorce, I let him talk me into a trial reconciliation. It only lasted a few weeks, but"—she glanced down at her bulging middle—"as you see."

"The jerk left you pregnant?" Jubal actually sounded angry.

"Not quite. By the time I found out I was expecting, he'd already married the current love of his life. I never told him about the baby. He still doesn't know."

"Is that wise?" He studied her, eyes narrowing. "The man has a responsibility—"

"I'm aware of that. But he doesn't deserve this child. And I don't want him in our lives. I can raise my little girl on my own."

"Having pretty much done that myself, all I can do is wish you luck. Being a single parent can be tough."

"Ben told me about your wife's accident. What an awful tragedy for you and Gracie. I'm so sorry, Jubal."

He leaned back into the couch, stretching his long legs out in front of him. His cowboy boots were scuffed and worn beneath the frayed hem of his jeans. This was a man who worked hard, with no need for vain trappings. He was who he was, no excuses, no apologies. Until now Ellie had never realized how much she respected him for that.

"I remember Laura from school," Ellie said. "She was a lovely girl—the perfect wife for you. I did you a favor by leaving."

"Did you?" He didn't look at her. "It's been four years since the accident. It's like it happened yesterday. There's not a morning goes by when I don't look at Gracie leaving for school and wish her mother was there to fuss over her and send her off looking pretty."

"But you've done a fine job with her. She's bright, caring, and respectful. And I get the impression she knows how to take care of herself." Ellie could scarcely believe it. They were talking, almost like old friends. But something told her this truce was too fragile to last.

Jubal gazed into the dying fire. He hadn't expected to enjoy having Ellie here, sharing his couch and catching him up on her life. He found himself wanting her to stay. But that wasn't going to happen—especially after she heard what he needed to say. Turning toward her, he forced himself to begin.

"Gracie's a tough little girl. But losing a mother is something no child survives without emotional scars. She was four when it happened—old enough to remember. She puts on a brave face, but that loss cut deep. It's made her hungry for a woman's affection—and set her up to get her heart broken."

Restless, he rose and stood looking down at her. "I won't see my daughter hurt again. That's why I'm asking you to back off. The more time you let Gracie spend with you and your dog, the more devastated she'll be when you leave. And you will leave, Ellie. You were never meant for Branding Iron. Nobody knows that better than I do."

Ellie didn't reply. She sat looking up at him, her face hauntingly beautiful in the firelight. He could almost imagine cupping that face between his hands, then bending down to brush her lips with his—except that a brush-kiss wouldn't be enough. Pregnant and all, damn the consequences, he wanted to devour her.

"Maybe you should think about getting married again, Jubal," she said. "Gracie told me there'd been ladies coming around—with cookies and meat loaf, she said. Surely there's at least one woman out there who could be a good wife to you and a loving mother to your little girl."

"As I recall, you said something along those lines ten years ago. 'Find yourself another girl to marry—a girl who'll be happy sharing your life.'"

A little smile played around her lips. "I did say that. And you found one. Are you afraid to try your luck again?"

Turning away from her, Jubal stared into the glowing bed of coals. He'd loved Laura, but theirs had been a practical kind of love, steady and solid, nothing like the breathless highs he'd known with Ellie. Lord, he'd never find anything like that blazing teenage passion again—and probably shouldn't try. He wasn't a high school kid anymore. At his stage in life, a homemade supper on the table and a warm bed at night ought to be enough.

But even that was more than he could offer a woman now.

"Well?" She was still looking up at him, waiting for his reply. As Jubal searched for a clever retort, something snapped inside him.

"Blast it, Ellie, don't push me!" He sank onto

the couch, cursing under his breath. "This isn't a good time to ask!"

"What is it, Jubal?" The weight of her hand on his shoulder was no more than the brush of a bird's wing. But he felt it in a deep place where no one but Ellie had ever touched him.

He'd sworn to keep his troubles to himself, but the story came spilling out—his father's mismanagement, his plans for the ranch, and the shocking discovery he'd made at the bank.

"The work I've done, the debts I've paid off, the things I've gone without—worse, the things *Gracie* has gone without. It's all been for the sake of a miserable piece of land I don't even own."

"You're sure?" Ellie's dark eyes were wells of sympathy—the last thing Jubal wanted from her. He was already wishing he'd kept quiet. Now it was too late for that.

"I checked the deed in the recorder's office. This ranch belongs to some outfit called Shumway and Sons Property Management. My father signed away the property the year before he passed. I might've paid more attention, but it happened right after Laura's accident. I was dealing with other things."

"And your father could do that? Sell the property without your signature?"

Jubal remembered then that Ellie had gone to law school. "The ranch was part of a family trust," he said. "As long as he was alive, my father, as trustee, had control. Yes, he could sell it or give it away or whatever the hell he wanted to do with it." Jubal raked his fingers through his hair. "Sorry, I'm still in shock. I know I've got to fight this. But right now I don't even know who or what I'm fighting. I've tried to learn more about the new owners, but it's like they don't exist—or maybe don't want to be found."

"That makes sense if they did something illegal to get the land."

"I've thought of that. But I've got no proof. I've got nothing."

"What I don't understand is why you're still here. Why hasn't the new owner evicted you and taken over the ranch?"

Jubal exhaled wearily. "I've thought about that, too. The best explanation I can come up with is that they're holding the property as an investment, hoping that, for whatever reason, the value will go up. If that's the case, it would be to their advantage to have somebody working the place."

"What about property taxes?"

"They're set up on autopay from the ranch account. And they've been paid every year. Evidently the new owners have no problem with my taking care of those."

"That's monstrous, Jubal."

"It's business. And I didn't invite you in to talk about it. It's my problem, not yours."

"Gracie doesn't know?"

"I'm hoping I can clear up this mess without having to tell her we're homeless." He stood, holding out his hand to help her up. "Come on, it's time you were getting home. I've burdened you enough."

She took his hand, her fingers silky smooth against his roughened palm as he pulled her to her feet. "I haven't forgotten what you told me about Gracie," she said. "Believe me, I understand. I don't want to hurt her either. I'll try to distance myself."

"Thanks." He walked her to the door and lifted her quilted jacket off the rack. As he held it open, so she could slip her arms into the sleeves, her subtle fragrance rose from the fabric—not perfume, only Ellie, creeping into his senses just as he remembered.

Her shoulder-length hair was twisted up and anchored with a clip, exposing the nape of her graceful neck. The urge to lean close and press his lips to her soft, white skin was so powerful that he almost groaned out loud. But he managed to control himself as he pulled the jacket up into place. "I'll walk you to your car," he said. "The front steps could be slippery."

"Thanks, I wouldn't want to take a tumble." She let him balance her as they crossed the porch. Partway down the steps, her foot slipped on an icy spot. With a little gasp, she pitched forward. Catching her shoulders, Jubal managed to stop her fall, but the move swung her around hard to face him.

For a heart-stopping moment, they froze, her parted lips a finger's breadth from his. *It would be so easy, so tempting to kiss her,* Jubal thought. But he knew better. One kiss would never be enough. Give in to his urges, and he'd be walking into a minefield of trouble—more trouble than he needed.

He found his voice. "Are you all right, Ellie?"

She nodded. Something glimmered in her eye. Was it a tear or just the reflected light from the porch? "Just a little shaky, that's all," she said.

"Will you be all right to drive home?"

"I'll be fine as soon as my nerves settle. I could've had a bad fall just now."

"Here, take my arm again." A dry wind had sprung out of the west. It whipped tendrils of hair around her face as he eased her down the remaining steps, saw her to her car, and opened the door. She slid her body carefully behind the wheel and fastened the seat belt low on her lap.

"Thank you for catching me." The car's dome light cast her face into stark light and shadow. She looked pale and tired, he thought.

"Be safe. Call me if you need anything. I mean it." Jubal closed the door. With his back to the biting wind, he watched as she turned the sleek car around and drove out of the gate. Had he overstepped, inviting her to call him? She'd looked so vulnerable that he'd felt the need to say it. Not that she'd ever take him up on it. She had family to take care of her, including a brother who was the county sheriff. Forget it, Jubal told himself. Ellie would be fine.

But something else was gnawing at him. By the time her taillights vanished down the lane, he was already regretting what he'd revealed to her about the ranch.

Why hadn't he kept his mouth shut? His problems were nobody's business but his own. But tonight the story had come pouring out of him. Now Ellie knew about the trouble—and if she mentioned it to anybody, the story would soon be all over town. And even if she didn't, it would color what she thought of him.

In the old days, he'd shared almost everything with her—his clashes with his father, his desire to improve the ranch and make it more productive, and his worries about the future. Back then they'd been more than just teenage lovers; they'd been good friends who could talk for hours about anything. Maybe that was why it had felt so natural to open up with her.

But it was no way to impress a sophisticated woman like Ellie. Maybe he should've put on an act—told her how well his plans were going and how much money the ranch was bringing in. But Ellie was no fool. One look around the place, and she'd have known it was all a lie. But even that would've been better than having her feel sorry for him.

Turning, he headed back up the steps and went inside. Tonight he would spend more hours online, searching for whatever he could find in the way of county records, tax lists, complaints to consumer agencies, trust laws—any clue that might lead to something he could use. So far he'd found nothing. But he couldn't afford to give up. There was too much at stake—including his future and his daughter's.

Christmas was only a few weeks off. If he

couldn't find a way out of this mess by then, there wouldn't be much to celebrate.

After checking both ways for oncoming headlights, Ellie pulled onto the main road and headed back to town. At this hour there was little traffic, but then, Branding Iron wasn't exactly known for its night life.

Clouds had darkened the face of the moon. Vaguely nervous, she switched her headlights to high beam and turned up the radio, which was still playing Christmas music. "Here Comes Santa Claus" boomed out of the BMW's state-of-the-art speakers. She tried singing along, as she had with Gracie, but soon gave up and switched the radio off. She wasn't in the mood. Her thoughts were with Jubal.

Seeing him tonight, talking like friends, had brought back the memory of old times and how good things had been between them. But they were different people now. She was about to have her ex-husband's baby. He was a single father struggling to save his ranch. The idea of anything more than friendship between them— if even that—was unthinkable.

So why had the thought crossed her mind?

She remembered the night of her high school graduation—the night Jubal had proposed. He'd been her date for the senior party, and afterward they'd driven out to one of their favorite spots, a wooded rise overlooking the moonlit sweep of the open plain. She'd already been admitted to the University of Texas and planned to leave for Austin that summer to find a job and, hopefully, an apartment with room-mates before school started in the fall. It was an option Jubal didn't have. His only choice was to stay in Branding Iron and help his father work the ranch.

They'd snuggled and kissed. Then, to her sur-prise, he'd taken a small velvet box out of his pocket and opened it to reveal a diamond en-gagement ring. The stone was tiny, but Ellie had known it had probably drained his meager sav-ings to buy it. She'd been moved almost to tears, but even before he spoke, she'd known what her answer would be.

"Say you'll wear this and come back to me, Ellie," he'd said. "I know you want an education, but for however long it takes, I'll be waiting for you. There'll never be anyone else for me."

Then she had broken his heart.

Something flashed in front of her—a deer, then another one, leaping into her headlights. Her foot groped for the brake. No way to stop in time. Instinctively she wrenched the wheel to the right. The car swung onto the graveled shoulder and kept going. Like a slow-motion nightmare, it careened down into the low barrow pit and crunched to a cornerwise stop against a steel fence post.

# Chapter 6

Ellie groaned as the shock wore off. The car was motionless and oddly slanted. Through the windows she could hear the howl of wind. Tree branches, bare of their leaves, lashed against the night sky.

*The baby!* Panic surged through her as she laid a hand on her belly. A healthy thump eased her fear. Thank heaven she'd read that article about how to wear a seat belt during pregnancy.

The accident had happened so fast that her memory was a blur. She recalled seeing the deer and swerving off the road. Then there was out-of-control motion, a sharp lurch, and a crash. Except for where she'd ended up, it was hard to believe it had been real.

She moved her hands, her arms, and legs. Everything seemed to work. But the sense of unreality lingered, as if she were about to wake up and discover that she'd been dreaming.

With luck, maybe her car would be all right. The air bags hadn't deployed. But the engine had stopped and the vehicle was tipped at a low angle toward the passenger side. The headlights were still on, so at least the battery was working. Maybe, if the car would start, she could manage to back out onto level ground and drive home.

After turning off the lights to save the battery, she shifted into neutral, switched the ignition off, then on again, and cranked the starter. The powerful engine purred to life. *So far, so good.* Everything was going to be fine, Ellie told herself.

Shifting into reverse, she floored the gas pedal. The engine roared. Wheels spun, tires screamed. The car didn't budge. With a sigh, she turned off the ignition and sank back in the seat.

Now what? It made sense to get out and look at the damage. But if she wanted to get out of the tipped car, she would have to push the door open and hold it against the wind while she crawled upward to get out. Ordinarily that wouldn't have been a problem. But with the added bulk of her belly, she could easily fall to the ground or get stuck partway. And even if she could make it out, what could she do except look? With bitter wind whistling around the car, her best option would be to stay inside and call for help.

Nine-one-one would get her the dispatcher in Cottonwood Springs, who would probably relay the message to Ben or one of his deputies. Sooner or later, somebody would show up. But she wasn't hurt, just stuck. And what if answering her call kept the responders from somebody's real life-or-death emergency?

Jubal was minutes away. His truck should be able to pull her car back onto the road. Things were still touchy between them, but there was nothing to do but swallow her pride and call him.

Her purse had fallen against the far door. Unfastening her seat belt, she reached across the seats, grabbed it, and fumbled inside for her phone.

As her fingers closed around it, the reality of the crash hit like a thunderclap. Dropping the phone in her lap, Ellie pressed her hands to her face. Her body shook as her nerves unraveled.


Jubal was at his computer, searching state corporate records for Shumway and Sons, and finding nothing, when his cell phone rang. His pulse skipped when he saw the caller ID.

"Ellie? Is that you? Are you all right?" He could've kicked himself for sounding so anxious.

"More or less." She didn't sound all right. He could sense the fragility in her voice. "I ran my car off the road to keep from hitting some deer. Now I seem to be . . . stuck."

"Where are you?"

"A couple of miles past the turnoff." She was making an effort to sound calm. "I can start the car, but it won't budge. I should probably get out and look at it, but it's cold, and I don't know if I can climb out by myself."

"Do you smell gasoline?" A picture flashed through Jubal's mind—Ellie's BMW exploding in flame with her trapped inside. "If you do, get out now."

There was a moment of silence. "I don't smell anything."

"And you're not hurt?"

"Not as far as I can tell."

"Then stay put. I'll be right there."

"Oh—bring a tow chain if you've got one."

Jubal ended the call and went for his keys and coat. He'd need to tell Gracie he was going. It would be a shame to disturb her, but he couldn't risk her waking up to find him gone. Even a note could be missed.

Leaning over the bed, he nudged her shoulder. She stirred and opened her eyes.

"Honey, I've got to go out for a while. Ellie just called. She's having car trouble. I'll be back as soon as I can."

"Is Ellie okay?" She pushed onto one elbow.

"She's fine. Just stuck. Go back to sleep."

Gracie lay back on the pillow and closed her eyes. She was accustomed to staying alone when Jubal was out during the calving season or when other ranch emergencies called him away at night. In case she needed to reach him, she had a cell phone by her bed. She would be fine.

Jubal buttoned his coat and shoved a pair of leather work gloves in the pockets. After locking the front and back doors, he went out to the shed and loaded the tow chain into the back of his truck. The rest of his tools, along with a good flashlight, were already there. Moments later he was flying down the graveled lane toward the main road.

By now it was almost 9:00, the dark roadway all but empty of traffic. After making the turn, Jubal slowed the truck and drove at a crawl along the right-hand shoulder of the road. Ellie had mentioned she was only a couple of miles past the turnoff. He should be able to find her in the next few minutes.

As he drove, the memory of another accident rose in Jubal's mind: the twisted heap of wreckage that had been Laura's car, the sirens, the flashing lights, the ambulance . . .

Ellie had told him she wasn't hurt. But what if she was? What if something had happened to her baby? Jubal's jaw tightened as he spotted the dark shape of the BMW below the road. He stomped the brake hard. Grabbing the flashlight, he jumped to the ground and strode down the slope. The cold wind raked his hair and whipped the old sheepskin coat, which had been his father's, against his body.

As he approached, the driver's side window rolled down. The flashlight beam took in the tipped car and Ellie's pale, frightened face. "Are you all right?"

"Fine . . . I think." Her voice was unsteady but she managed a feeble smile. "Thanks for showing up. I'll need a hand getting out of this car."

"Come on." Setting the flashlight down, he

opened the door, bracing it against the wind. Clutching her purse with her right hand, she offered him her left. He pulled as she squeezed out from under the steering wheel, worked her feet around to the opening, and climbed out onto the grassy slope. Her quilted jacket was too thin for the weather. As the cold wind struck her, she shivered.

"Here." Jubal shrugged out of his sheepskin coat and wrapped it around her. She was still shaking. He felt a little shaky himself. Only now did he realize how scared he'd been for her.

Without conscious intent, his arms went around her. Still quivering, she nestled close. Years had passed, but holding her felt as natural as it had in the old days. Even with her rounded shape between them, she seemed to fit in all the ways he remembered.

He ached with the urge to bend his head and warm her chilled lips with his. But that would be a bad idea. He and Ellie had traveled too far, in opposite directions, to go back to where they'd once been.

"You're sure you're all right?" he asked.

She looked up at him, her dark eyes melting into shadows. "I'm fine now. Just shaken up, that's all."

"And the baby? Do we need to get you to the hospital?"

Without a word, Ellie took his hand and moved it downward beneath the coat to rest low on her belly. Jubal felt flutter kicks against his palm, followed by a solid thump. He struggled to keep his emotions in check.

"Frisky little thing, isn't she?" he said. "But I still think you ought to get checked at the clinic in the morning."

"Good idea." She drew away from him with a nervous laugh. "Right now, let's see about getting my car out of here. Did you bring the tow chain?"

"I did, but it might not be enough. Let's take a look."

Wind bit through Jubal's flannel shirt as he picked up the flashlight and walked around to the low passenger side of the car. It didn't look good. The right front fender had crumpled against the solid fence post. The wheel trapped beneath it was bent at a cockeyed angle, the tire flat and peeled partway off the rim.

"It doesn't look good." He used the flashlight beam to show Ellie the damage. She muttered a few choice curses under her breath—that, too, was the Ellie he remembered.

"Even if I could pull your car out, you wouldn't be able to drive it," Jubal said. "For now, let me take you home. In the morning you can call Silas to pick it up with his tow truck. Your insurance should cover the tow and repair."

It was good advice. Silas Parker, who'd run Branding Iron's only garage and body shop for the past twenty years, was as honest as he was capable. Ellie knew she could trust him.

She swore again, then sighed. "All right. Would

you get Beau's booster basket for me? If I have to rent another car, I'll need it. It's hanging on the back of the passenger seat.

"Sure. But let's get you into the truck first."

"Take your coat." She slipped Jubal's sheepskin coat off her shoulders and handed it to him.

"Thanks." The coat held her warmth and her aroma. He helped her into the truck, retrieved the dog's booster basket, and headed for town.

On the road, Ellie was silent. Jubal thought about turning on the radio but neither of them would be in the mood for Christmas music.

As the Christmas lights on Main Street came into view, she finally spoke. "My car is a BMW, Jubal. How am I going to get it fixed around here?"

"Don't underestimate Silas," Jubal said. "It might take time to get your parts, but he's got connections. If he can get the fender and wheel components from a junkyard, it'll save you time, and any money over what your insurance will pay. And you know Silas. His work will be first rate."

"Could I get it fixed in Cottonwood Springs?"

"I wouldn't bet on it. You'd probably have to haul it to a bigger city. They could put you through the wringer and you'd never know what they'd done to your car or where the parts came from. But Silas would never cheat you. He'd probably even lend you one of the loaners he keeps around so you won't have to go to the hassle and expense of renting a car. Think about it."

"I will. Thanks." She touched his shoulder as they turned onto her street. Jubal felt the contact like a gentle electric spark through his coat. He cursed silently. Against his better judgment, he was letting the woman get to him.

He pulled into her driveway, climbed out of the truck, and went around to open her door. She took the arm he offered to help her to the ground. Wind whipped around them as they stood face to face.

"One thing, Ellie," he said. "What I told you about losing the ranch. Let's keep that information private for now, all right?"

She nodded, clutching her jacket around her. "But if you talked to Ben, he might be able to help you."

"I'm not talking to anybody yet. Not until I know more about what happened and who's responsible. Understand?"

"I do. Not a word." Her teeth were chattering. "I'd invite you in, but I know you need to get home to Gracie."

"Sure." Again, he resisted the crazy urge to pull her into his arms and kiss her until the past ten years vanished into nothing. "Now get inside before you freeze."

She turned and fled toward the porch. Jubal watched until she was safely in the house. Then he climbed back into the truck and headed out of town.

*Damn! Damn! Damn!*

He would never have chosen to have Ellie

back in his life. In the old days, she'd led him on for a couple of years, telling him she loved him, and proving it in ways every boy dreams of. She'd let him believe she was his for life. Then, just like that, she'd stomped his heart to dust under her feet, packed her things, and left.

Now here she was again, with her fancy car and big-city ways, her silly fluff of a dog, and another man's baby in her belly. The crazy thing was, it felt as if she'd never left.

The woman was reeling him in like a fish on a line, with her beauty, her damned vulnerability, and all the little ways she'd gotten to him in the past. But this time he was wise to her. She'd humiliated him once. If he let her, she'd do it again. But that wasn't going to happen. He was smarter and tougher now, and he had more pressing concerns than Ellie and her problems.

No more, Jubal vowed as he turned down the lane to the ranch. He and Ellie were history—over and done.

After her appointment, Ellie crossed the clinic parking lot to the space where she'd left the purple '95 Ford Escort with the dented bumper and mismatched door. The loaner car Silas had given her to drive was no prize, but it ran, and the good man wasn't charging her for the use of it. She'd already named it the Purple People Eater after the old fifties song.

The hinges squawked as she opened the door and squeezed her body onto the threadbare

seat. Beggars couldn't be choosers, she reminded herself. At least the aging Ford was getting her where she needed to go. Still, on this,
the second day she'd driven it, she'd found herself slumping in the seat in the hope that nobody would recognize her. Fat chance of that.
The good folks of Branding Iron must already
be wagging their tongues and laughing. Ellie
Marsden, who'd driven into town with her fancy
car and her nose in the air, had clearly come
down in the world.

Even Beau, when she'd taken him out for a
ride, had seemed to know that something wasn't
right. Instead of his usual pawing against the
window and barking at every dog he saw, he'd
hunkered down in his booster basket, peering
over the edge as if ashamed to be seen.

She shifted into neutral and cranked the
starter. The old engine fired right up. It ran
fine, despite a noisy muffler that announced her
coming a block away. But Ellie hadn't driven a
stick shift since the days when Jubal had taught
her how on his old pickup. She'd ground the
gears a few times before getting the hang of it
once more.

At least, on her follow-up visit to the clinic,
she and the baby had checked out all right. Dr.
Ramirez's chattiness might have crossed the
boundaries of professional conduct, but for Ellie,
the friendly patter was a welcome change from
the impersonal manner of most city doctors.

*"Say hello to the* mango *for me."* As she drove up
Main Street, Ellie remembered the doctor's teas-

ing farewell. But it didn't appear she'd be saying hello to Jubal anytime soon. She hadn't heard from him, or from Gracie, since Monday night. It was surprising how much she already missed them. But Gracie would be in school, she reminded herself. And Jubal would be dealing with the loss of his ranch. If only she could find a way to help him. But how could she even begin, when he'd ordered her to keep his secret?

Main Street was aglow with old-style Christmas lights, probably the same ones Ellie remembered from her girlhood. Tinsel draped the shop windows, and Christmas carols boomed from a hidden speaker somewhere. Ellie could hear "Deck the Halls" through the crack at the top of the passenger side window. There could be no escape from Christmas in Branding Iron.

Silas's garage was just off Main Street. Ellie parked and went in to check on her BMW. She found it up on a rack, the fender and wheel removed.

"I've got good news and bad news." Silas was tall and lanky, with graying hair, a long jaw, and an easygoing manner. "The good news is, I've located a wrecked car, in Wichita Falls, same make, model, and color as yours. The wheel and fender you need are in good shape, and the price should be fair—cash up front, but you said that wouldn't be a problem."

"And the bad news?" Ellie asked.

"They're backed up on orders. It'll take a couple of weeks to get them here, and at least a week for me to get the work done—that's if they send all the parts and they all work."

Ellie sighed. "So you think, maybe, by Christmas?"

"Maybe. I'll do my best." Silas rubbed the back of his neck. The creases in his fingers were stained black with oil. *Never trust a mechanic with spotless hands,* Ellie remembered her father saying.

"That old Ford workin' okay for you?" he asked.

"Fine. It gets me around."

"You let me know if you have any trouble with it." His gaze flickered to her belly for an instant. "Wouldn't want a lady like you gettin' stuck somewhere at the wrong time."

Ellie thanked him and left. Silas was honest to the bone, but he couldn't work miracles. Since, as she'd learned, the only car rental agency in Cottonwood Springs had gone out of business, she would just have to make do with the Purple People Eater a few weeks longer.

One errand remained. Her mother needed a prescription picked up at the Shop Mart pharmacy. She turned back onto Main Street and headed south to the big-box store at the far end of town.

It was barely midmorning, but with a big holiday sale going on, the parking lot was already crowded. Ellie took the only spot she could find, in the last row. The walk would do her good, she told herself. And at least, this time, she shouldn't have any trouble finding her car.

She was just closing the car door when a voice called her name. She turned to see a woman in a fur-trimmed leather coat loading groceries into the back of a late-model SUV.

"My stars! Is that really you, Ellie?"

The woman, a classmate from high school, had dyed her hair and gained a few pounds, but the voice was unmistakable.

"Krystle!" Ellie remembered the name just in time. The two of them had never been friends. In fact, Ellie had once suspected Krystle Martin of spreading some vicious gossip about her. But that was in the past. No reason not to be friendly now.

Krystle's green eyes took in Ellie's car and her expanded waistline. "My goodness, Ellie, I never expected to see you back in Branding Iron. Last I heard of you, you'd left us for the good life in San Francisco. What a surprise!"

*Surprise, my foot!* Ellie thought. Unless Krystle had changed, she'd be up on the latest dirt and eager to spread more. "You're looking good, Krystle," she said. "How have you been?"

"Oh, just dandy! I married Phil Remington—he owns the Chrysler dealership in Cottonwood Springs, but we both wanted to raise our family here, in his parents' old home—you know what a lovely place that is. We have two girls and a boy." She gave Ellie's middle a look that couldn't be missed. "Your first?"

"That's right."

"And you plan to keep it?"

"Of course I do." Ellie felt a rising prickle of annoyance. "Just so you won't need to ask, the baby's father is my ex-husband."

"Oh!" Krystle's eyebrows went up. Evidently this was news, more grist for the gossip mill.

"And the car's a loaner from Silas, while my BMW is in the shop." Ellie could have kicked herself. Why should she need to justify herself to this woman?

"You probably know Jubal McFarland is widowed," Krystle said. "The two of you were pretty hot and heavy back in the day. Any plans to get together?"

It was the last straw. "Right now my only plan is to have my baby. Nice to see you again, Krystle. Now if you'll excuse me, I have errands to run." Clutching her purse, Ellie hurried off toward the store.

"Merry Christmas!" Krystle called after her. Ellie pretended not to hear. If this was the kind of reception she could expect from the good people of Branding Iron, maybe coming back had been a mistake.

But with a baby on the way and no one else to be there for her, where could she have gone except home?


Jubal faced the loan officer across his polished walnut desk. "All I'm asking for is your help," he said. "I need to talk with the people who bought the ranch—maybe I can make some kind of deal with them, or at the very least find out why my father sold it. But I've searched every record I can find, and there's no trace of a Shumway and Sons Property Management. There must be something you can tell me."

Clive Huish shook his balding head. Middle-aged, with faded blue eyes, a ruddy face, and a thickening middle, he'd married a Branding Iron girl, settled in Wichita Falls, then moved to his wife's hometown six years ago. Since then he'd become one of the town's leading citizens. He'd even run for mayor in the last election, but lost.

"Sorry, Jubal, but I don't know any more than you do," he said. "We didn't find out about the transfer until we checked the title before approving your loan. It was almost as much of a shock to us as it must've been to you."

"Was there a title company involved? They'd have to know."

Huish shrugged. "Not necessarily. If the title was clear, a witness and a notarized signature would've been enough. I'm a notary myself. But I know I didn't notarize your dad's signature. If I had, I would certainly have remembered."

"And you don't have a copy of the bill of sale?"

"All we have is a copy of the registered deed from the county recorder. You've seen that."

Jubal stood, reining in the frustration that seethed like a volcano inside him. "Then I guess I'll just have to keep looking," he said. "Believe me, I'm not done with this, and I'm not giving up."

He left through the bank lobby, forcing himself not to punch the front door on his way out. All his instincts told him a criminal wrong had been committed. But without proof, he was nowhere. Anytime they chose to, the ranch's new owners could evict him from the land without notice.

Somewhere there had to be an answer—or at least a clue that would give him a leg up on the truth. He'd learned nothing online, at the recorder's office, or at the bank. He had sorted through the papers in the office alcove and had yet to find anything helpful. The one place left to look was the mountain of letters, invoices, receipts, and miscellaneous paperwork he'd emptied out of his father's desk and boxed away. The search would be long and tedious. But it was his last, best hope.

He walked to his truck, the fresh air chilling his face. From farther down Main Street, the loudspeaker was playing "White Christmas." Jubal didn't feel much like Christmas today. In fact, he hadn't felt like Christmas since Laura's accident. For Gracie's sake, he'd gone through the motions, but his heart hadn't been in it. This year would be even more dismal, knowing it might be the last Christmas on the ranch where he'd grown up and had planned to spend the rest of his life.

He drove down Main Street beneath strings of twinkling lights. This morning, before catching the school bus, Gracie had asked him again when they were going to get a Christmas tree.

Preoccupied with his own worries, he'd put her off. A year ago they'd waited too long and had to settle for the last scrawny tree on the lot. Gracie had done her best to smile as they decorated the crooked, needle-shedding pine. But he knew she'd been disappointed.

The truck's front tire crunched through a frozen pothole, jarring Jubal's thoughts back to the present. Losing the ranch wasn't just his own tragedy, he reminded himself. It was Gracie's, too. If they were forced to move, she'd even have to give up Jocko, her beloved horse. Damn it, it was time he stopped feeling sorry for himself and thought about his little girl, who deserved better than a half-dead stick of a tree and a father who could barely manage a smile. If this was to be their last Christmas on the ranch—or even if it wasn't—he would make it the best ever. His heart might not be in it, but he would do it. Whatever it took, he would give Gracie a Christmas to remember.

# Chapter 7

Jubal had planned to stop at Shop Mart on the way out of town. He needed a few groceries. Picking them up now would save him a trip later on.

He'd left the truck and was crossing the crowded parking lot when Ellie came out of the store. Today she'd worn her hair loose. It fluttered like dark silk as she paused to gaze out over the sea of vehicles.

She hadn't seen him yet. If he was smart, he'd stay back and just let her leave. But he hadn't heard from her since Monday night and, truth be told, she'd been on his mind far too often. He was curious to know what she'd done about her car, and there was a favor he'd meant to ask of her. Running into her now, by chance, would be less awkward than a phone call.

She caught sight of him walking toward her. A smile brightened her face. "Hi," she said.

"How's the car?" He felt like a fool kid at his first dance.

She laughed, the same laugh he remembered. "My carriage has been transformed into a pumpkin. Walk with me and I'll show you."

He fell into step with her, offering an arm to steady her on the uneven asphalt. "I saw that your car was gone from the barrow pit," he said. "Did you get Silas to tow it?"

She nodded. "He's already tracked down some parts. But it'll take a couple of weeks to get them. Meanwhile, he lent me another car to drive. Step right up, folks. Here it is."

Jubal found himself staring at the ugliest car he'd ever seen. It was painted a lurid, metallic purple with a sagging bumper and a mismatched yellow driver's-side door. Silas was known for patching up old cars to use as free loaners for his customers. This one was a masterpiece.

"I've christened it the Purple People Eater," Ellie said. "It's what I've been driving all over town."

Jubal chuckled, shaking his head. It felt good, standing here joking with her—maybe *too* good. "There are no words," he said. "Your reputation is made."

She giggled. "Yes, I'll be known as the purple pregnant lady forever."

"Or at least for as long as you stay in Branding Iron." And she wouldn't be staying long, Jubal reminded himself. "While you're here, I could use your help with something—Gracie's hair."

"Is something wrong with her hair?"

"Not really wrong. But she loved that braid you did so much that she tried not to sleep on it Monday night so it would look nice for school the next day. This morning she tried to fix her hair that way again. She couldn't do it. She wound up in tears and had to go to school with her hair in pigtails again."

Jubal sighed, remembering. At the time, he'd found himself wishing Ellie had left his daughter's hair alone. But then he'd realized how pleased Gracie had been with her new look and how confident it had made her feel. "I was hoping you could show her how to do the braid herself," he said.

"I'd be happy to try," Ellie said. "But it won't be that easy for Gracie to braid her own hair. It was my mother, not me, who French-braided Gracie's hair. She used to do my hair that way when I was in school. I know how to do it—I used to braid my friends' hair. But I never could fix my own hair that way. I'd try, but it never went right. Something tells me Gracie would have the same problem."

"Too bad. She'll be disappointed. But at least I can tell her I asked you."

Ellie studied him, a thoughtful smile on her face. "I can think of one way this would work. I could teach *you* how to French-braid Gracie's hair."

"Me?" Jubal choked on his own surprise. "I can't braid hair!"

She grinned. "Sure you can. Remember that summer when we braided your mare's mane and tail for the July Fourth parade? It's the same idea."

"That was a long time ago. And I'm not a damned hairdresser."

"No, you're the solo parent of a sweet little girl. And learning to do her hair would be an act of love."

She had him, roped and tied. "I guess it wouldn't hurt to try," he said. "But don't expect much."

"You'll be fine. When do you want the lesson?"

"How about we invite you to dinner tonight at the ranch? Gracie would be over the moon to see you. Six o'clock?"

"Fine. I'll watch out for deer on the road. And I won't forget what you told me."

Jubal's mind went blank for an instant; then he realized she was talking about his admonition not to encourage Gracie's friendship. "Thanks, I appreciate that," he said.

"Six, then." She climbed into the Purple People Eater and started the engine. The muffler growled as she pulled out of the parking slot.

Jubal watched her drive away. Only Ellie could pull off a car like that with so much class. Even pregnant, she was out of his league. Not that he was in the market—and even if he were, it wouldn't be Ellie. Branding Iron might be a temporary refuge for her. But she was a city woman, elegant, sophisticated, and accustomed to the best.

So what would be up to her standard for din-

ner? Lobster? Coq au vin? Never mind, Ellie
would have to settle for pot roast with carrots
and potatoes. It wouldn't be fancy, but he knew
how to make it good.

Was he doing the right thing, inviting Ellie
back into his life, and into his daughter's? Ellie
Marsden was a package of heartbreak tied with
an elegant silk bow. But right now his lonely little daughter needed something more than he
could give her.

Whether he liked it or not, maybe that something was Ellie.

It was dark by the time Ellie turned onto the
graveled lane and headed for Jubal's ranch.
She'd driven with care, keeping a sharp lookout
for deer. So far, she'd seen none.

"I guess no self-respecting deer would risk
being hit by the Purple People Eater," she said
out loud. "What do you think, Beau?"

Hunkered in his booster basket, the tiny poodle gave her a nervous yip. He wasn't much for
dark roads and old cars steeped in unfamiliar
smells. But Ellie knew that if danger threatened
he would spring to protect her.

Bringing Beau along had been a last-minute
decision. She hadn't asked Jubal for his approval. But Gracie would love seeing the little
dog, and Beau would enjoy the attention she lav-
ished on him.

Back in San Francisco, good manners would
have required that she bring a bottle of wine to a

dinner party. Since that wasn't practical tonight, Ellie had whipped up a batch of chocolate chip cookies that afternoon. It had been a long time since she'd baked anything from scratch, but her mother's old recipe was as tasty as ever.

As she pulled up to the porch, Jubal came outside to open her car door. She handed him the box of cookies, tucked her purse under the seat, and lifted Beau out of his basket.

Jubal raised an eyebrow. "You didn't tell me you were bringing a guest."

"Sorry, I didn't think you'd mind. You know how Gracie loves him." Ellie climbed out of the car and locked the door with the key, which she put in her pocket.

"Yes, I know. She's been wanting a little dog for a long time. I might give it some thought as a Christmas present, but the timing isn't right."

His eyes met hers, and she caught the flash of pain and worry in them. Gracie wouldn't know about his struggle to salvage the family ranch, or what would happen if the mysterious new owners chose to take possession.

"Come on in," he said, offering his arm. "Dinner's almost ready. I hope you like pot roast."

"I love it." She inhaled the aroma that drifted through the open front door. "If it tastes as good as it smells, I'll be in heaven."

"Careful." His free hand steadied her going up the front steps.

"You make me feel like an invalid—or a very old woman," Ellie said.

"Sorry, but nothing's going to happen to that baby, or to you, on my watch."

That was true, Ellie remembered. Jubal had always kept her safe. No one else had ever made her feel so protected.

Gracie came bounding in from the kitchen, where she'd finished setting the table. Tonight there was a blue tablecloth with carefully folded cloth napkins and nice white dishes that matched.

"Hey, you brought Beau!" She reached out and took the little poodle from Ellie's arms for a frenzy of wagging, licking, petting, and giggling.

Jubal had taken Ellie's coat to hang on the rack. Now he stood in the entrance to the kitchen watching his daughter, his expression a stoic mask.

"Can I help with dinner?" Ellie asked.

"There's not much to do except put the food on," Jubal said. "I can do that. Gracie, you'll need to wash your hands."

Still holding Beau, Gracie turned to Ellie. "Can I put him on the floor?"

"Sure. But you might want to close the doors to places where he shouldn't go. He likes to explore." Taking her cue, Ellie followed Gracie into the bathroom to wash her hands as well. "Thank you for having me here tonight," she said.

"I hope you like dinner." Gracie rinsed her hands and dried them on the towel. "My dad's a pretty good cook, but I made the salad."

"I'm betting it will be wonderful." Ellie washed

and followed Gracie back to the living room, where they found Beau happily sniffing out a corner behind the rocking chair. The crackling blaze in the fireplace lent a warm glow to the plain room with its timbered ceiling and time-worn furnishings. *Cozy.* That was the word for it, Ellie thought. Compared to this lived-in home, her San Francisco condo had been about as welcoming as the display window in a high-end furniture gallery.

"Come and get it," Jubal called from the kitchen. He'd put the pot roast, salad, and freshly warmed bakery rolls on the table. Everything looked and smelled delicious. As they took their seats, it struck Ellie how much time and effort had gone into making this meal for her. She'd sat down to plenty of lavish dinners in San Francisco, but she'd never felt more like an honored guest than she did tonight.

Was that what she wanted—to be important to this good man and his love-hungry little daughter? Or was she letting herself be drawn into a trap of her own making?

As she listened to Gracie's murmured blessing on the food, she could feel the baby kicking. An unexpected ripple of contentment swept over her. This was almost like being family, she thought.

This was what she'd run away from, far and fast, when she'd left Branding Iron ten years ago, for a different life.

Gracie's happy chatter filled what might have been awkward silences, making the meal a pleasant time. They finished off with vanilla ice cream to go with Ellie's chocolate chip cookies. Then, when the dishes were cleared away, it was time for the hair braiding lesson.

Gracie sat on a kitchen chair, holding Beau in her lap, while Ellie brushed out her hair and began the demonstration, starting at the crown of her head with a few strands and weaving in more as the single braid progressed. Jubal stood by watching, occasionally muttering and shaking his head.

Reaching the bottom of the braid, Ellie brushed it out again. "Your turn now," she said to Jubal. "You'll see. It's not that hard."

"You can do it, Dad." Gracie added her encouragement. "You can do anything."

"You start like this." Ellie stood close, guiding his big hands as she struggled to ignore the heat that the intimate contact—and the memories— stirred in her body. Little by little he began to get the knack of it. The first braid he finished was somewhat lopsided, but he had the technique down. Gracie and Ellie clapped their hands as he finished.

"I'll do better next time." His face wore a grin of accomplishment. "What do you think of it, Gracie?"

Gracie handed Beau to Ellie. Standing, she felt the braid with both hands. Then, with a happy laugh, she flung her arms around her father's waist and hugged him tight. "I'm proud of you, Dad," she said.

A rush of tears caught Ellie by surprise. She

blinked them away. She could have hugged Jubal herself, he looked so pleased—and yet the worry was there, a shadow in his eyes. With what was looming, how was he going to provide all the things his daughter would need?

"This calls for a celebration!" he said. "Ellie, how would you like to go with us to buy the prettiest, greenest Christmas tree on the lot?"

Ellie had been about to make her excuses and leave, but Gracie was jumping up and down. "Oh, please come with us, Ellie! It'll be a lot more fun with you and Beau along."

How could she not say yes?

"Of course, I'll come along." Ellie put Beau down long enough for Jubal to help her on with her coat. When all three of them were bundled up, they headed out to the truck.

The Christmas tree lot was at Hank's Hardware, on the near side of town. Ellie let Gracie hold Beau on the way, while the radio blared Christmas music—loud, with all of them singing along, the way Gracie wanted.

The tree lot was crowded with families. Ellie's heart sank as she realized that showing up with Jubal and his daughter was going to cause some talk. Jubal glanced at her as he pulled the truck up to the chicken wire fence.

"If this is going to be too much for you, you can wait in the truck," he said.

Was he talking about the strain of being on her feet too long or the discomfort of facing the towns-people? Either way, Ellie decided, it wouldn't hurt to be a good sport.

"I'll come with you," she said, tucking Beau under her coat. "If I get tired, I can always go back to the truck. Oh—and I won't plan on coming in when we get back to the ranch. By then I'll be ready to head home."

The weather was clear tonight, the breeze little more than a whisper. Ellie unbuttoned her coat far enough for Beau to stick his head out. The little poodle squirmed and whimpered, wanting to get down.

"No, you don't," Ellie told him. "Those trees aren't for you."

She glanced up to see Jubal smiling at her. "He's all dog, isn't he?" he said.

"He is," Ellie said. "And this place, with all these trees, would be heaven for him. But no way is he getting loose."

Gracie tugged her father's hand. "Come on, Dad, let's get a tree!"

Ellie let them get ahead, following at her own slower pace. All around her, the air was filled with the scent of fresh evergreens and the sounds of excitement as families searched for the perfect tree.

What would it be like, she wondered, being part of a real family with a husband and children? Christmas in San Francisco, with Brent, had been a series of parties with casual friends and business associates. Being married to him had never felt like family to her. This year . . . Ellie's gaze wandered across the lot to where Jubal was holding up a tree for his daughter's approval. They'd brought her along as a friend tonight, but she wasn't family. She didn't belong.

She'd be all right after Christmas, she told herself. The holiday would be behind her and she could look ahead to having her baby. But for now, even with her mother and Ben and Jess around, this Christmas would be fraught with loneliness and anxiety.

"Ellie! Come look!" Gracie had darted back to pull at her hand. "Come see the tree we found!"

Aware of the curious glances she was drawing, Ellie followed Gracie to where Jubal was standing with a perfect tree. It was a foot taller than his head, with a lovely natural shape, fresh, full, and green on all sides. She glanced up at the price posted on the row of trees. It was expensive—probably more than Jubal, in his present circumstances, could afford to pay.

"So this is the one for sure?" he asked Gracie.

"Yes! It's perfect! I love it!"

"Then it's yours. Keep an eye on it." Removing the tag, Jubal took it over to the counter and fished his wallet out of his hip pocket. Ellie, who happened to have a few bills in her pocket, was tempted to offer her help in buying the tree. But she knew better. Jubal wanted to do this for his daughter.

Minutes later he was back, his face flushed with cold and pleasure. "It's ours. Let's get it home." He hefted the tree onto his shoulder and headed out the gate to the truck. Gracie followed, dancing with excitement, with Ellie, weary on her feet, trailing behind.

"Please, can we put the tree up and decorate it tonight?" Gracie asked as they drove back to the ranch.

"Not tonight," Jubal said. "You've got school in the morning, and it's already close to your bedtime. The tree will be fine on the porch for a couple of days. What do you say we decorate it this Friday?"

"Yes!" Gracie hugged Beau so tightly that he squirmed. "Ellie, can you come and help us? It'll be lots more fun with you there."

Ellie's gaze met Jubal's across the truck cab. In the glow of the dash lights, she read a look of warning. She imagined them putting Laura's decorations on the tree, remembering past Christmases when Jubal's wife was alive. She shook her head. "I'm sorry but I've got other plans. You two have a good time. I'm sure your tree will be beautiful."

Gracie deflated into a silence that lasted until the truck pulled through the ranch gate and stopped at the foot of the porch. Jubal climbed out and came around to help Ellie out of the high passenger seat. "Give the dog back to Ellie," he told Gracie. "Then run on inside and get ready for bed. I'll be in after I walk Ellie to her car and unload the tree."

Gracie climbed the porch steps and turned at the door. "Good night, Ellie," she said. "Thanks for coming."

"And thanks for dinner," Ellie said. "It was yummy, especially your salad. Sleep tight."

When Gracie had gone inside, Jubal took

Ellie's arm and walked her to where the car was parked. A chilly wind had sprung up. Beau was shivering. Ellie opened the passenger side door, put him in his booster basket, and tucked his blanket around him. Closing the door again, she turned back to Jubal.

"Thanks for a lovely time," she said. "I mean it. You went to a lot of trouble to make me feel welcome."

He was looking down at her, his eyes in shadow. "Thanks for the hair braiding lesson. I just hope I can remember how to do it in the morning."

"For what it's worth, I think you're a great father," Ellie said. "Gracie's a wonderful kid."

"She deserves a lot more than I can give her." He exhaled with a ragged breath. "Oh, damn it, Ellie, why did you have to come back at a time like this?"

Cupping her chin between his hands, he captured her lips in a kiss that was as fierce as it was tender—a kiss that felt as natural as opening buds in springtime. Ellie's eyes closed. She stretched on tiptoe, straining upward to deepen the rough velvet contact of his mouth with hers. She breathed him into her senses, knowing the whole time that this was wrong and that it had to end. Once they'd been young enough to believe in fairy-tale endings. They would never be that young again.

As she'd known he would, Jubal released her and took a step back. His face wore a stricken expression.

Ellie spoke first, knowing what had to be said. "We can't do this, can we?"

He shook his head. "We aren't kids anymore. We can't go back to where we were—and we shouldn't try."

She blinked back welling tears. "Neither of us needs more craziness in our lives right now, do we?"

He walked around the car, took her key, and opened the driver's side door. "Good night, Ellie. Watch out for deer."

"Thanks, I will." She slid her bulk beneath the steering wheel. By the time she got the car started, Jubal had closed the door and walked away.


Later, lying in the darkness, he allowed himself to relive the kiss he'd shared with Ellie. It had been a crazy impulse, but he wasn't sorry. Even after ten years, the way her sweet lips molded to his was just as he remembered. And the response that had sent heat surging through his body was as urgent as ever.

But it was over and done. They'd both moved on, and there could be no going back. Ellie didn't belong in Branding Iron. And he would never belong anywhere else. She'd said as much the day she left him.

Tonight's kiss had proved that the old chemistry still simmered. But chemistry wasn't enough to hold two people together. He'd learned that ten years ago, and the lesson was worth remembering.

Holding that thought, he drifted into sleep.

Friday night, true to his promise, Jubal cleared a corner of the living room, lugged the tree inside, and set it up in the stand. Gracie was beside herself with excitement. She put a CD in the small boom box and danced around the room as he added water to the stand and opened the big box of decorations he'd brought down from the attic.

"Just smell that tree!" she said, hugging him around the waist. "The whole house smells like Christmas!"

Jubal lifted out the strings of colored lights. With Gracie helping, he laid them out along the floor and plugged them into the wall to make sure they were working. Then they draped them over and around the tree. Lit, in the darkened room, the effect was magical.

"Want to leave it like this for a night or two?" Jubal suggested. "We can always add the ornaments and tinsel later."

"Let's get it all done tonight," Gracie said. "If it takes a while, I can stay up past my bedtime. Tomorrow is Saturday."

Jubal opened the smaller boxes, holding the carefully packed ornaments that Laura had chosen and loved—shiny gold balls, glittery snowflakes, and little figures of elves, angels, reindeer, and Santas. This was the fifth Christmas without her, but hanging these small treasures never seemed to get any easier.

This year Gracie was tall enough to stand on a step stool and decorate even the higher parts of the tree. Jubal handed her the ornaments and steadied her balance while she fastened the wire hooks to the lush, green branches.

"This is nice," she said, "but it would be even nicer if Ellie was here."

"Ellie has her own family. They'll have their own Christmas tree at home."

"She just has her mom. And Beau. They could all come over and have fun helping."

"That's not how it works, Gracie." Jubal hoped to hell she wouldn't ask him to explain because he wouldn't know where to begin.

Gracie was silent while he helped her climb off the stool. "It seems like you and Ellie kind of like each other," she said. "Maybe you should think about getting married."

The glass ball Jubal was holding dropped from his hand and shattered on the hardwood floor. "Get me the broom and dustpan out of the kitchen," he said, hoping the subject would be forgotten. But he should have known he wouldn't be that lucky.

"Did you hear what I said?" Gracie handed him the broom and dustpan. "I said maybe you and Ellie should get married."

"Ellie and I are just friends." Jubal began sweeping up the shards of broken glass. "Besides, she's about to have a baby."

"Uh-huh." Gracie sat on the step stool to keep

her feet out of the way. "It's a little girl. She told me. That would be all right. I'd like having a baby sister."

"Maybe so. But I'm not the baby's father." Jubal was digging himself in deeper and deeper. Gracie was a farm girl so she knew the basics. But she might not have figured out how they applied to humans, and this was no time to tell her.

"That doesn't matter," Gracie said. "If you took care of the baby and loved it, you would be the father."

Wise words. Jubal felt the sting as he emptied the broken glass into the waste bin. "There's something you need to understand about Ellie," he said. "She grew up in Branding Iron. But a small town was never where she wanted to be. She left as soon as she was out of high school, and she only came back to visit her family."

He would leave out part of the story—how Ellie had chosen to leave town for good rather than marry him and spend her life on the ranch. "After her marriage ended, she found out she was going to have a baby. Because she didn't want to be alone, she came home to Branding Iron."

"So her mom could help her."

"That's right. But Ellie only came home to have her baby. As soon as she's ready to take care of the baby on her own, she'll leave."

"But where will she go?" Gracie's eyes were large and sad.

"Most likely to some big city. That's the life

she likes—lots of people, lots of things to do. She'd never be happy in Branding Iron."

"How do you know?" Gracie asked.

"She told me ten years ago, when she left for the first time. And I don't think there's anything you or I could do to change her mind." He put a hand on his daughter's shoulder. "I just don't want you to be sad when she leaves. Okay?"

"Okay." Gracie climbed off the stool. Taking a length of tinsel from the box, she began draping it over the branches of the tree. Following her lead, Jubal took another strand and started higher up.

This tree would be as pretty as any they'd ever decorated. But a bit of the holiday magic had faded.

# Chapter 8

On the following Tuesday night, Ellie had invited Ben's family over for dinner. With Clara, they crowded around the kitchen table and feasted on spaghetti with salad and garlic bread, topped off with chocolate ice cream for dessert.

Although she hadn't planned it that way, the dinner turned out to be a celebration. Jess and Ben had just learned that they were going to be parents. Happiness overflowed at the small table.

"So your little girl will have a cousin to grow up with." Ben gave Ellie a grin. "Think how much fun that will be, the two little nippers running around together, getting into all kinds of mischief."

Ellie avoided her brother's eyes. Didn't Ben understand that she planned to leave Branding Iron? Or was this his way of coaxing her to stay?

True, with family here, the town would be a good place to raise her child. But merciful heaven, how would *she* stand it? She couldn't just sit around watching her baby grow up. She needed something to do. She needed friends and most likely a job—things that would be easier to find in a city where she didn't stand out like a sore thumb.

Ethan nudged his father. "Dad, may I be excused to go and play with Beau?"

"Sure. Did you thank Ellie for dinner?"

"Thanks, Ellie, the spaghetti was great." Ethan slid out from his chair and left the kitchen to look for the dog. At the week's end, when school was out, he'd be leaving for Boston to spend the holidays with his mother and her new family. Ben was happy with the new custody arrangement that allowed his son to go to school in Branding Iron, but not having Ethan here for Christmas was going to be hard on them both.

"So . . ." Ben leaned back in his chair, his lawman's gaze fixed on Ellie. "How's it going with Jubal?"

*Jubal again.* Ellie shook her head.

"Honestly, Ben, will you stop teasing me? I haven't heard from him or his little girl since last week. There's nothing going on between us—nothing at all."

The memory of that searing kiss flashed in her mind. She'd felt the shimmering heat all the way to her toes. But it couldn't be allowed to mean anything. Jubal had understood that as well as she had.

The fact that Gracie, who had her own cell phone, hadn't called her was a clear sign of where things stood between them. That was best for everyone, Ellie told herself. But she already missed Jubal and his daughter.

She worried about them too, knowing what Jubal was facing with the loss of his ranch. There had to be some way to help him. She was tempted to involve Ben, but she'd promised to keep Jubal's secret. For now, at least, she couldn't break that promise.

"I've been working on Gracie's dress for the Christmas Ball," Clara said. "I need to fit it on her before I do any more. Could you get her over here sometime soon? The ball is a week from this Saturday, so we don't have much time."

Ellie had almost forgotten about the dress. Had Gracie told her father about the plan for her to go with them to the ball in the gown Clara was making? What if he viewed the whole idea as "charity" and refused to let his daughter be involved?

In that case, Ellie thought, she would give him a piece of her mind. But Jubal was proud, not cruel. It would be more like him to insist on paying for the dress and Gracie's ticket.

"I'll invite Gracie over again," she told her mother. "I know she'll be excited about the dress."

"Speaking of Christmas," Ben said, "with Ethan gone, it won't be much of a Christmas at our little house. We were thinking, before he leaves, we'd like to stick with tradition and put a nice tree up here. Then Jess and I could come over on Christmas Day to celebrate together. What do you think?"

"Why that would be lovely," Clara said. "Our first Christmas with Ellie since she got married to that . . ." She paused, weighing her words. "Oh, never mind."

Her mother had never liked Brent, Ellie recalled. When Clara had voiced her feelings privately to Ellie, before the wedding, the rift between them had lasted for years. But all that was in the past. At least Clara had never said, *I told you so.*

"That sounds great," Ellie said. "Maybe I can be Santa Claus. I've certainly got the figure for it."

"Good one, sis." Ben grinned at her.

They were finishing dessert when Ben got a call about a drug bust and had to leave. Ellie and Jess shooed Clara into the living room and went to work cleaning up the meal.

"I'm so happy for you!" Ellie hugged her sister-in-law. She already knew how much Ben and Jess had wanted to start a family.

"It was quite a surprise when we saw that pregnancy test," Jess said. "Ben's over the moon."

"How about Francine? How do you think she'll take the news that she's going to be a grandma?"

"She'll be tickled pink. She's been hinting for a grandchild almost since the wedding. But we may wait a few weeks to tell her. You know Francine. She won't be able to keep it quiet."

"What about you?" Ellie opened the dishwasher and began loading it. "After all, you're the one who's actually going to have this baby."

Jess was covering the leftovers, putting them in the fridge. "Me, I'm a little scared. Oh, I'm thrilled about the baby, but it's all so new. When I think about what's ahead, especially giving birth, all I can do is pray that I'm up to it."

"Let me tell you a secret," Ellie said. "When you've been pregnant for almost nine months and you're as big as a cow and so miserable that you can barely get around, you'll be ready to go through *anything* to get that baby into the world. Believe me, I'm there. It's being responsible for this brand-new little life that scares me now."

"I'll remind myself of that," Jess said. "And speaking of babies, don't forget your shower is this Saturday."

"Are you sure anybody will want to come?" Jess had seen the guest list. More than half the nineteen names on it were women she didn't recognize. At least one—her former classmate, Krystle Martin Remington—had no reason to be friends with her.

"Oh, they'll come," Jess said. "I sent the invitations with an RSVP, and fifteen of them have already accepted. It's a good thing we're having it at the B and B. Plenty of room and plenty of chairs. And you do need a baby shower, Ellie. You're going to need a lot of things for your little one."

"I already have quite a few," Ellie said. She really did feel prepared. Ben had found her old bassinet in the basement, dusted it off, and hauled it up to her room, along with the mattress and the little sheets Clara had carefully boxed away years ago. Last week, when Ellie had driven to Cottonwood Springs for her meeting with the obstetrician and her precheck at the hospital, she'd dropped by the mall afterward, bought some Christmas gifts, and stocked up on baby clothes, including some pajamas and some darling little girly outfits complete with hair bows and tiny slippers. And diapcrs. She'd bought a couple boxes of those, too, in newborn size.

"You'll get some useful items—and good practical advice—from the women who've had babies," Jess said. "They'll know what works and what doesn't. Trust me, you'll be glad you listened."

"I know I will." Ellie gave her sister-in-law's shoulders a squeeze before closing the dishwasher. "Thanks for doing this—I really mean it."

*When your turn comes, I'll do the same for you.* Ellie bit back the words she'd been about to say. She didn't believe in making promises she couldn't keep. By the time Jess and Ben's baby was due, she could be anywhere.

Anywhere except Branding Iron.


That night, with the baby's acrobatics keeping her awake, Ellie lay on her side, gazing at the moon through the gauzy curtains. Worries churned in her mind—handling motherhood, the baby shower, her future plans . . . But every thread of thought circled back to Jubal. Over the years, she'd convinced herself that their teenage romance was history. But that kiss had awakened all the old flutters and urges. The feeling was like being seventeen again.

But it wasn't just the kiss that had moved her. It had been the little things—like watching Jubal braid his daughter's hair and seeing him pay more money than he could afford to buy her the Christmas tree she wanted. It had been remembering the boy she'd loved and left behind, and now seeing the man he'd become.

When Jubal had told her about the loss of the ranch and his vain search for answers, Ellie had shared his frustration. There had to be some way she could help him without breaking her promise. She rolled onto her back, thinking hard as she rested her hands over her shifting baby. If the Shumway corporation, whoever they were, had illegally cheated Seth McFarland out of his property, there had to be a reason. That reason could be the key to Jubal's quest.

With little to do except help her mother and wait for the baby, she had plenty of time to spare. The library kept archives of the local newspaper, the *Lone Star Reporter*, which was published in Cottonwood Springs. The older copies were stored on microfilm, the newer ones on DVDs or thumb drives. She would visit the library tomorrow and spend several hours looking. She had nothing to go on except a few dates and names, and perhaps a hunch or two, so it was a long shot at best. But if it paid off, it could make all the difference.

Still mulling possibilities, Ellie eased back onto her left side. Beau, who'd been curled in a nest of pillows on the floor, jumped onto the bed, licked her face, and settled down beside her. Snuggling her little dog close, she drifted into sleep.

When the Branding Iron Public Library opened at 10:00 the next morning, she was waiting to walk through the doors. Since her mother had been city librarian during Ellie's growing-up years, the place was like a second home to her. She knew exactly where to go and what to ask for. Fifteen minutes later, she was in the library basement, seated at one of three aging computers with cases of DVDs containing newspaper editions dating from the last two years before the McFarland ranch was transferred to Shumway and Sons, and from the year after.

For a moment, the task she'd taken on seemed overwhelming. If she checked out every item, she was going to be here a long time. Even if the out-of-date software had a search function, finding useful information wasn't going to be easy.

She had barely started when she heard footsteps and a familiar voice.

"Ellie? I saw your car outside. What are you doing here?" Jubal, wearing his sheepskin coat and carrying a notepad, stood behind her.

"I'm trying to help you," she said.

He eyed the cases of DVDs. "So that's why I was told that the news files I wanted were checked out."

"We must've had the same idea," Ellie said.

Jubal didn't look too pleased. Maybe she'd overstepped. Maybe he was about to tell her to mind her own business.

"You don't have to do this," he said. "It isn't your problem."

"I have time on my hands," she said. "I might as well make myself useful. Working together we can cut the load in half. And who knows? We might even find something important. So sit down and let's get going."

He hesitated. Then, with a long exhalation, he shed his coat, sat down, and brought up the computer next to the one Ellie was using. "Fine. I'll start with the oldest editions and work forward. You can start with the more recent and work backward."

"Makes sense." Ellie passed him the DVDs with older dates, and they went to work. "I'll be looking for any mention of Shumway and Sons, or any reason somebody might want to steal your land."

"You're assuming it was stolen," Jubal said. "My father made some reckless financial moves in his last years. He could've signed away the ranch for reasons of his own. But I've searched through all his papers. There's no bill of sale, no clue to what happened."

"Maybe we'll find something." Ellie touched

his arm in a gesture of reassurance. He glanced toward her, his eyes a flash of galvanizing blue in the shadows of the low-ceilinged room. Then he looked away.

"Let's get to work," he said.

Side by side, they scrolled through the contents of one disk after another. They said little, but Ellie could hear his breathing and feel his presence inches away. The awareness created a pleasant pool of heat low in her body.

Did he feel something, too? But what a silly question. Her pregnant figure wouldn't stir a tingle in any man—let alone a man as preoccupied as Jubal.

"Look at this." His voice startled her in the silence. Ellie shifted her chair for a view of his computer screen. The print on the scanned page was hard to read, but she could make out the date—a few weeks before the time of Laura's accident—and the headline.

*OIL FIELD RUMORED SOUTH OF BRANDING IRON*

Ellie shook her head. "There can't be any oil around here. I haven't seen so much as a single pump jack."

"True," Jubal said. "But I remember the rumor and all the fuss about it. Some big company was supposed to come out here and sink a few experimental wells. The months went by, and it never happened, but people were mighty stirred up for a while. They were buying property right and left where the oil was supposed to be."

"What about you?"

"I never set much stock in it. Neither did my dad. We figured if there was oil around here, somebody would've already found it. Besides we had a ranch to work. And then, after Laura died, it was all I could do to get through one day at a time. I wasn't paying much attention to oil rumors."

Their eyes met in a flash of understanding— as if they knew, without speaking, that they'd both come to the same conclusion.

"There's no proof either way," Jubal said. "But those oil rumors could've given somebody reason to swindle my dad into signing over the ranch."

"And they never took possession because the oil boom never happened," Ellie said. "As things stood, it made more sense to just let you keep working the ranch."

"They wouldn't have needed to take physical possession. If the oil had been there, all they'd have needed to do was sell the mineral rights to the oil company. The bastards would've been sitting pretty."

"They couldn't have just taken over the ranch," Ellie mused, thinking out loud. "Coming into the open would've exposed them to suspicion—especially if it turned out to be someone you knew—and especially if they'd done the same thing to other people."

"Damn it, Ellie!" Turning in his chair, he seized her shoulders. His grip was almost painful, his eyes feverish with excitement. "This has to be the answer. It makes perfect sense!" He released her, his hands falling to his sides. "But we don't have a blasted shred of proof!"

"Maybe we can still find proof."

Jubal eyed the stack of unexamined DVDs. "So we keep digging in the haystack, hoping we'll find the needle."

"Do you have a better idea?"

Jubal's only response was to turn back to the computer screen and start scrolling down the page.

"Are you sure your father wouldn't just sell the ranch outright? You said he'd become reckless."

"If he did, I don't know what he did with the money. When I took over the finances I found a mountain of unpaid loans and bills. Come to think of it, he did give me five thousand dollars to pay for Laura's funeral expenses. At the time, it didn't occur to me to wonder where it came from. But he'd have gotten a lot more than that if he'd sold the ranch." Jubal's mouth tightened. "We need to track down Shumway and Sons. That would be our best chance of finding whether the transfer was legal."

They spent the next two hours on the computers. By the time they'd finished going through the files, they were bleary-eyed and mentally exhausted. Worse, they'd found nothing else useful.

"At least I saved you some time. Wish me luck getting up. My back and shoulders are killing me." Ellie moved forward to push her ungainly body off her chair.

"Stay put. Maybe I can make it easier." Standing, Jubal stepped behind her. His big, rough hands rested on her shoulders, thumbs working the tight muscles on either side of her spine.

Ellie closed her eyes. Her breath emerged in a blissful sigh. "Oh, that feels heavenly. Please don't stop."

His hands kneaded her shoulders with gentle skill. He chuckled as she moaned with pleasure. "Let me know when you want me to quit," he said.

"How about never?"

Only when he failed to answer did Ellie realize what her words had implied. Ten years ago those words might have pleased him. Now they were bittersweet.

The library basement was dim and silent. His fingers gentled on her shoulders, his touch becoming a caress. She battled the urge to reach up and stroke his hands—or even to turn and raise her face to his kiss.

*Oh, Jubal, how did we get here—you widowed, me divorced and pregnant, both of us so unhappy? What if I'd said yes? Where would we be if I'd promised to come home to you?*

Ellie knew better than to voice the thought. Whatever was happening here, it mustn't go on. She broke the silence with a forced laugh. "I think I'll be all right now," she said, getting up. "Thanks for the massage."

His mouth twitched in a half smile. "You earned that and more. How about I treat you to lunch?"

Ellie was about to decline. Then she remembered that she still needed to invite Gracie over to have her dress fitted. It would be easy enough to bring it up over burgers and shakes at Buckaroo's.

After turning in the files at the reference desk, Jubal escorted Ellie outside to the Purple People Eater. He'd asked to drive the old car to Buckaroo's, and she'd gladly let him.

"This is great," he said. "Cruising down Main Street, with the muffler roaring and a pretty girl by my side, I feel like a teenager again."

Laughing, Ellie laid a hand on his knee. The Christmas lights were glowing, the music was playing, and he'd discovered a possible clue to the loss of the ranch. It wasn't much to go on, but for the first time in weeks, he felt a spark of hope. The ride was a short one, but Jubal enjoyed the feeling while it lasted.

With the lunchtime rush over, Buckaroo's was quiet. They settled in a corner booth, and Jubal ordered cheeseburgers, fries, and double chocolate shakes—Ellie's old favorite—for them both. He'd have preferred beer himself, but he knew she wasn't drinking because of the baby. Service was fast. They had their order in a few minutes.

Ellie sat across from him, her body barely fitting between the seat and the edge of the table. Her face was flushed with cold, her hair loosely twisted and anchored at the crown with a silver clip. Tired shadows framed her dark brown eyes—he guessed she wasn't sleeping well. Even so, she looked beautiful.

It struck Jubal how alone she was. Even with her family here, she was taking on a heavy burden, having this baby by herself. But he was in no position to help her. And even if he were, Ellie was bound to go her own way—and break his heart again, along with Gracie's.

"How's it going with your daughter's hair?" she asked.

"Fine. The first morning I did the braid, she was late for the bus and I had to drive her to school. But I'm getting the hang of it—and we've got her hair looking good. No more pigtails ever again, she says."

"That's great." She sipped her shake, getting chocolate on her full lower lip. Jubal fought the temptation to bend close and lick it off—as he might have done years ago.

"I don't know if Gracie has told you," she said, "but my mother is making her a Western gown for the Christmas Ball. She wants Gracie to come by the house and try the dress on so she can finish it."

The request came as a surprise. Jubal had always encouraged Gracie to be honest with him, but she'd said nothing about a gown or even about the Christmas Ball.

"I didn't even know she was going," he said.

"Ben and Jess said they'd take her. And my mother offered to make the dress. Gracie's excited about going. I hope you won't spoil things for her."

Ellie's words stung. Why would she think he'd spoil a happy celebration for his little girl?

"Is it all right?" she asked.

"Of course it is. I just wish I'd known about it, that's all. I'll pay for her ticket, of course. And the dress, too."

"The dress isn't costing a cent," Ellie said. "My mother already had the fabric, and she loves to sew. As for the ticket, why don't you buy one for yourself, too, and come with her? Gracie would love that."

Jubal sighed. True, Gracie would be happy if he took her to the ball. But with so much worry bearing down on him, he was hardly in the mood to go to a party. "I haven't been to the Christmas Ball in years," he said. "After Laura's accident, there didn't seem to be much point in it."

"So Gracie hasn't gone to the ball either?"

"I always take her to the Saturday morning Christmas parade. She's never said it wasn't enough."

"But everybody goes to the Cowboy Christmas Ball, even kids. Surely she's heard her classmates talking about it at school. I know you want to give her a good Christmas, Jubal . . ." She paused, then added, ". . . .and I know why."

"Damn it, Ellie, nobody could say no to you." Jubal pushed his empty plate to one side. "All right, I'll buy Gracie a ticket. She can wear the dress and go with your family. Are you happy now?"

"This isn't about me. It's about Gracie. And I think she'd be even happier if you went to the ball with her."

"Don't push me." Jubal took a bill out of his wallet and laid it on the table to cover the meal and the tip. "Let me know what time's good for you, and I'll bring Gracie to your mother's place to try on the dress."

"I'd be glad to pick her up after school and bring her home." Ellie shrugged into her coat, which she'd slipped off her shoulders in the booth.

"I'll bring her. I want to thank your mother for the dress and pay for the ticket."

"Fine. How about tomorrow night? You're welcome to come and have supper with us if you like."

"Thanks, but that's a lot of bother for you. We'll eat at home and stop by around seven. All right?"

"Sure. See you then." She accepted the hand he offered to help her squeeze out of the booth.

In the parking lot, she took the wheel so she could drop him off at his truck. Jubal studied her silent profile as she drove back up Main Street, under the strings of colored Christmas lights. Snow was falling in airy flakes, brushed away like scraps of lace by the creaking windshield wipers. Ellie's eyes gazed ahead. Her mouth was set in a determined line. Jubal knew that look. She wasn't happy with him. Maybe he should have agreed to come to supper, or promised to go to the Christmas Ball with Gracie. But he'd never been much of a socializer. And right now he had more worries than he could mask with a friendly smile. He just couldn't do it.

At the library she pulled up next to his truck and kept the engine running while he climbed out of the car. "So, we're on for tomorrow night around seven?" she asked.

"Right. And thanks. I mean it, Ellie. You were a lot of help this morning."

"You're welcome and thanks for lunch." She sounded like a polite stranger.

Jubal closed the car door and watched her drive away through the falling snow. During the few years he'd been married to Laura—and they'd been good years—he'd managed to convince himself that he was over Ellie. But he'd been wrong. She was back—like a remembered song that had never stopped playing in his head.

And the timing couldn't have been worse.

# Chapter 9

Ellie and Clara had warmed up last night's leftover spaghetti and finished it for supper. Ellie was clearing the table when Ben, Jess, and Ethan came in through the front door, trailing the aroma of pine. Only then did she remember that they'd talked about putting up the Christmas tree tonight.

"The tree's on the porch," Ben said. "Ellie, you'll want to get your pet rat out of the way before we bring it in. He'll be all over it."

"Oh, thanks." Ellie ignored her brother's joke. "Ethan, would you find Beau? We don't want him running outside while the door's open, or getting underfoot while you're putting up the tree."

"I've got him," Ethan said. "He came right to me." He opened his jacket to reveal the little poodle snuggled against his chest. Until two weeks ago, Beau had never been around children. But he'd taken to Ethan and Gracie like instant best friends.

"Take him upstairs and shut him in my bedroom," she said. "We'll let him out again once the tree's up."

As Ethan vanished up the stairs with the dog, Ellie remembered once again that Jubal and Gracie were coming at 7:00. Unless they'd been delayed or changed their minds, they'd be here in a few minutes. Jubal wouldn't be expecting a crowd, let alone a family celebration. He might feel uncomfortable. But that, Ellie reminded herself, was his problem, not hers.

Jubal had always been a loner. Now, after losing his wife, his father, and possibly his ranch, he seemed to have become even more solitary. Maybe being with Ben's happy family would be good for him. He might even open up enough to talk with Ben about the loss of the ranch. If a crime had been committed, who better to involve than the local lawman?

That would be the sensible thing to do. But Jubal didn't operate on sense. He operated on pride.

Jubal McFarland was the most stubborn person Ellie had ever known. She'd be smart to turn her back and let him solve his problems in his own mule-headed way. After all, she had her own situation to worry about. The trouble was, she couldn't help feeling his pain. And she couldn't help caring about the man and his adorable little girl.

Her thoughts scattered at the sound of Jubal's

old truck pulling up in front of the house. She would know that sound anywhere. Back in high school it had set her pulse skipping when he came by the house to pick her up for a date. But that had been a long time ago. Their whole world had changed since then.

"All clear!" Ethan announced, coming down the stairs. "I found the stand in the closet. Let's get our tree in."

Through the open doorway, Ellie glimpsed the truck's headlights going dark and the doors opening. Moments from now, for better or for worse, Jubal and Gracie would be coming up the walk.

When Jubal had pulled up to the curb and seen Ellie's brother's family on the porch, he'd been tempted to keep driving. Not that he had anything against the sheriff. Like most of Branding Iron's citizens, he had nothing but respect for Ben Marsden. But he'd hoped to make a quick stop, let Gracie try on the dress, and be on his way. Now things were looking complicated.

*They've got a lot going on here. Let's go and come back another night.*

The words had been on the tip of Jubal's tongue. But Gracie had been so excited about coming here, he couldn't bear to disappoint her. He switched off the engine and lights and climbed out of the truck.

As they mounted the porch steps, it occurred to Jubal to wonder if he'd been set up. What if

Ellie had arranged all this to get him talking to the sheriff about the ranch—something he wasn't ready to do? What if she'd broken her word and told her brother already?

Ben was wrestling an enormous Christmas tree through the front door. "Hey, Jubal," he said with a friendly grin. "Care to give me a hand?"

"Sure. Stay back, Gracie." Jubal stepped up to help maneuver the eight-foot tree bottom first through the open doorway. He'd never known the sheriff well. Ben had been two years ahead of him in high school, so they'd never run with the same crowd. And unlike Ben, Jubal had never played team sports. He was a natural athlete who loved to ride and swim, but with the demands of the ranch, he'd had no time for the extra hours of practice that being on a team required.

While Jubal was dating Ellie, Ben had been a football star in college. By the time Ben returned to Branding Iron, his NFL hopes shattered by a knee injury, Jubal and Ellie were history. Only one encounter with the sheriff was seared into Jubal's memory. It was Ben Marsden who'd knocked on the door that cold December night to bring him the news of Laura's fatal crash. Ben's manner had been professional and compassionate. But Jubal had avoided him after that. For a time, the sight of Ben's face had been enough to stir the painful memory. But that had been four years ago.

Now, taking care not to break the branches,

Jubal and Ben managed to get the heavy tree through the entry and into the living room. Meanwhile, Jess and Ethan had cleared a space in front of the window and put the metal stand in place. With Jess giving directions, the two men centered the tree, lifted it, and lowered the base of the trunk into the stand. Ethan wriggled underneath to tighten the bolts that would hold it in place.

Ben gave a low whistle of relief. "Thanks, Jubal. I swear the trees we choose get bigger every year. Or maybe I'm just getting older."

"No problem. Glad to help." Catching his breath, Jubal glanced around the room. He hadn't been here since Ellie had broken up with him, but not much had changed. *Cozy* was the word for the small room, with soft chairs and pillows, green plants, and a shelf-full of well-worn books, mostly discards from the library where Clara had worked. A love of reading was something he and Ellie had shared from the beginning.

Turning, he saw her sitting next to her mother on the flowered sofa. For the space of a breath their gazes locked; then her attention shifted to Gracie, who'd followed the tree inside and closed the door behind her.

"Hi, Gracie," she said. "How nice your hair looks. Would you like to help decorate our Christmas tree?"

Hesitant, Gracie glanced at Jubal. "We just came by so I could try on the dress," she said. "Where's Beau?"

As if in answer to her question, the sounds of

scratching, barking, and whining came from the upstairs room. Gracie looked stricken. "Is he all right?"

"He's fine," Ellie said. "We locked him in my room to keep him safe while we put up the tree. You can go upstairs and see him if you want. Just be careful not to let him out."

"Is it all right, Dad?" Gracie asked.

"Just for a few minutes," he said. "We don't want to be a bother."

"Nobody's being a bother." It was Clara who spoke. "Let her enjoy the little dog, Jubal. She can try on the dress when she comes downstairs. Meanwhile, we've got some cold apple cider in the fridge. Let me get you a glass."

"I'll do it. Stay where you are, Mom." Ellie was on her feet. "Anybody else?"

"I'll take some as long as you're going," Clara said. "Bring it out on a tray with some glasses. Then folks can help themselves."

Gracie had gone upstairs. Ellie was glad she'd taken time to put the drawing of Beau in a spare frame and hang it on her bedroom wall, where Gracie would see it.

"Take off your coat and have a seat, Jubal." Clara spoke as Ellie vanished into the kitchen. She'd always been nice to him, Jubal recalled. But then Ellie's mother was nice to everybody. If Branding Iron had a queen, it would be Clara Marsden.

Ellie returned with a jug of cider and a tray of glasses, balanced against her burgeoning belly. Setting her burden on the coffee table, she filled the glasses and passed them out to Clara, Jubal, Jess, and Ben.

Ethan had dashed upstairs again. Now he was making his way down with an awkward grip on the box of Christmas tree lights. The box didn't look heavy but it was so big the boy could barely see over it. He had to negotiate each step by feeling with his feet.

"Got it." Jubal put down his glass and lunged for the box, grabbing it just as it was about to topple. "You must be anxious to start decorating," he said, setting it in front of the tree.

"Dad used to have the tree up before I got here," Ethan said. "This year I get to help. It'll be fun."

"Sit down, son," Ben said. "After we finish our cider we can string the lights. After that, I'll help you bring the other boxes down."

Jubal finished his cider and glanced toward the stairs. There was no sound from the upper floor of the house. A good fifteen minutes had passed since Gracie had gone upstairs to greet the dog. What could be keeping her?

Ellie was watching him, as if sensing his unease. "Maybe I'll go up and check on Gracie and Beau," she said, as if it were her idea. "Things are a little too quiet up there."

"Thanks." Jubal remained on his feet. Gracie had been taught the way to behave in other people's homes. But she was a curious little girl. He'd feel better if he knew she wasn't getting into mischief. It would be like Ellie to understand his concern.

*Strange how well she read him,* he thought. *Even after ten years, some things didn't change.*

Ellie reached the top of the stairs, a little breathless from the climb. A lot had changed since the days when she'd raced home and taken those steps two at a time.

The door to her bedroom was closed. No sound came from inside. Maybe Gracie had gone to sleep. Ellie knocked lightly, then eased the door open.

Gracie sat cross-legged on the floor with Beau in her lap. Surrounding her was the collection of stuffed toy animals that Ellie had shoved into the back of the closet. There were teddy bears, an elephant, a unicorn, a tiger, a rabbit, a monkey, and several others that Ellie had accumulated over the years and displayed on her bed as a teenager.

Gracie started and glanced up, guilt written all over her small face. "I'm sorry, Ellie. Beau ran into the closet, and when I went after him I found these. I just had to get them out. They're so wonderful!"

She put Beau on the bed and scrambled to her feet. "Please don't be mad at me! I'll put them back right now!"

"I'm not mad, Gracie." Ellie sat on the side of the bed. "I'm glad you found those animals. Nobody's played with them in a long, long time. Who knows, maybe they were lonesome."

Ellie had planned to donate the toys to a charity, but she'd never gotten around to it. It would be a pleasure to give Gracie the whole batch of them. But something told her that Jubal, in his pride, wouldn't stand for it.

But surely he wouldn't mind just one, if it would give his daughter joy . . .

"I had a teddy bear when I was little," Gracie said. "All the stuffing fell out of him and we had to throw him away. But these animals are nicer. And all different kinds. They're beautiful."

"Do you have a favorite?" Ellie asked. "Which one do you like the very best?"

Gracie hesitated only a moment before picking up a white poodle. "I like him," she said. "He looks like Beau, only he's a lot bigger."

"Then he's yours," Ellie said.

Gracie's blue eyes widened in disbelief. "Really? I can just take him?"

"That's what I said. He's yours."

"Thank you!" Gracie flung her free arm around Ellie's neck and hugged. "I love him! And I love you!"

Something jerked around Ellie's heart, tightening until it hurt. Blinking back tears, she eased the little girl away from her. "Now that he's yours, he needs a name. What are you going to call him?"

Gracie hugged the toy dog tighter. "I'm going to call him Big Beau."

"Perfect." Ellie reached for Beau, who was pawing her arm for attention. "Now that the tree's up, shall we take our dogs downstairs?"

"Okay." Gracie skipped to the door, then turned back with a worried look. "I'll have to ask my dad if I can keep him. What if he says no?"

*He wouldn't dare,* Ellie thought. *Not if he's anything like the man I remember.*

"We'll ask him together," she said. "Come on."

They were halfway down the stairs before Ellie recalled where the white plush poodle had come from. Jubal had given it to her on their first Valentine's Day, with a big red bow around its neck.


Jubal recognized the stuffed dog as soon as he saw it. Sixteen-year-old Ellie had pined over it in the window of a local gift shop. He'd emptied his wallet to buy it for her as a Valentine surprise. Now here it was, minus its red ribbon and clutched in his daughter's arms.

"Look, Daddy." Clasping the toy, she walked up to Jubal, with Ellie behind her. "His name is Big Beau. Ellie said I could keep him."

"I hope it's all right." Ellie stepped in quickly. "Gracie found my old stuffed animal collection. I let her choose the one she liked best."

"Can I keep him? Please?" Gracie's eyes were bright with hope, but Jubal saw the worry there. She was afraid he'd say no. But how could he refuse such a simple thing that would make his little girl so happy?

He nodded. "I guess you can. Just make sure you thank Ellie."

"She already did." Ellie's eyes met Jubal's. He wondered if she'd forgotten where that dog came from.

Clara rose from her chair. "Gracie, do you want to try on the dress now? It's in my sewing room."

"Sure!" Gracie thrust the toy dog into Jubal's arms. "Take care of Big Beau for me till I get back, okay, Daddy?"

"Okay." Jubal watched her skip down the hall, following Ellie's mother. He sat there, holding the stuffed dog and feeling like a fool. Ellie placed her tiny poodle on the couch and busied herself putting the empty glasses back on the tray. When she carried it into the kitchen he followed her.

"Sorry if I overstepped." She put the tray on the counter next to the sink, then turned to face him. "I know you don't appreciate gifts. I just wanted to make her happy."

"Don't apologize, Ellie. I wish you'd asked me first, but it's done."

"Would you have said no?"

"Probably not. How could I?"

"Anyway . . ." She opened the dishwasher and began putting the glasses inside. "You're the one who paid for that dog, all those years ago when you gave it to me."

Jubal forced a chuckle. "I can't believe you remember, or that you kept the silly thing all these years."

"I've got a whole menagerie, saved from my

teens. Gracie could have them all if you'd let her."

"If I'd let her?" Jubal's voice lowered to a growl. "Damn it, Ellie. It's not that I don't want Gracie to have toys and nice things. It's that I want to be the one providing them. That's what I've worked for—paying the debts on the ranch so I can upgrade to a good, moneymaking operation. I want Gracie to have nice clothes and music lessons like other girls, maybe art classes, too. When she's ready, I want to send her to college. But right now . . ." He let the words trail off. There was no need to say more.

Ellie finished loading the dishwasher and straightened to face him. "I know what you must be thinking. But I haven't said a word to Ben about your situation. And no matter how it looks, I didn't set you up tonight. I'd forgotten they were coming when I asked you to bring Gracie here." She stepped closer, her voice dropping. "I'll do anything to help you, Jubal. But only if you want me to."

Flecks of copper burned in her deep brown eyes. If he hadn't been in her mother's kitchen, with her family in the next room, Jubal would have been tempted to seize her in his arms and ravish her mouth with kisses. But even thinking about it was a bad idea. The sooner he closed the door on that notion, the better.

Still, he couldn't stop himself from looking at her. Those haunting eyes and kissable lips triggered memories of other times, when she'd been his girl and there'd been almost no limits to their love—or so he'd thought. But he wasn't going down that road again.

"Look, Dad! Look, Ellie!" Gracie stood in the doorway to the kitchen, looking like a little doll in blue flowered calico. She made a turn to show off the dress—long, with a ruffled hem, puffy sleeves, and ties that made a bow in back. Jubal's throat tightened as he looked at her. So pretty.

Ellie clapped her hands. "It's perfect!" she said. "Look how the color matches her eyes!"

Clara appeared in the doorway behind Gracie. "Isn't it lovely on her? The seams are still pinned at the sides. But now that she's tried it on, I can finish the dress tomorrow."

Jubal found his voice. "Thank you, Mrs. Marsden. It's a beautiful dress. I'd like to pay you for the material and your time."

"Oh, nonsense, Jubal!" Clara gave a vehement shake of her silvery head. "The dress didn't cost me a cent to make and I enjoyed every minute. Just seeing your little girl so happy is payment enough."

"Well, thanks. If there's anything I can do for you—"

"You can accept a gift with pleasure. Just that." Clara spoke as if she were scolding a noisy child for talking in the library. "Come on, Gracie, let's take the dress off. Then you can help us decorate the tree." She turned around and walked toward the hall with Gracie skipping after her.

When Jubal looked back at Ellie, she was smiling. He forced a chuckle. "I never was a match for your mother," he said.

"Nobody is. But she always liked you. On the day of my wedding to Brent, she told me that you were the one I should've married."

Something jerked in Jubal's chest. "I can't believe she liked me *that* much," he said.

"I guess we'll never know. But she couldn't stand Brent. And in the end she was right—at least about him." Ellie fell silent, maybe wondering whether she'd said too much. Her gaze dropped to her bulging middle, covered by the loose black sweater she wore. Then she looked up and smiled, ending the awkward moment.

"Well, we might as well go back and help finish the tree," she said.

Jubal rethought the excuse he'd been about to make. After all, what did he have to go home to? "I hadn't planned to stay. But Gracie seems set on decorating, so I guess it won't hurt to stick around a little longer."

"Did you get your own tree done?"

"We did." Assuming a relaxed expression, he followed Ellie into a room alive with Christmas cheer and talking, laughing people.


An hour later, Jubal managed to get Gracie into her coat and out of the house. As they climbed into the truck and pulled away, they could see the tree, a glory of sparkling lights in the living room window.

By the time they reached the outskirts of town, a storm was blowing in. Jubal drove carefully, a hard wind battering the truck. Beside him, buckled into the passenger seat, Gracie clutched her precious stuffed dog. She'd had a wonderful time tonight, helping trim the tree and playing with Ellie's tiny poodle. It had done his heart good to see his little girl so happy.

But Jubal's thoughts were still centered on the theft of his ranch—if that's what it was—and what it could mean to their future. He had never felt more frustrated in his life. There had to be something he could do.

More than once during the evening, he'd been tempted to pull Ben aside and ask his advice. But he'd stopped himself. Going to the sheriff without a shred of evidence would only make him look like a fool. He needed to find something solid, like a copy of the contract—or whatever it was—his father had signed to transfer the ownership of the ranch. And he needed to identify the people who'd drawn it up.

But did such a document even exist? He'd searched the desk and spent hours going through boxes of his father's papers. There was no place else to look.

"Are you all right, Daddy?" Gracie's touch on his sleeve pulled him back to the present.

"I'm fine, sweetheart," he said. "Just tired, that's all."

"You don't look fine. You look sad. Is something wrong?"

"Not really." The white lie was necessary. He turned off the highway onto the graveled lane. Snow had begun falling in soggy flakes that slid down the windshield. Jubal switched on the wipers. Playing with a sudden idea, he glanced at his daughter.

"I want you to use your imagination, Gracie," he said. "If you had to hide something important, something you didn't want people to see, where would you put it?"

"Something important? You mean like a treasure?"

"No, more like a letter, maybe. Or a picture. Or even money."

Gracie thought for a moment. "I don't know. Once I saw a TV show where people hid some money in their bed, under the mattress. I guess I could put it there, if it wasn't too lumpy to sleep on."

"That's a good answer," Jubal said. Come to think of it, one place he hadn't checked was his father's old bedroom. Seth McFarland had died of a stroke in the barn. After the burial, his room had been tidied up and closed. Jubal had meant to haul out the old furniture, repaint the walls, and make it into an office or den, but he'd never found the time. Except for the bedsheets and the old man's clothes and shoes, which had been donated to a shelter in Cottonwood Springs, the room was pretty much as he'd left it three years ago.

"What do you want to hide, Daddy?" Gracie asked.

"Nothing. I was just thinking, that's all."

"Oh." She yawned. Through the falling snow, Jubal could see the glow of the porch light he'd left on.

"Bedtime for you, as soon as we get inside," he said.

"Can I take Big Beau to bed with me?" She hugged the stuffed dog tighter.

"Sure." He pulled around to the open shed to park the truck out of the snow. That done, he boosted Gracie out of the seat and carried her into the house through the back door. She scurried off to get ready for bed.

A few minutes later, when he came to tuck her in, he found her already asleep, curled under the blankets with Big Beau in her arms.

Leaving her door ajar, he walked down the hall. His father's old bedroom was at the very end. An uneasy prickle stole over him as he opened the door and switched on the overhead light. He'd always felt like an intruder coming in here, especially when his father was sleeping off one of his headaches. Maybe that was the real reason he hadn't followed through with his plan to refurbish the room.

The closet and the dresser drawers had been emptied, but Jubal checked them anyway, finding nothing. The hardwood floor, even under the furniture, showed no sign of a loose board that might hide a secret cache. That left Gracie's idea—the bed.

The brass bed frame was old and tarnished. The bare mattress, covered in blue and white ticking, bore a hollow where the old man had slept. Faint odors of sweat and tobacco lingered in the fabric.

Steeling himself for disappointment, Jubal

crouched next to the bed and slid an arm between the mattress and the box spring. His hand moved cautiously over the surface. It might have been smarter to lift the mattress off the bed and look underneath. Anything could be lurking under here—spiders, mice, even a weapon.

He was about to do just that when his fingers touched something. It was paper—several sheets, folded like a letter. Jubal's pulse slammed as he withdrew them into the light and saw what they were.

# Chapter 10

Ellie sat at the breakfast table in her bathrobe, doing her best to enjoy the eggs that Clara had scrambled for her. She knew her mother meant well, but all she really felt like this morning was coffee.

"Bad night?" Clara looked up from her morning crossword puzzle with a sympathetic smile.

"Not great. The baby was tap-dancing, and I swear Beau jumped up and barked every time the wind rattled that loose shutter outside my window. He must've thought somebody was trying to get in, and he needed to protect me."

"I'll ask Ben to fix it. Where's Beau now? I don't see him."

"He was so tired from guarding me all night that, when I got up, he went to sleep in my bed." Ellie sprinkled pepper on her eggs. "Sorry to be such a grump. I'm aware that every woman who has a baby goes through times like this, when she's as big as a house and all she wants to do is lock the door and bawl her eyes out. Sometimes I can't wait to have this baby. Other times, when I think about it, I'm scared to death."

"That's perfectly normal, dear. Believe me, you'll be fine. One look at that sweet little girl, and you'll know exactly what to do."

Ellie forced down another bite. Her mother wasn't helping.

"Remember, tomorrow's your baby shower," Clara continued. "The ladies there will have lots of good advice to offer you, along with their nice gifts."

Ellie sighed. Jess had gone to so much work to plan the shower and send out the invitations. She should be looking forward to it. Instead she was dreading the event, sitting there looking like a fat, pregnant heifer in front of women who'd all brought her presents, even though they scarcely knew her. How could she be so ungrateful? What was wrong with her this morning?

"Cheer up, sweetheart, it's almost Christmas," Clara said. "A week from tomorrow will be the Christmas parade, with the ball that night, and everyone celebrating."

"Don't count on me for the ball," Ellie said. "Something tells me I won't feel up to going."

"That would be a shame," Clara said. "If you don't want to be on your feet, I know they could use help at the ticket table. By the way, I finished Gracie's dress early this morning. There wasn't much left to do, just the side seams. If you don't have other plans, maybe you could drop it off for her at the ranch."

"I have a ten o'clock appointment for a checkup at the clinic. I could go after that, I suppose, but I'm not sure anybody's going to be home. Jubal could be working on the ranch, and Gracie's in school."

"You could call Jubal." Clara gave her a knowing look. "Something tells me he'd be glad to see you."

"Mother—"

"What? I'm not blind. I saw how you two were looking at each other last night."

"Jubal and I are friends—and barely that. After the way I treated him, he'll never trust me again. I'm surprised he's even speaking to me."

"But you've given it some thought, haven't you?"

"I'm not even going to answer that question."

"If you don't mind my speaking frankly—"

"Has that ever stopped you before?"

"Listen, I've got to say this, Ellie. You could do worse than Jubal. Your baby's going to need a father, and Gracie needs a mother. Anyone can see that little girl adores you."

"Gracie's a darling. But it's Beau she adores, not me. She wants a dog, not a mother." Ellie rose to her feet and began clearing the table. "If you want to give me the dress, I'll take it with me. But it may or may not get delivered today."

"Fine. I'll have it waiting for you when you're ready to leave. Be careful out there. The roads will be slick from the storm."

Ellie loaded the dishwasher and went upstairs to get ready for the day. She loved her mother. Either of them would rush into a burning building to save the other. But like most mothers and daughters, they didn't always agree with one another. When Clara pushed a little too hard, Ellie tended to push back. There'd likely be more pushing once the baby arrived. But never mind that, Ellie told herself. She was home, where she'd chosen to be—and where she felt safe and loved.

"Everything's looking good. You're all set to go." Dr. Ramirez gave Ellie a parting smile. "See you in a week. Say hello to the *mango* for me."

That *mango* bit was getting old, Ellie thought as she walked out to the Purple People Eater. Maybe she should let Jubal know the perky Latina had a crush on him.

*Good grief, could she be jealous? What was wrong with her today?*

With a sigh, she climbed into the old car. She'd stopped by the garage on her way to the clinic. Silas was still waiting for the parts to fix her BMW. "Any day now," he'd told her. Maybe she should have had the car towed to a big-city dealership and paid through the nose to have it repaired there. Either way, the insurance would have covered most of it. But Silas was doing his best, and it was too late to change her plans now.

The box with Gracie's dress in it lay on the backseat. She had plenty of time and not much to do at home. There was no good reason not to call Jubal and deliver the package.

Last night's fast-moving storm had left a glaze of sleet on the ground. Earlier the driving had been slippery, but by now the main roads had been salted, the slush cleared by morning traffic. Driving to the ranch shouldn't be a problem.

Before starting the car, she found her cell phone and scrolled to Jubal's number.

He answered on the second ring. "Ellie?" There was something in his voice, a shadow of tension that put her on alert.

"Is everything okay?" she asked.

"Fine, it's just that . . ." He took a breath. "I've found something."

"Can you tell me more?" Ellie's pulse skipped.

"I'd rather show you—but not anybody else until I'm sure of what I've got. I could use some input from your legal mind."

"I can meet you somewhere. Are you at the ranch?"

"Yes. Do you mind coming here?"

"Not at all. If you're worried about gossip, I've got the excuse of having Gracie's dress to deliver."

"I'm not worried about gossip. But be careful on the road."

"You sound like my mother."

He chuckled at that. "Take your time."

"See you." Ellie's sour mood lifted as she ended the call and started the car. Jubal had asked for her help. He valued her opinion. Today, when she needed a boost, that made all the difference. Maybe she could actually help him find a way to save his ranch.

Jubal was waiting on the front porch when she drove up to the ranch house. Motioning for her to stay put, he came down the steps to help her out of the car. "How were the roads?" he asked as if nothing unusual was on his mind.

"Not that bad. Gracie's dress is in that box in the backseat."

"I'll get it after you're safely inside. That's precious cargo you're carrying." He took her arm to balance her as she climbed the steps. That was the Jubal she remembered, always looking out for others. Maybe her mother was right. Maybe she should have married him. But then everything would have been different. He wouldn't have married Laura and had Gracie. She wouldn't have married Brent. And she wouldn't be carrying this baby.

*Who would she be now if she'd chosen to stay in Branding Iron? Who would Jubal be?*

Inside, he slipped off her coat and hung it on the rack. Gracie's Christmas tree, with its cherished decorations, stood in the corner. The lights weren't on, but the flames that crackled in the fireplace lent warmth and cheer to the room. The fresh logs were barely burnt, as if Jubal had kindled the fire only after learning that she was on her way.

"Have a seat. I'll get the box out of your car."

Ellie settled on the couch, basking in the warmth of the fire as he strode outside, returned with the dress box, and took it down the hall to Gracie's room. Moments later, he reappeared with a plain manila envelope.

"I found these papers under my dad's mattress. Take a look." He sat next to her, opened the envelope, and laid three sheets of paper on the coffee table. "Before I give you my ideas, I want you to read them and let me know what you think. Tell me everything that comes to mind, even what's obvious."

Ellie picked up the first page, which appeared to be a loan contract, and studied it.

She voiced her thoughts for Jubal's benefit. "I see that it's between your father, Seth McFarland, and Shumway and Sons, for the amount of five thousand dollars. The date, December nineteenth, four years ago this month." She glanced up, meeting his gaze. "You told me that when Laura died, your father gave you five thousand dollars to pay for her funeral."

"He never told me where he got the money," Jubal said. "And given what I was dealing with, I didn't think to ask. I just took the cash and paid the funeral home."

"Had he ever been that generous with you before?" Ellie remembered the hard-bitten curmudgeon who could barely spare a smile, let alone anything beyond the essentials, for his son.

"Never. But he'd always liked Laura. It hit him hard when she died. I guess he wanted to help any way he could. The old man must've had a heart after all."

Ellie scanned the page, thinking aloud as she

read. "From what you've told me about his bad credit, I'm guessing the bank wouldn't lend him any money. So he found a loan shark that would."

She was making assumptions now, she cautioned herself. But that was where her thoughts were leading her—that Shumway and Sons, whoever they were, had somehow used the contract to swindle Jubal's father out of the ranch. Willing herself to focus on the complicated legal language, she pored over the next page. The print was so minuscule she could barely read it.

"Interest rate . . . That's high, really high. Did you find any evidence that your father made payments?"

"No cancelled checks, no receipts for cash. Nothing. He insisted on handling the ranch accounts right up to the end of his life. He was in the ground by the time I found what a mess our finances were in. I can't imagine he paid anything on this loan."

Ellie scanned down the page. Buried amid a jumble of fine print, she found the sections on repayment terms and collateral. As she took her time to read these parts in detail, a sick rage rose inside her. Whoever they were, these lenders had taken full advantage of a grieving, irresponsible old man.

"I take it you're thinking what I'm thinking," Jubal said.

Ellie gripped the page so hard that her hand shook. "This is like one of those title loans people can get on their cars. You see the ads on TV—give the lender the signed title to your car, and you get a pile of cash. What the ads don't tell you is that unless you repay the loan, along with an obscene amount of interest, by the due date, they keep your title and take your car."

"Agreed," Jubal said. "But my father didn't borrow five thousand dollars on a car. He put up the title to the ranch for a ninety-day loan at twenty percent compound interest. Then he gave me the money and pretended it had never happened—I'm guessing that's why he hid the contract under the mattress, so I wouldn't know what a crazy thing he'd done to help me. Maybe he meant to pay it back and couldn't. Or maybe he just ignored it, like he did so many debts. Lord, Ellie, if I'd realized how far gone his judgment was, I'd have stepped in and taken over. This mess is at least partly my fault."

Ellie laid a hand on his sleeve, feeling hard tension through the fabric. "He was your father. You'd grown up with him taking care of things. You'd just lost your wife, and you had a little girl to take care of. You can't blame yourself, Jubal. If you have to blame somebody, blame the crooks who took advantage of the poor man."

When he didn't reply, Ellie turned her attention back to the contract. This time she focused on the signatures at the end. "You're sure it was your father who signed this?"

"If he didn't, it's a damned good forgery. I'd know his handwriting anywhere. And why would he have the contract if he hadn't signed it? For now, let's assume he did."

"And the lender—J. D. Shumway?" The spidery letters were barely readable. They looked as if the signer might have been very old or ill. "Have you ever heard of this person?"

"I've lived here all my life. I've never known any Shumways. I do recognize the notary who witnessed the signing, old Charlie Bergeson. But he died a couple of years ago."

"So where do you take this now?" Ellie asked.

Jubal exhaled, his breath ragged with emotion. "This is why I asked you to come, Ellie. I need to know whether a crime was committed, or whether my father signed a contract that was unfair but legal."

Ellie studied the document, rereading the parts that had allowed the lender to take the ranch. She'd been barely halfway through law school before she'd quit to marry Brent and move to San Francisco. With so much riding on the legality of this contract, how could she even offer a guess? What if she turned out to be wrong?

"This is too important to hang on my opinion," she said. "I think it's time we shared this with Ben. He's not a lawyer, but he has access to the county prosecutor's office and to several judges. One of them should be able to look at this and tell you whether you have a case. Or you could take it to Cottonwood Springs and find a lawyer who'd offer a free first-time consultation—"

"That would be begging, Ellie. I'm not ready to do that."

She stared at him. "How can you say such a

thing, Jubal McFarland? You need real legal help. Get it."

His jaw was set, his eyes steely. "A lawyer who offers a free consultation is hoping for a lawsuit that'll make him some money. With nobody to sue, I can't offer that—and right now I can't afford to pay for legal advice. As for bringing in your brother and asking him to get help, that would not only be begging, it would mean going public. My father was respected in this town. I've done my best to honor his memory and keep his problems private. Until I know there's no better choice, I'd rather have things stay that way."

"So what is it you want?" Ellie struggled to contain her frustration.

"I want the bastards who did this to my father, to me, and to Gracie. I want to face the Shumways, whoever the hell they are, and demand justice for what they did to our family. Most of all, I want our ranch back."

Ellie shot to her feet, her temper boiling over. "Then swallow your blasted pride and get some help! If you had any sense, Jubal McFarland, you'd realize you can't do this on your own— and don't look at me like that. I'm no help at all. Not the kind of help you need."

"Ellie, calm down." He was on his feet, facing her. It crossed her mind that the wretched man might try to take her in his arms. That had worked in the old days when she was peeved with him. But it wouldn't be a good idea now. Not while she was mad enough to punch him in the face.

"Listen to me," he said. "I know you're running out of patience, but I've got to do this my way."

"Fine." She stepped back, half turning. "Do it any way you want. Just leave me out of this mess. I've had enough."

With that she strode toward the door, grabbed her coat off the rack, and headed out onto the porch. Jubal wasn't there in time to help her down the steps, but there was a rail. Gripping it tightly, she made it to her car without stumbling—even though, by then, her eyes were blurred by tears.

"Ellie, come back here! We can talk this out!" She could hear his voice from the porch, but she didn't look around. If she did, she might not be able to leave.

Proud, stubborn, impossible Jubal! He hadn't changed since their school days. But she had. She wasn't his girl anymore. And she didn't have to put up with his mule-headed ways.

She managed to drive all the way to the turnoff before she broke down, crying so hard that she had to pull off the road. She couldn't do this anymore. Dealing with Jubal, his problems, and his refusal to get help was like riding an emotional roller coaster. And her conflicted feelings for the man only made things worse.

She had to back off while she still could. No more discussions. No more playing detective. Jubal could handle his issues without her help. She already had enough on her plate.

She'd had it. She was through with him. Finished.

Jubal's gaze followed the old purple car until it vanished down the lane. He could still feel the sting of Ellie's words. Maybe she was right. Maybe he shouldn't be too proud to ask for help. But pride wasn't the only thing holding him back. The thought of the story getting out, the gossip spreading like wildfire, was more than he could stand. Even kids—they had big ears, and they could be cruel. Sooner or later the story would reach Gracie, and not likely in a kind way.

He wanted to protect her as long as possible. If he could find a way to save the ranch, his daughter would never have to know what her grandfather had done. And he would never have to break the news that they were in danger of losing their home.

Jubal's mood darkened as he walked back into the house and closed the door behind him. With Ellie gone, the house seemed too big, too quiet. Even the fire had lost some of its glow.

Damn the woman, even after ten years she had a way of lighting up a room, then leaving it dim and empty when she was gone. That had never changed. A lot of things hadn't.

Jubal swore under his breath. He'd known it as soon as he'd seen her at that Saturday morning breakfast—even when he'd realized she was pregnant. He still had feelings for the woman.

Not that it made any difference. He was a

bumpkin rancher with barely enough money to buy his daughter a burger and fries. She was a sophisticated city woman with a fancy little dog and a BMW in the shop. And her baby had a father—a man Ellie had loved enough to make that last-ditch attempt to save their marriage. She hadn't gotten pregnant by herself—and there was a good chance that having her baby, and loving it as he knew she would, would reawaken feelings for the child's father.

Shrugging into his work coat, he headed for the back door to clean out the stalls in the barn—a job that fit the mood he was in. Walking out on him ten years ago was the smartest thing Ellie had ever done, he told himself. The life he'd offered could never have made her happy.

The baby shower was set for 3:00 on Saturday, late enough to give Jess and Francine time to clean up after Saturday's breakfast buffet and decorate the B and B with a baby theme. Ellie had offered to help, but her sister-in-law wouldn't hear of it. Jess had insisted that Ellie and Clara stay away until everything was ready.

Ellie had made sure it was all right to bring Beau. When left home alone, the little poodle tended to get anxious and chew on things like shoes and pillows. Jess had promised that while the party lasted, Beau's nemesis, Sergeant Pepper, would be shut in the basement.

Ellie had never attended a baby shower and wasn't sure what to expect. "Just let yourself go,"

Clara told her on the way up the walk. "It'll be good, silly fun. Expect that, and you'll do fine."

The guests were still arriving when Jess ushered Ellie and her mother inside. The room was decorated like a fifties prom with pink and blue crepe paper streamers dangling from the ceiling. There were pink and blue balloons and pink plastic cloths on tables decorated with little plastic babies in diapers. Tacky, but maybe that was the whole idea, Ellie thought. And she had to give Jess and her mother credit for going all out. Glasses of sweet tea and plates of cookies had been set on the tables. The décor and food must've involved a lot of work and more than a little cash.

If she was still around next summer, Ellie knew she'd want to return the favor for Jess. But how could she hope to pull off anything like this?

She remembered the story, how Jess had come to town a year ago, a stranger searching for her birth mother. Now Jess was part of the community—the sheriff's wife and the owner of Branding Iron Bed and Breakfast. She seemed to know everybody in town, and they all seemed to like her. Ellie had grown up in Branding Iron. But now she was the one who felt like a stranger.

"Sit right here. You're the guest of honor." Jess motioned Ellie to a table at the front of the room and seated Clara next to her. "You'll know a lot of the ladies. I'll introduce you first. Then we'll play a little game, have some refreshments, and let you open your gifts. After that, there'll be time to mingle and visit."

Gifts were stacked high next to the Christmas tree. The women who'd come today had been more than generous. With Christmas around the corner, most of them wouldn't have had it easy coming up with money for a baby gift. Ellie couldn't help feeling touched. Some of these ladies didn't even know her. How could she thank them all?

The tables had been arranged in a circle with everyone facing the middle. Conversation buzzed, filling the room with a happy babble. Glancing around at the seated guests, Ellie recognized a few of them. Pretty, blond Kylie Taggart, married to Ben's friend Shane, was there with her great-aunt Muriel, who had a farm on the edge of town. The two of them gave Ellie a smile and a friendly wave. Two white-haired ladies at a side table were old friends of Clara's. The stern-looking woman next to them was Maybelle Ferguson, who'd been a substitute teacher at the high school. Krystle, the schoolmate she'd met days ago at Shop Mart, was there, too. She was dressed to the nines, her hair and nails salon fresh.

Ellie recognized Silas's wife, Connie, and her daughter, Katy, coming in the door. They went everywhere together. Katy, who had Down syndrome, had been a sunny little girl when Ellie left town. Now she was a confident young woman. Ellie had seen them at the wedding and remembered them both.

Catching sight of Ellie, they crossed the room

toward her. "I have some good news for you."
Connie had graying hair and a patient smile.
"Silas got word your car parts are on the way.
They should be here early next week."

"That's great!" Ellie said. "Does he have any
idea when my car will be done?"

"He'll know when he's seen the parts. If everything he needs is there, in good condition, it
shouldn't take more than a few days."

"Thanks for the good news. I won't be sorry
to see the last of that old purple car."

Katy noticed Beau, who'd poked his head out
of Ellie's bag. Her eyes lit. "I love your little dog!
Can I pet him?"

"Let him smell the back of your hand," Ellie
said. "If he acts friendly, it's fine."

Beau responded to Katy's hand with licks and
wags. Ellie lifted him out of her bag and placed
him in Katy's arms. Katy giggled when the little
poodle licked her face.

"You can hold him for a while if you want,"
Ellie said. "When you've had enough, just bring
him back."

Still cuddling the dog, Katy followed her mother
to a seat at a nearby table.

Jess was talking to a woman who'd just walked
in the door. Tall, fashionably thin, and dressed
in a red designer pantsuit, she appeared to be in
her mid- to late forties. Her sharp features were
crowned by short, professionally streaked hair,
which made her look like a younger Jane Fonda.
She carried a small, wrapped gift, which she
handed to Jess to put with the others.

Ellie nudged her mother. "Do you know that woman?" she asked in a whisper.

"She looks familiar," Clara said. "I think her husband ran for mayor in the last election. But I don't remember being introduced to her."

Now Jess was ushering the woman over to their table. "I'd like you to meet Donetta Huish," she said. "Her husband works at the bank. They're the ones who sold me this old house for the B and B. It had belonged to Donetta's grandfather."

Clara smiled. "I feel as if I already know you, Donetta," she said. "When I was a little girl, I had a friend who lived here. I used to play with her until the family broke up and her mother moved away with the girls. My friend's name was Beatrice. By any chance, could she be your mother?"

Donetta shook her elegant head. "Beatrice was my aunt. Her sister Florence was my mother. Sadly, they're both gone now."

"So how long have you and your husband lived in Branding Iron?" Clara asked. "Forgive me, I don't get out much anymore."

"We came here six years ago to look after my grandfather. We'd tried to manage things long-distance—paying to keep the heat and water on and the house in decent repair. But Grandpa had become reclusive in his old age and we needed to keep an eye on him. Two years ago he passed away and left me this house."

"I remember your grandfather quite well," Clara said. "He was a nice man, but he became depressed, I think, after his family left. So sad the way he shut himself in. The kids used to call him the Vinegar Man, after the old poem they'd read in school. As time went by, I don't think they even remembered his real name. Heavens, what was it?" Clara paused to think. "Now I remember. It was Shumway. Jacob Shumway."

# Chapter 11

Ellie looked up at the woman she'd just met and arranged her face into a smile. "What a pleasure, Donetta. Thank you so much for coming to my baby shower." She mouthed the polite words, her thoughts spinning like windmills in a Texas tornado.

Was Jacob Shumway the man who'd signed the loan contract with Jubal's father?

But how could that be? The contract was only four years old. According to both Donetta and Clara, the man had been a bitter recluse for the latter part of his life, shutting himself in his house, refusing to let people through the door. Surely such a person wouldn't have been in the business of lending money.

True, Jacob Shumway had been alive when the contract was executed. And the wavering signature suggested an infirm hand. But no theory Ellie could come up with made sense—especially now that all parties to the contract, including the notary, had passed away.

She had to talk to Jubal—as soon as she could get away from here.

Clara's discreet nudge startled her back to the present. The buzz of conversation had ceased. Donetta Huish had taken her seat, and Jess, standing next to the table, was speaking to the guests.

"When I sent out the invitations, I asked each of you to bring a piece of advice for the new mother. To get the party started, we'll go around the room. When your turn comes I want you to tell Ellie your name—even if she already knows it—and give her your advice. Katy, we'll start with you."

Katy was still snuggling Beau in her arms. She beamed. "Katy Parker. Give your baby lots of love."

Her mother was next. "Connie Parker. While you're taking care of the baby, don't forget to take care of yourself."

Sitting next to them, in a beautiful handmade sweater, was a tiny, alert woman who appeared to be in her eighties. "Merle Crandall. Find something to laugh about every day. It'll keep you young—and sane." Laughter rippled around the room. Only then did Ellie remember who the woman was. She ran Merle's Craft and Yarn, around the corner from the B and B.

"Children are never too young to learn proper table manners." That was typical advice from Maybelle Ferguson, who had no children of her own.

"Fix your hair and put on your makeup every day. It'll do wonders for your mood." That tip came from Ellie's old schoolmate, Krystle.

There was more advice. Some of it was practical, such as never go anywhere without at least three diapers, a packet of wipes, and two clean outfits for the baby. Some was funny. Kylie Taggart advised her, "When you take your baby anywhere, wear colors that won't show spit-up. Floral prints are best. Black is out." Ellie, dressed head to toe in her customary black, joined in the laughter.

She found herself relaxing a little. These were nice women. They all seemed to wish her well. Most of them would become her friends if she reached out to them. She was even beginning to have a good time  except that her thoughts kept flying back to what she'd learned about Jacob Shumway and the need to contact Jubal. After their last parting, she'd sworn she was finished with the man and his problems. But this chance discovery could be the key to everything. It was too important to put aside.

The game that followed, "Pin the Diaper on the Baby," was pure silliness, but Ellie did her best to be a good sport as she was blindfolded, spun, and given a paper diaper to pin on a poster of a bare-bottomed infant. To the accompaniment of hysterical giggles, she missed the target by a good eight inches.

When the time came for refreshments, Katy
brought Beau back to Ellie, who gave him a treat
and tucked him into her bag. The little poodle
settled down and went to sleep. By then Jess and
her mother were bringing in the light luncheon
they'd prepared.

Francine, a masterful cook, had outdone herself with fruit salad, stuffed croissants, and miniature apricot tarts, served on pink paper plates.
Ellie made a mental note to thank Jess's mother
with something nice, like flowers or really good
chocolates, if she could find anywhere to get
such things in Branding Iron.

Now it was time for the gifts. Katy accepted
the job of taking each wrapped package from
beside the tree and bringing it to Ellie to be
opened. Most of the baby clothes were practical—pajamas, nightgowns, and onesies. There
were bath sets, disposable diapers by the case, a
silver baby spoon from Donetta Huish, and from
Jess, Ben, and Francine a car seat that attached
to a folding stroller. Gazing at all the things
she'd been given, Ellie felt overwhelmed—not
only by the generosity of these women, but by
the thought that one tiny baby would have so
many needs.

Katy brought the last gift and placed it in
Ellie's hands. The dress-sized box was wrapped
in white tissue paper and tied with a pretty bow
of pink yarn. Ellie tore off the paper, lifted the
lid, and gasped.

Inside was a lacy white baby shawl, hand-
crocheted from angora yarn so light and silky

that when she unfolded it, the shawl almost seemed to float. The pattern of flowers and butterflies was exquisite.

"It's a christening blanket," Connie said. "Merle makes them and sells them in her shop."

"It's just lovely," Ellie said. "Thank you, Merle. This is a treasure. I've never seen anything like it, not even in San Francisco."

The petite, white-haired woman smiled. "My mother taught me how to do the pattern when I was a girl. The yarn comes from a friend in Lithuania. You can't find it in this country."

Ellie refolded the shawl with care and replaced it in the box. "Did you also make that beautiful sweater you're wearing?" she asked Merle.

"I did. Come by my shop when you're not busy. I'd be delighted to show you around."

"Thank you so much," Ellie said. "I'd love to—"

A bedlam of barks, hisses, and yowls drowned out the rest of her words. The uproar came from the back of the kitchen. Ellie didn't need to check her bag to know that Beau had escaped and gone exploring.

Ellie jumped to her feet, but Francine, who was closer, made it into the kitchen ahead of her. "It's all right, honey," Francine called. "Beau and the sergeant are just having a little to-do through the door."

Ellie burst into the kitchen to find Beau barking at a half-inch crack under the closed basement door. The threatening yowls and the dagger claws that stabbed through the crack left no doubt as to who was on the other side.

"Honestly, Beau, don't you have any sense? That cat could have you for lunch!" Ellie scooped up the little poodle. From the safety of her arms, he yapped even louder, giving Sergeant Pepper a piece of his doggy mind.

Ellie carried him back into the dining room and put him in her bag while she thanked each of the guests. By then most of the women were getting ready to leave. They had families at home, errands to run, and no more time to spare. Once they were gone, Ellie helped clean up and load the gifts in the back of Jess's SUV. Then she thanked Francine, and let Jess drive her and Clara home.

Twenty minutes later, with the gifts put away and Clara napping on the couch, Ellie finally found the time to try to reach Jubal. Sitting at the kitchen table, she called his cell phone. No answer.

What a time for him to be out of touch, when she was bursting to tell him what she'd learned. If he called her back, she could give him her news over the phone. But it would be better if they could talk it over and come up with a plan. That would mean meeting face to face. For now, all she could do was leave him a brief message.

"Jubal, I've learned something that could be important. I need to talk to you. Call me. Maybe we can meet."

They hadn't parted on the best of terms yesterday. What if he was ignoring her call, to show her he didn't care? She'd known men who would do that. But Jubal wasn't that kind of person. She'd never known him to play those games. If he knew she was calling him, he would answer.

Why hadn't he answered his phone? Was he all right? Ellie's worry instincts kicked in. She stood, her anxiety surging. She could call Gracie's phone. But if Gracie wasn't with him, the call could worry the girl. Besides, Ellie didn't want to give the impression that she was stalking the man. Short of showing up at his house, she could only wait for Jubal to call her back.

Beau pawed her leg, begging to be picked up. Ellie reached down for him and gathered him into her arms. He wiggled with pleasure and licked her chin with his wet pink tongue. Ellie blinked back tears of exhaustion. Physically and emotionally, the afternoon had worn her out.

Slipping her phone into her pocket, she walked into the living room and curled into a cushiony armchair. Clara had switched on the Christmas tree lights before lying down for her nap. They glowed softly in the fading afternoon light. Beau snuggled against Ellie's shoulder, a tiny bundle of warmth and comfort. Within minutes they'd both dozed off.

Jubal had resolved to put his worries aside for the day and spend time with his daughter. After he'd done the morning chores, braided her hair, and made her French toast for breakfast, they'd put on their coats, climbed into the truck, and headed for Cottonwood Springs to do some Christmas shopping.

Most of Gracie's Christmas gifts would be clothes. Jubal knew she'd be happiest with the ones that she'd picked out herself and given him to wrap and put under the tree.

They parked at the mall and walked into a wonderland of glittering decorations, Christmas music, and mouthwatering aromas. Christmas trees stood at every corner, trimmed with dazzling lights and ornaments. Tinsel garlands hung overhead. Shoppers bustled in and out of stores filled with a myriad of things to buy. One look at Gracie's sparkling eyes, and Jubal knew he'd done the right thing bringing her here.

In the center of the mall, a plump, bearded Santa sat in a big red chair, with parents and children lined up to perch on his knee and have their photos taken.

"Would you like to tell Santa your Christmas wishes?" Jubal asked his daughter.

Gracie wrinkled her nose at him. "I'm getting too old for that, Dad. Besides, you can tell his beard is fake."

Jubal sighed. Where had his wide-eyed little girl gone?

He'd promised Gracie she could choose whatever she wanted in the way of clothes. He'd brought his credit card, free of debt, and had been prepared to splurge if it would please her. But he should have known she'd make sensible choices—she was Laura's daughter, after all. Gracie came to the counter of the preteen shop with some nice basics for school—sweaters, a skirt, jeans, and two pairs of the patterned leggings Jubal had seen young girls wear. The one extravagance was a pair of smart little fleece-lined leather boots, which he was happy to buy her.

"You'll need a new coat, too," he said.

"It's all right, Daddy," she replied with a heart-melting smile. "The coats will go on sale after Christmas. We can buy a nice one then."

Jubal swallowed the lump in his throat. His daughter hadn't had an easy life, but that life had made her wise for her years.

He knew what she really wanted—a little dog like Ellie's poodle. The fact that she didn't press him for one was a reflection of her maturity. He'd never told her about the loss of the ranch. But she seemed to sense that something was wrong  something that made this a bad time to ask for a high-maintenance pet.

"I want to get a present for Ellie, too," Gracie said. "She's been really nice to me."

Jubal sighed, remembering how Ellie had stormed out of the house yesterday. Even if he'd known what a sophisticated woman like Ellie might like, buying her a Christmas present would be an awkward gesture. In the end, because Gracie was so keen on getting something, they settled on a half-pound, gold-wrapped box of gourmet chocolates and a packet of home-baked puppy treats for Beau.

After eating Chinese at the food court and wolfing down hot fudge sundaes, they spent time strolling around the mall, taking in the decorations and the stores. Jubal had turned his cell phone off that morning. He'd needed a day free from distractions and bad news, a day when the ringing phone wouldn't interrupt his time with his daughter.

This good day was worth it.

But shutting off his thoughts wasn't as simple as shutting off his phone. Ellie had been on his mind all day. He'd done his best to push her aside, but now, driving home in the truck with Gracie asleep beside him, he couldn't fight her any longer.

Yesterday, when he'd refused to follow her advice, she'd been frustrated and hurt. Jubal knew her well enough to understand. Ellie was a passionately caring person. She'd wanted to help him, but he'd turned a deaf ear. He couldn't blame her for walking out on him. But, damn it, he had to do this his way—and that included not asking for help until he could put together a solid case against the Shumways, whoever the hell they were.

Maybe his quarrel with Ellie was for the best— a clean break for both of them. These games they were playing—the phone calls, the intimate conversations, and that one sizzling kiss—were only leading them down the path to regret. Forget the past and move on. That was the sensible thing to do, for Ellie as well as for him. And for Gracie. For Gracie most of all.

By now it was getting dark. Jubal switched on his headlights. A glance at the gauge on the dashboard told him the truck was running low on gas. A mile ahead, at the next highway junction, was a gas station where he could fill up. With luck, he could do it without waking his daughter.

She was still asleep a few minutes later when he pulled up to the gas pump, climbed out of the truck, and closed the door softly behind him. The December wind was brisk and bitter. Jubal stood in the cold waiting for the slow pump to fill the tank. It seemed as good a time as any to take his cell phone out of his pocket, turn it on, and check for voice messages.

There was only one. Jubal played it once, then again, struck by the undercurrent of excitement in Ellie's voice. He'd spent the past half hour convincing himself to forget her. But nothing could have stopped him from calling her back.

She answered on the first ring. "Jubal? Are you all right?"

"My phone was turned off. I just got your message." He could explain more later. "You found something?"

Wind howled under the protective awning that sheltered the gas pumps, muffling her reply. "Can't hear you," he said. "I'm on the road. Gracie's asleep. Let me call you when I get her home. Maybe I can meet you somewhere."

She said something he couldn't make out above the keening sound of wind. "I'll get back to you," he said, then ended the call and put the phone back in his pocket. Inside the truck, Gracie was still asleep. Jubal started the engine and pulled back onto the road. He'd been fighting to stay alert before the call. Now he was wide awake, adrenaline surging.

Ellie said she'd found something new—maybe something that could make a difference. But that wasn't all that made his pulse race. Unwise as it might be, he had a reason to see her again.

Ellie put her phone in her purse and reached for her coat. Jubal had said he was on the road, headed home with Gracie. She couldn't be sure how close he was, but waiting for him to call back and arranging to meet would not only take time, but for him it would mean leaving Gracie alone. If she could go now and meet him at the ranch, it would save time and trouble.

"Where are you off to in such a hurry?" Clara glanced away from her favorite TV crime drama.

"Just an errand. I shouldn't be long. Would you keep an eye on Beau for me?" The little poodle had left the armchair and was sprawled under the Christmas tree, fast asleep.

Clara raised an eyebrow. "Not a problem. But you're being very mysterious. Is everything all right?"

"Everything's fine. See you later." Ellie escaped out the door, found her keys, and climbed into the Purple People Eater. The engine fired up on the first try. The old bucket of bolts had served her well. But she wouldn't be sorry to trade it in for her BMW.

Wind gusts slammed the sides of the old car as she drove through town. Maybe another storm was blowing in. But for now the twilight sky was clear, the roads dry. She switched on the radio. Nothing but Christmas music, but it was better than hearing the howl of the wind outside.

She'd reached the last stop sign before the main highway and was about to make the right turn when Jubal's truck passed in front of her, headed in the direction of his ranch.

She would know that truck anywhere. He was pushing the speed limit, probably anxious to get home. She'd hang back a little, give him time to get there and get Gracie settled. By the time he phoned her again, she'd be pulling up to the house.

Turning onto the main road, she drove slowly. Far ahead now, the familiar taillights of Jubal's truck were fading into the near-darkness. After the way she'd stormed out on him the day before, seeing him again might be awkward. Maybe she should apologize. But no, in the light of what she had to tell him, a petty argument wasn't worth remembering.

A few minutes later she turned off the highway and onto the gravel lane that led between the fields to Jubal's ranch. Outside, wind battered the car and shook the ancient cottonwoods that grew along the roadside. The towering trees swayed like spooky goblins, their branches bare and dark against the moonlit sky.

Ellie was gripping the wheel with both hands and humming along with Elvis Presley's "Blue

Christmas" when, above the wind, she heard a shattering crack. She glanced to her right, just in time to see a huge limb break loose from the nearest tree. Crashing through the weaker branches beneath, it plummeted right toward her.

Ellie stomped the gas pedal to the floor. The car shot forward. Broken twigs and small branches showered down as the limb struck the ground behind her with a deafening thud.

The car had come to a stop, Elvis still singing on the radio. Shaken, Ellie geared down and tried to pull forward, but something was blocking the wheels. Switching off the ignition, she braced against the wind, shoved open the door, and climbed out of the car.

The limb that had fallen behind her was as long as a bus and at its base almost as thick as a man's waist. It lay across the road, one heavy side branch resting against the car's rear bumper. Loose twigs lay all around the car, littering the hood and trunk. One broken branch lay across the road, blocking the front wheels. For all that, the Purple People Eater appeared undamaged.

Ellie sagged against the side of the car, her knees shaking. If that massive limb had landed on the car, she could have died, and the baby, too. Either she was the luckiest woman alive or she'd just experienced a miracle.

From inside the car, her cell phone was ringing. She yanked the door open against the wind, sank onto the seat, and grabbed the phone out of her purse.

"Ellie?" The voice was Jubal's. Her lips moved

in an effort to reply, but the only sound that emerged from her throat was his whispered name.

"What is it? Are you all right?"

Willing herself to be calm, she struggled to tell him. Her voice shook as she related what had happened. "I'm not hurt. Just . . . I don't know . . ."

"Stay in the car. I'm coming," he said.

"Will Gracie be all right?"

"Gracie's in bed. She'll be fine. Stay put." The call ended.

Ellie closed the door and slumped against the seat. The baby was stirring. She felt the poke of a tiny foot beneath her sweater. The answering surge of love brought tears to her eyes. What if something had happened to harm her precious baby?

She'd been told that she would love her baby as soon as she saw it. At the time, Ellie hadn't understood. But she did now. She loved her little one already, with a fierce protectiveness that was unlike anything she'd ever known. She thought about her own mother's constant fussing and worry and how it had always annoyed her. Now, for the first time, she knew how Clara must feel, and how anxious she was to keep her beloved child safe. That motherly urge to protect never went away.

Wiping her eyes, Ellie peered through the litter-covered windshield. The ranch was close. Jubal couldn't be more than a few minutes away. But an eternity seemed to pass before she saw the truck's headlights coming down the lane. She retrieved her purse and climbed out of the car. The wind whipped her coat around her as she waited.

The truck stopped a few yards away. Leaving the headlights on, Jubal opened the door and sprang to the ground. "I'll be damned, lady. Rescuing you could get to be a full-time job." He made a feeble joke, recalling the recent night when she'd swung her BMW off the road to miss a deer.

The smile vanished from his face as he took in the broken branches around the car, and the massive limb that could have crushed the vehicle as easily as an eggshell. "Oh, my Lord, Ellie!" he muttered. "You could've died right here."

Ellie took a step toward him but her legs refused to hold her. She stumbled, almost falling. Jubal reached her in two long strides. His arms caught her and cradled her close. She felt his strength supporting her, his body adapting to her awkward shape as if it were the most natural thing in the world for him to hold her that way.

Racked by dry sobs, Ellie buried her face against his open coat. He smelled of hay and horses and clean, honest sweat, and right now she needed him.

"Oh, damn it, Ellie . . ." Muttering incoherent curses, he used his thumb to tilt her face upward. His kiss was rough and hungry, driven by a need as deep as her own. As the contact deepened, she felt the years melting away as if they'd never been apart—as if they were young and so much in love that nothing could come between them. The feeling wouldn't—and couldn't—last. But in that moment, with the wind whirling around them, there was nothing but Jubal, nothing but his strong arms and the raw sweetness of his mouth on hers.

They broke apart, Ellie trembling, Jubal making a visible effort to pull himself back to reality. "We've got to get you back to the house," he said.

"The car—"

"It'll have to wait for morning. You can call your mother when we get there." Jubal put a sheltering arm around her shoulders as he led her to the truck and helped her climb in. Huddled beside him, with wind gusts pummeling the truck cab, Ellie kept silent as Jubal drove back to the house. She'd come here to tell him something important, she reminded herself. The fallen limb, Jubal's dizzying kiss—they were nothing more than distractions. They couldn't be allowed to make a difference between them.

He helped her up the steps, into the shadowed living room, then went out again to put the truck in the shed. Ellie hung up her coat, then tiptoed down the hall to check on Gracie. In the glow of a night-light, Jubal's daughter lay fast asleep, her arm cradling the toy dog Ellie had given her. Ellie couldn't help smiling. The little girl was a heartbreaker. It was impossible not to love her—even knowing how much it would hurt them both when the time came to leave.

Returning to the living room, she plugged in the Christmas tree lights, settled on the couch, and used her cell phone to call her mother.

"Ellie? Did you have another accident? Are you all right?" Clara's voice shook with alarm.

"I'm fine, Mom." For once, Ellie didn't feel annoyed by her mother's concern. She could imagine herself asking her own daughter the same questions.

"So why are you calling? Where are you?"

"I'm at Jubal's."

"Oh . . . really?" Ellie could imagine her mother smiling.

"I just needed to tell him something. I was planning to come right home, but a big tree limb blew down across the lane. I can't leave here until it's cleared away tomorrow morning." Ellie knew better than to mention how close that limb had come to crushing her car.

"So you'll be there all night?" *How delicious,* Ellie could almost imagine Clara thinking.

"Relax, Mother. Gracie's here, so you don't have to worry about a scandal. I'll probably spend the night right here on the couch."

"You don't have to explain, dear. That's really none of my business. But think about it. Maybe that limb fell off the tree for a reason."

"Honestly, Mother—" Ellie's patience was frayed to the snapping point.

"You're still in love with him, aren't you?"

The memory of that electrifying kiss flashed through her mind. She couldn't lie to her mother. "All right! Maybe I am still in love with him! And I adore his little girl. But nothing's going to happen. There are too many . . . issues."

"Issues? Like what?"

"Like me being pregnant with my ex-husband's baby. Like all the reasons I left in the first place. Like—"

She broke off at the creak of a floorboard behind her. Glancing around, she saw that Jubal was standing in the kitchen doorway.

# Chapter 12

Jubal had come inside through the back door, which opened off the kitchen. He hadn't meant to overhear Ellie's exchange with her mother, but here he was, caught in the act.

He'd done some serious thinking after he'd left her to put the truck away. The kiss they'd shared had made him feel like a giddy teenager again. Holding her in his arms had brought back all the surging hormones and pulse-pounding thrills of the old days. But that kiss had been a mistake. He was already dealing with a plateful of trouble. The last thing he needed was to get jerked around by Ellie again.

Now, as if things weren't complicated enough, she'd just confessed to her mother that she loved him. In the awkward silence that followed, Jubal knew he had to put the brakes on this scene. The last time Ellie had said she loved him, she'd ended up damn near destroying him.

He wasn't about to let it happen again, especially now that Gracie was involved and could be hurt.

At the same time, he had no desire to embarrass Ellie, especially since she'd come to help him. For now, the simplest strategy would be to pretend he hadn't overheard.

She had ended the call to her mother. That was Jubal's cue to stride into the living room, rubbing his hands as if to warm them. "That howling wind is brutal," he said, moving toward the fireplace. "My ears are ringing so loud I can barely hear."

*If she bought that line, he could probably sell her some nice oceanfront property in Nevada. But at least it gave her an out.*

"In that case, you should probably warm up before I give you the news I brought." She was playing along, but something told Jubal she wasn't fooled.

"How's that again?" Crouching by the hearth, he turned toward her. His hand cupped his ear. "Give me a minute to light this fire and I'll be right with you."

He struck a match. The stack of dry kindling, crumpled newspaper, and logs, which he'd laid earlier, caught the flame and swiftly became a cheerful blaze.

Straightening, Jubal turned back to face her. Ellie was huddled in a corner of the sofa, her cell phone still in her hand. She'd been through a hell of a time tonight. Still, she looked beautiful, with windblown hair framing her face and firelight dancing in her dark eyes. It was all he could do to tear his gaze away from her.

"Thanks for plugging in the tree," he said. "The place should be warming up in the next few minutes."

"How are your ears?" Was it a jab or just a polite question?

"Better, I think." He joined her on the couch, needing to change the subject. "So what's the big news?"

She told him, then, about the baby shower and meeting Donetta Huish, the loan officer's wife, who'd sold Jess her grandfather's house— the house that became the B and B. The awkwardness between them fell away as he listened.

"I didn't think twice about it," she said. "Not until my mother remembered the name of the old man who'd lived there. It was Jacob Shumway."

*Jacob Shumway.* A memory flashed in Jubal's mind—a stoop-shouldered, wild-eyed old man standing in his ratty bathrobe on his moonlit porch, shrilling curses at the young hooligans who'd disturbed his sleep.

"The Vinegar Man?" He shook his head in disbelief. "I remember that old grump. We kids used to dare each other to knock on his door and run away before he could open it. I can't believe I lived in Branding Iron my whole life without caring enough to even know the old man's name."

"I didn't know it either," Ellie said. "That's pretty sad when you think of it."

"So what are the chances that it's his signature on that loan document?"

"He was still alive at the time the document was dated, but he'd have been very old. And to shut himself up the way he did, the poor man must've been mentally ill. I remember Donetta saying that she and her husband moved here to keep an eye on him."

Jubal stretched his legs, resting his boot heels on the edge of the time-scarred coffee table. He took a deep breath to calm his galloping pulse. "For now, let's assume he did sign the contract. A sick old man like that, how would he even know what he was signing? He could've been duped into writing his name."

"Unless he was sharper and meaner than we give him credit for. What if he was in on the scheme?"

"Either way, since he was a recluse, he'd need a go-between on the outside. Somebody he trusted." Jubal swung his feet to the floor, stood, and strode to the desk in the alcove. Coming back with the contract, he took the three pages out of the manila envelope, spread them on the coffee table, and switched on a nearby reading lamp.

The blue-inked signatures and the old-fashioned notary seal looked genuine, but the document itself had been photocopied on cheap, slick paper. The lender had probably kept the original and given Jubal's father a signed copy.

Jubal sat down again and studied the copied letterhead at the top of the first page. It had an

old-fashioned look to it, with leafy scrolls surrounding the company name. The original paper
may have been embossed—the design had that
quality look about it.

Jubal had already done some checking. The
only address on the letterhead was a post office
box in Cottonwood Springs, which had long
since been rented to different customers. Below
the post office box was a phone number, which
Jubal had called. He'd reached a woman, also in
Cottonwood Springs, who'd told him she'd had
the same number for twenty years and had never
heard of the Shumways. Dead end.

*Shumway and Sons.* Jubal frowned at the name
on the letterhead. "It would help to know whether
Jacob Shumway had any sons."

"I could ask my mother," Ellie said. "But I only
heard about two daughters, both deceased now.
Since Donetta's mother was one of the daughters, and since it was Donetta who inherited the
house, I'm guessing there were no sons—or at
least none who outlived him."

Ellie leaned in close, studying the letterhead.
"This is strange," she said. "There's a phone number here, but no fax number or email address.
Jubal, what if the property management business was old—really old, like fifty or sixty years—
maybe even older? That would explain why we
couldn't find it online or in the county records.

"This is what I'm thinking." She gripped his
arm, her eyes sparkling with excitement. "Maybe
Jacob Shumway didn't have any sons. Instead,
he could have *been* one of the sons—maybe the

last one living. If the business was still a legal entity—or even if it only appeared to be—he would have the right to sign the document and not have it questioned. And he could easily have kept a supply of the old company letterhead stationery."

"Give me a minute." Jubal leaned against the back of the couch and closed his eyes; his thoughts were spinning so fast that it made his head ache.

"So my father wanted to borrow five thousand dollars to pay for the funeral. He went to the bank. They turned him down because of bad credit. So somebody steered him to Shumway, used the old letterhead paper to draw up the loan contract, then had the old man sign it with a notary present. Somewhere along the way my father turned over the deed to the ranch and got his five thousand dollars. And we know the rest of the story." Jubal sighed. "It makes sense—but the puzzle still has a couple of missing pieces. If the old man was too far gone to know what he was signing, who was behind the plan? And who owns the ranch now?"

Ellie stayed silent, giving him a chance to reason things out. Jubal appreciated her for that. She'd always been a smart girl—smart enough to know when to talk and when to listen. He'd bet money that she'd already figured things out, but she wanted to make sure his conclusion matched hers.

"The registered owner of the ranch is Shumway and Sons," he continued, still thinking aloud.

"But if old Jacob was the last of the Shumway men, the business would have died with him, or gone to his heirs . . .

"I'll be damned!" Jubal swore as the last puzzle piece fell into place. One look at Ellie told him she'd reached the same conclusion. Jacob Shumway's heir was Donetta Huish. She and Clive, her lying banker husband, had carried out the scam and taken the ranch.

But even if it was true—and it made too much sense not to be—there was no paper trail to tie the couple to the crime. And there was no way to prove the transaction hadn't been perfectly legal.

Jubal stacked the pages of the contract, slid them back into the envelope, and reached up to turn off the reading lamp. The flickering firelight deepened the shadows in the room. What they'd done tonight felt good. Working together, they had solved the mystery of the stolen ranch. But now they'd run flat into a wall.

"Maybe it's time to get some help," she ventured. "We could talk to Ben—"

"Not yet. The sheriff's job is to arrest criminals. We can't even prove there was a crime." He stared into the fire, his fists resting on his knees. "I'm not giving up, Ellie. Who knows, there might have been other folks who were cheated in the same way. Some of them might not even know they've lost their land. First thing Monday I'm going back to the county recorder's office and search the records for any other property registered to Shumway and Sons."

"Will they let you do that?"

"They should. It's public information. If not, that's when I'll talk to your brother."

"I'll help, too. If we work together we can save time." Ellie's eyes glowed with enthusiasm.

Jubal cursed silently, knowing what had to be done. She was so damned beautiful. He couldn't even look at her without remembering how he'd loved her, and how she'd left him cold. Now she was getting to him again—and he couldn't let it happen. It was time to push her away and close the door before she left his heart, and Gracie's, in ruins.

Turning, he placed his hands on her shoulders, holding her at arm's length. "Your help has made all the difference. But you've done enough. Please understand, this isn't good for either of us, or for Gracie. You need to get ready for your baby and let me finish this on my own."

His words struck her like a slap in the face. Ellie had been so excited about what they'd discovered tonight. They might not have found a way to get the ranch back, but for the first time in years she'd felt like she was making a difference. Brent had treated her like property, an ornament to have on his arm at parties, someone to act as his hostess, charm his friends, manage his home life, and satisfy his needs in bed. It hadn't been enough—either for her or for him.

But tonight she'd felt like a different person. Being with Jubal had reawakened emotions she hadn't felt in years. He'd made her feel needed and protected. With him, she'd felt alive again. Now he was taking it all away.

Steeling her resolve, she lifted his hands off her shoulders and clasped them between hers. "Jubal, we were always able to talk. We could say anything to each other as long as it was honest."

"We could."

"I only hope we still can, and that we're still friends."

"That's pretty much up to you, Ellie." He stirred, looking vaguely ill at ease. She took a breath, forcing herself to go on.

"Ten years ago, I was nothing but a crazy kid with big dreams. I'm a grown-up now and things are different. But I still care about you. And I care about Gracie, too. That's why I want to help you get your ranch back."

"Then listen to me. This is hard to say." His hands shifted, trapping hers, now, between his big, rough palms. "I care about you, too. But the more time I spend with you, the greater the chance of my falling head over heels all over again and making a fool of myself. That kiss tonight was like going back in time. It pushed me to the edge, almost over. But I can't let that happen. Not to me and not to Gracie. You almost killed me when you left. I can't let you do it again—especially to a little girl who already thinks you hung the moon. That's why I'm calling this enough. I can finish this job on my own. You need to go home, have your baby, and move on to whatever comes next."

Ellie pulled her hands away. He'd cut her deeply, just like she'd done to him ten years ago. "I guess I deserved this," she said, fighting tears she was too proud to shed. "Fine, I'll go—first thing tomorrow, as soon as that limb's cleared out of the road."

His expression was a rigid mask. "One more thing. Please thank your mother for Gracie's dress. And tell your family I'll be taking my daughter to the Christmas Ball myself. That's the least I can do for her." He stood, looming above her. "Now get some rest. You can have my bed. I'll sleep out here—or in my dad's old room."

Ellie stood. "You don't have to do that. I can take the couch."

"Just go, Ellie. The bathroom's across the hall. You probably know that."

"All right." Ellie was too tired to argue. "Wake me early." She turned away and walked down the hall to the bedroom, feeling swollen and achy and miserable. He'd finally paid her back for leaving him. She could only hope he was happy. As for her, like Scarlett O'Hara, she would think about it tomorrow. Right now, all she wanted to do was close her eyes and shut down.

Having nothing to sleep in, and not wanting to undress, she unfolded the quilt at the foot of the bed. Leaving her shoes on the rug, she lay down in her clothes and wrapped the quilt around her. Minutes after closing her eyes, she was fast asleep.

* * *

Feeling like a first-class jerk, Jubal lingered on the sofa, watching the fire die and listening to the howl of the wind in the chimney. Part of him ached to walk back to the bedroom, wake Ellie, and apologize. But no, cutting off their relationship had been the right thing to do. She'd be better off in the long run. So would he.

Forcing his thoughts in another direction, he opened the manila envelope, slid out the three pages of the loan contract, spread them on the table, and reread every line. His mind circled and analyzed, weighing every possibility. Only one conclusion felt right—the one he and Ellie had reached together. Clive and Donetta Huish had taken advantage of his father's need and failing mental capacity to steal the ranch. Using old man Shumway's business name and signature had enabled them to keep their own names out of the scam.

Had they stolen other people's land the same way, or had Seth McFarland given them a single perfect opportunity? Either way, their involvement would be hard to prove—especially if the contract was legal.

But what if proof wasn't what he needed? Jubal's pulse lurched as a new idea struck him— an idea so simple that he could scarcely believe he hadn't thought of it sooner.

Pushing off the couch, he began to pace. Carrying out the plan would take guts on his part. True, there were risks involved. But as things stood, he had nothing to lose.

He'd be going it alone. Ellie was out of the picture—he'd made damned sure of that tonight. But there was no way he could have gotten this far without her. If he got his ranch back, he would have Ellie to thank for it.

So why hadn't he told her that? Ellie had come clean about her feelings for him, and his response had been like slapping her lovely face. If he'd wanted revenge, he had it. But the fleeting satisfaction it had given him only left a bitter taste behind.

He didn't want revenge. He didn't want satisfaction. All he really wanted was Ellie.

*Ellie, her baby, her fool dog, the crazy highs and lows—the whole damned adorable package!*

But it was too late now. Tonight he had closed the door on his chances.

The fire had burned down to coals. Jubal picked up the contract and slipped the pages back into the envelope. Then he unplugged the Christmas tree lights, kicked off his boots, and stretched out on the couch. The night wasn't going to be comfortable, but he didn't plan to sleep much.

*Ellie moaned in her sleep, her dream so vivid that it might have been real. It was Christmas Eve. She was back with Brent in their high-rise luxury condo with a view of the Golden Gate Bridge. Dressed in a black designer cocktail gown with diamond earrings, she was flitting back and forth between the kitchen and the formal dining room, where the table was elegantly set for eight. Brent, who was expected home any minute, had told her he was bringing some important guests, and everything had to be absolutely perfect.*

*Pausing by the table she checked the fold of each linen napkin, inspected each wineglass for any spot left by the dishwasher. The silver and china gleamed in the glow of the crystal chandelier above the long dining table.*

*In the oven, the crown rack of lamb, to be served with organic greens and an airy potato cheese soufflé, was done to perfection. The crème brûlée she'd prepared for dessert was ready for its touch of flame. The condo was spotless, everything polished and perfect.*

*Except for the Christmas tree. It stood in the corner, by the window, without a single light or ornament. Brent was going to be furious. Grabbing a box of decorations out of the closet, she began flinging them on the tree. She could smell the food burning in the oven. She rushed to take it out. The lamb was singed to blackness and the soufflé had fallen. And when she tried to open the vintage wine bottle, she dropped it on the marble floor. Glass shards and red wine spattered the kitchen.*

*Brent picked that moment to walk in the door, trailed by six of his women friends dressed as strippers. He gazed around the room, taking in the ruined food and the haphazardly decorated tree. "How could you let me down like this?" His lip curled in a snarl. Raising his hand, he smacked the flat of his palm across her face.*

Ellie woke with a jerk. Her whole body was shaking. She was fine, she told herself. It had only been a dream. But where had that awful dream come from? What was it trying to tell her?

She'd never burned a company dinner or forgotten to decorate a Christmas tree. But Brent had found other excuses to punish her. She'd retreated into denial about his abuse. She'd told herself she loved him. And she'd made excuses for him—he was working too hard, he wasn't sleeping well, she just needed to be more understanding, and everything would be all right. Even when she'd gone back to him for that trial reconciliation, she'd been in denial. But she'd come out of it knowing two things—Brent's problems weren't her fault, and he would never change.

She lay on her back, feeling the baby move. She was safe. So was her little one. Brent would never hurt either of them again.

Little by little, she drifted back into dreamless sleep.

The distant sound of a chain saw jerked Ellie awake. She thrashed free of the quilt and sat up. A confused moment passed before she remembered where she was and why she was there. She hadn't expected to get much rest, but she felt as if she'd barely stirred all night. Even that disturbing dream was a dim memory this morning.

Gray sunlight filtered through the blinds. She glanced at the bedside clock. Seven-thirty, and it sounded as if Jubal was already working on the

fallen limb. Good for him. After last night, all
she wanted was to climb into the Purple People
Eater and go home.

"Hi, Ellie." Gracie stood in the open doorway.
She was dressed in faded jeans and a red sweat-
shirt, her French-braided hair mussed from sleep.
"My dad told me you were here. I'm really glad
that old limb didn't hit your car. Can I make you
some coffee?"

"You make . . . coffee?" Still muzzy from sleep,
Ellie stretched cautiously and slid her legs off
the bed.

"Sure. We have a machine. My dad taught me
how to use it. I already made some for him. I can
cook you a toaster waffle, too, if you want."

"Coffee will do. Thanks. Give me a minute."
Ellie pushed to her feet and found her shoes.
With the baby doing a Ginger Rogers number
on her bladder, she made it across the hall to
the bathroom. She emerged a few minutes later,
face splashed, hair finger-combed, teeth rinsed
with the mouthwash she'd found. With her
makeup gone and her hair cow licked from sleep,
she probably looked like an extra from a zombie
film, but that couldn't be helped. At least she
had no more reason to impress Jubal.

The aroma of fresh coffee beckoned her to
the kitchen. As Ellie took a seat, Gracie lifted the
carafe from the coffeemaker and filled a blue
stoneware mug without spilling a drop, no mean
feat for an eight-year-old.

"Milk and sugar?" she asked.

"Just a little milk. I'll pour it." Ellie took the

cup, added milk from the carton on the table, and took a sip. "This is really good. You're one amazing girl. I'll bet you can do lots of things."

"Thanks." Gracie poured herself a glass of milk and mixed in some powdered chocolate. "My dad says coffee is for grownups so I don't drink it. But that's okay because I think it tastes awful."

Ellie sipped her coffee. From the direction of the road, she could hear the chain saw starting, stopping a moment, then whirring up again. The sky was clear through the kitchen window, the morning calm and windless.

"Why didn't you bring Beau?" Gracie asked.

"I'd only planned to stay a little while," Ellie said. "I left him with my mother. I didn't know I was going to be stuck here overnight."

"Dad says that limb is really big. It might take a while to cut it up and pull it out of the road. While you're waiting, would you like to see my horse?"

"I'd love to," Ellie said. After last night, Jubal might not approve of her spending time with his daughter. But she wasn't about to hurt the little girl.

"I'll get your coat!" Gracie darted into the living room. By the time she came back, Ellie had finished her coffee. Shrugging into her coat, she followed Jubal's daughter outside.

The sun had risen, flooding the yellowed pastures with light. A flock of blackbirds rose from the bare branches of an old apple tree, twittering as they soared against the sky.

At Gracie's approach, two scruffy-looking brown dogs bounded out of the barn to greet her. They wagged their tails, tongues lolling as she patted them. "This one's Pearl and that one's Ruby," Gracie said. "They're sisters. Dad says they're the best cattle dogs ever."

The dogs turned to Ellie, wagging and sniffing. As she stroked them cautiously, she found herself wondering how well the pair would get along with Beau. But why should it matter? She wouldn't be bringing her little poodle here again.

"What breed are they?" she asked Gracie.

"Just mutts. We got them from the shelter in Cottonwood Springs, so we don't know for sure. They look like they might be Border collie and Australian shepherd. Dad likes girl dogs. He says they're smarter, and they're less apt to fight with other dogs. These two are fixed, so they won't have babies." Gracie glanced up at Ellie. "Is Beau fixed?"

"He is. I didn't want him chasing after the ladies."

"You should bring him the next time you come. I bet Ruby and Pearl would like him. They'd probably think he was their puppy."

"Maybe." Ellie didn't have the heart to say she wouldn't be coming back. "Hey, where's your horse?"

"Come on!" Gracie led the way into the barn with the dogs tagging behind. The place had changed little in ten years. Ellie even recognized

one of the three horses as the one Jubal had let
her ride in the old days. The gentle bay mare
was showing her age now, but Ellie was glad to
see that she was still here. The second horse, a
tall, spirited buckskin, was new, as was the third,
a small brown and white paint gelding. "Here's
Jocko." Gracie walked into the stall and wrapped
her arms around the little horse's neck. "Isn't he
beautiful? Dad says he's all mine."

Ellie thought of the shadow that was still
hanging over the ranch. If Jubal lost the place
and had to leave, what would happen to these
animals and the little girl who loved them?
Knowing Jubal, he'd probably lain awake nights
asking himself the same question.

"I can't take Jocko riding alone until I'm
older," Gracie said. "But I ride him with Dad
when we go out to check the cattle. Jocko's not
very big but he's fast and smart. I'm going to
train him to barrel race so we can compete in
rodeos."

"That sounds like a great idea." Ellie stroked
the satiny neck. She'd done all she could to help
Jubal save his ranch. Now he'd pushed her aside,
determined to finish the fight on his own. She
could only wish him the best, for his sake and
for Gracie's.

Walking out of the barn, Ellie could still hear
the distant whirr and whine of the chain saw.
Abruptly the sound stopped. Now, faintly, she
heard the ring of calling voices.

"That must be our neighbor, Travis," Gracie

said. "He bought the old place up the lane. I bet he'll help Dad move the limb. Hey, let's go watch!"

Not a bad idea, Ellie thought. Her car wasn't that far, even to walk. The morning was cold but sunny. And if she was there she could leave as soon as the road was clear. "That's fine, Gracie," she said. "But would you run into the house and grab my purse off the rack? That way I won't have to come back for it."

"Sure. I bet Beau is really lonesome for you." Gracie flashed into the house. A moment later she caught up with Ellie partway down the drive. "Here's your purse. I'll carry it for you." She slung the strap over her thin shoulder and led out as they set off down the lane.

They hadn't gone far when Ellie spotted the two pickup trucks parked one behind the other. She recognized Jubal's old red Ford in front. The one behind looked almost as old and was a rusty black. Coming closer, she could see Jubal at the rear of the purple car, sawing side branches off the fallen limb. A tall, wiry stranger was gathering up the limbs and stacking them in the dry grass at the roadside. His arms were full of wood, but he paused to nod a greeting.

"Good morning, Miss Gracie." He'd taken off his coat to work. His body was all lean-roped muscle, with part of a tattoo showing below the left sleeve of his T-shirt. Beneath the battered felt hat he wore was a face that could've starred in a Clint Eastwood Western—long-jawed, with a hard mouth and narrow eyes that spoke of having seen too much.

"Travis, this is my friend, Ellie." Gracie made the introductions. "Travis's dad is Hank, the man who has the Christmas tree lot."

He balanced the armful of limbs for the briefest tip of his hat. "Hope you won't mind keepin' that bit to yourself, ma'am. My old man and I, we don't have much use for each other."

"Of course," Ellie said. "And thank you for your help."

He glanced at the Purple People Eater. "Yours?"

"In a way. I need a bumper sticker that says MY BMW IS IN THE SHOP."

Seemingly unimpressed, he shrugged and rebalanced his load.

"Hey, Travis!" Jubal was not at his best this morning. "Are you going to stand around all day? We need to get this limb moved so the lady can head back to town."

Travis dumped his load and ambled back to the rear of the car. The huge limb had been lightened enough to drag to the side of the road, but it was going to take two men to do it. With Gracie cheering them on, Jubal and Travis lifted the limb and pivoted it on its shattered base until it lay along the edge of the lane. Pushing and pulling, they dragged it into the grass, clearing the way for Ellie to leave.

Travis surveyed the limb and the stacks of cut and broken branches. "Looks like a pile of winter firewood on the hoof," he said. "Hope you won't mind me cutting some of it up to haul home."

"Be my guest," Jubal said. "And tell anybody else you know that they can help themselves."

Ellie took her purse, fumbling for her keys as she walked to the mismatched driver's door. She was grateful that Gracie and Travis were there. After last night, saying good-bye to Jubal alone would have been painful.

Moving to her side, he opened the door for her and lent his arm for balance as she eased behind the wheel. When she looked up and met his gaze, his eyes were surprisingly warm. But she was still hurting from last night, when he'd made it clear that he wanted no part of her. Whatever he was selling this morning, she wasn't buying it.

"Thank you, Ellie," he said. "I mean it."

"Good-bye, Jubal." She closed the door, started the car, turned around, and drove away.

# Chapter 13

For Jubal, the hours of Sunday had crawled past. After seeing Gracie off to church with a neighbor family, he'd spent part of the morning cutting firewood with Travis and an hour wrapping the gifts Gracie had chosen at the mall. It saddened him that he had no surprise for her on Christmas morning, like the new saddle he'd given her last year. But until this business with the ranch was cleared up, that would have to wait.

He'd burned with impatience to do more checking at the county recorder's office and pay another visit to Clive Huish at the bank. But since neither would be open until Monday, he'd settled for making dinner, then saddling up and taking Gracie for an afternoon ride around the ranch. Usually, being on horseback, his gaze sweeping over the yellowed pastures, helped to calm his nerves and put his world in order. But the thought that this land was no longer his had only torn at his heart. And the memory of his parting with Ellie, sending her off hurt and angry, had haunted his every waking moment. She'd been wounded by one man she'd cared about. Now he'd hurt her, too.

He remembered how she'd braved that terrible windstorm, almost dying, to bring him the vital information he needed. She'd been so eager to help him, and when he'd taken her in his arms, she'd seemed so ready to love him again. But the thought of letting her into his life only to watch her walk away had thrown up a wall of fear. He hadn't meant to be cruel. He was only trying to protect himself.

*Protect himself.*

What a stupid, cowardly fool he'd been! He'd spent a restless night, lying on the pillow where she'd slept, her subtle fragrance triggering dreams of holding her, loving her, and sinking into desolation as he watched her disappear. Now it was finally Monday morning, and his mind was made up.

It was time to stop backing away and fight for the woman he loved. Maybe he couldn't convince her to stay, but he'd never know if he didn't make the effort.

It would take time to win back her trust and forgiveness. But he had to try. Convincing Ellie to stay would be worth whatever it took.

He was tempted to call her this morning and try to mend some fences. But it was too soon for that. She needed time to simmer down. Maybe later he'd have some news for her, and a better excuse for his behavior.

Christmas vacation had begun, so Gracie didn't have school. Jubal settled her with a stack of library books, her art supplies, and her cell phone, and made the drive into town.

He drove straight to the county recorder's office. For starters, he looked up the property that was now the B and B. Scanning the old records, he was able to verify that the old man who'd owned it was indeed J. D. Shumway, and that his signature, except for differences due to age and ill health, matched the one on the loan contract. And it was Donetta Huish, as his heir, who'd signed the deed to the old house over to Jess. So far, so good.

Jubal spent the next two hours searching the records for properties owned by Shumway and Sons. Aside from his own ranch, there were none. That was a disappointment. Finding other landholders who'd been swindled would have strengthened his case. He could have contacted them and worked up a plan to confront Clive Huish together.

But that was not to be. Evidently the crime against Seth McFarland had been one of opportunity—a desperate man with bad credit willing to put up his ranch for a small loan and not sharp enough to understand the terms. Jubal's father had played right into their greedy hands.

Jubal would be dealing with the slimy banker on his own.

This morning he was out of time. He needed

to get home to Gracie. In any case, he knew better than to go charging into Huish's office angry and unprepared. He needed a sensible plan. And he was going to need Ellie. After the way he'd treated her Saturday night, he could only hope she'd agree to help him.

*So help me, if she mentions the* mango *again . . .*

Dismissing the thought, Ellie dressed, slipped on her coat, and prepared to leave the exam room after her routine weekly checkup. She'd been in a black funk since yesterday, when she'd driven away from the ranch. Even Beau's antics had failed to cheer her. How could Jubal lead her on, welcome her help, give her that toe-curling kiss, and then just cut her out of his life? Had it all been a scheme to get back at her for leaving him ten years ago?

"Are you sure your due date is January third?" Dr. Ramirez asked as she returned to the room.

"Pretty sure, within a week or so." Even though her periods had never been regular, that final reunion with Brent hadn't lasted long enough to leave much of a window.

"Not knowing that, I'd have guessed you were a little farther along. From the looks of things, you could deliver anytime."

"As long as it happens after the holiday weekend, I'm good," Ellie said. "I don't fancy spending Christmas in the hospital."

The doctor laughed. "It'll happen when it

happens. But I'd stay close to home if I were you. I'll see you next Monday, same time. Oh— and say hello to the—"

"I'll see you then. And thanks." Ellie cut her off and left the clinic before the perky woman could finish her sentence. If she never saw Jubal again, it would be too soon—although she was bound to run into him, especially since he planned to bring Gracie to the Cowboy Christmas Ball this Saturday. Ellie had let Clara talk her into helping take tickets. But that didn't mean she couldn't change her mind. There were plenty of people who could take her turn at the ticket table.

The more she thought about staying home that night, the better Ellie liked the idea. Why not just spare herself the discomfort? Surely her mother would understand if she didn't feel up to a big, noisy party.

She drove down Main Street, under the glowing light strings that crisscrossed overhead. Even with the windows up, she could hear the speakers blaring "Silver Bells."

Growing up, Ellie had always looked forward to Christmas. Even after her father died, her mother and the community had made it a magical time. But this Christmas in Branding Iron just plain sucked. Ellie had never felt such a dearth of holiday spirit in her life. Even last year in San Francisco, with her marriage falling apart, there'd been friends and shopping and dressing up for glittering parties to distract her. Here, there was little more than too much time on her hands, her worries over Jubal, and her anxieties about becoming a mother.

She was still feeling down as she approached the corner where Merle Crandall had her craft and yarn shop. Remembering the woman's stunning gift, and the invitation to pay her a visit, Ellie braked and pulled up to the curb. She'd been hoping to find something extra nice for her mother. This quaint little shop, which looked like something out of the early 1900s, might have just the thing.

A string of hanging bells jingled as Ellie walked in the door. Merle was just bidding good-bye to a woman with a wrapped bundle. As her customer left, she turned to Ellie with a welcoming smile.

"Hello there. I was hoping you'd stop by." She was wearing gray slacks and another beautifully patterned sweater, different from the one she'd worn to the baby shower.

"After seeing that lovely baby shawl you gave me, how could I resist your invitation?" Ellie returned the smile, her sour mood evaporating as she looked around the little shop. It was a charming place, the walls decorated with antique photos, the shelves and display cases stocked with skeins of silky, beautiful yarn in a rainbow of soft colors. One shelf held an assortment of knitting needles, crochet hooks, and books of patterns and instructions. Another set of shelves held finished pieces—exquisite sweaters, hats, scarves, and baby shawls like the one Merle

had brought to the shower. An old-fashioned, or-
nate brass cash register stood on the counter. A
lighted candle wafted the scent of bayberry into
the air.

"What a delightful shop you have!" Ellie exclaimed. "You must do a lot of business this time
of year."

Merle replied with a sad smile and a shrug.
"Look around you. Do you see many customers?
The new Shop Mart here and the mall in Cottonwood Springs have all but run me out of business. If I didn't own this building and have my
apartment upstairs, I'd never be able to stay
open."

"But you have such lovely things here. I've
never seen anything like these yarns and the
things you make. They're heirloom quality."

Merle sighed. "Thank you, dear. But I can't afford to sell them at Shop Mart prices. And the
people around here aren't wealthy. If they can
get something made in a Chinese sweatshop for
a lower price, that's what they'll go for."

Ellie glanced around, thinking. "But there are
people out there who'd love these things and
could afford to pay your prices. Have you tried
selling online?"

"You mean on the Internet?" Merle rolled her
eyes. "Goodness, I don't know anything about
that newfangled technology. I wouldn't know
where to begin!"

"I could help you!" Seized by a sudden idea,
Ellie couldn't talk fast enough. "In San Francisco I had a friend who sold her cookbooks on-

line. I helped her set up her business—learned how as I went along. Facebook, Pinterest, eBay, even a simple Web site. I know how to do them all."

"You could do that for me?" Merle's blue eyes were wide with wonder.

"I'd love to try."

"That would be wonderful! Oh—" Her smile faded. "I'm sorry. It's a fine idea, but I'm afraid I couldn't pay you enough for it to be worth your time."

"You wouldn't have to pay me—at least not right away and not out of pocket. Once we have the business set up, I could take a percentage of what we sell online."

"We?" Merle's smile had returned. "Are you talking some kind of partnership?"

"That would be up to you," Ellie said. "Think about it. It would take a few weeks to get started, but I really think we could make this work."

"I could say yes right now. But"—Merle glanced down at Ellie's baby bump—"you're about to have a little one. That's going to be a full-time job."

"I'm sure I can manage it. Babies do need to sleep sometime."

Merle laughed. "You'll need sleep too, as you'll find out, dear. New babies can really wear you out. But in any case, since I wouldn't be paying you up front, I'd have nothing to lose by trying this, would I?"

"I'll tell you what," Ellie said. "Let me draw up a business plan, showing how it all could work.

Then, after you've looked it over, you can tell me yes or no, or make suggestions."

"Fair enough." Merle extended a small, wrinkled hand for Ellie to shake. Her fingers were surprisingly strong.

Ellie was about to leave when she remembered her reason for coming here in the first place. After some browsing, she chose a dusky blue-gray angora shawl for her mother. It would be silkily warm, and the color would look stunning with Clara's silver hair.

With the gift-wrapped box in her arms and her head buzzing with ideas, Ellie walked out to her car. Helping Merle sell her beautiful yarns and finished pieces would be just the challenge she needed. If she could grow the online business, it would give her an income and a job she could do right here in Branding Iron, without leaving her baby. Later on, when it came time to move, she might even be able to work long-distance.

Lost in thought, she didn't notice the truck that had pulled up behind her car until she heard Jubal's voice.

"Ellie. Glad I caught you."

He was out of the truck, striding up the sidewalk toward her. She stood in place, saying nothing. Only now that she could see him—so tall and rugged, his face ruddy with cold beneath the battered felt Stetson—did she realize how much his earlier rejection had hurt her.

"I was going to call you later," he said. "Then I saw your car. We need to talk."

Ellie gave him a chilling look. "I can't imagine we have anything left to talk about."

His shoulders rose and fell as he released a long breath. "I deserve that, and I'll take my whipping if you want to give it to me. But the truth is, I've come to ask a favor. I need your help."

The man had no shame. Ellie had every reason to walk away, but she couldn't help being curious. "What kind of help?" she asked.

"I have an appointment with Clive Huish at the bank tomorrow at ten. My plan is to confront the bastard, show him what I've found, and demand that he return my property. I need you to be there with me."

There was a moment of stunned silence as she caught her breath. Then her confusion exploded. "What for?" she demanded. "You said you didn't need me anymore. You told me to back off and let you finish this business on your own. Now you say you need me there. Why, Jubal? And why me?"

She fell silent as he held her gaze. His eyes were deep blue in the cold December sunlight. "Because I don't want to do this without a witness," he said. "And because you're the only one I trust."

She stared up at him. "You actually trust me? After those awful things you said?"

"Blast it, Ellie . . ." He shook his head. "It wasn't about trust. It was all those old feelings that were starting up again. I was plain scared. I couldn't stand the thought of what I'd go through when you left again, and what it would do to Gracie.

I'm still scared. Scared as hell. But I hope I can still trust you to be honest, and to help me as a friend."

*As a friend?* A mist of tears blurred Ellie's vision. She'd never loved a man the way she'd loved Jubal back in the day. Now something told her that, even if it was too late for them, she'd never love anyone that much again.

But what if it wasn't too late? What if she could really make a life here? There had to be some part of her that wanted to. Why else did she keep finding reasons to stay, like helping Merle?

Jubal was looking down at her, as if waiting for her answer. Ellie cleared her throat but couldn't hide the quiver in her voice. "That was quite a speech," she said.

He forced a chuckle, lightening the mood between them. "It was, wasn't it? So what do you say? Can I count on your help?"

Knowing there was only one possible answer, Ellie took a deep breath. "What do you need me to do?"

"Nothing much. Just be there, keep still, and listen. Okay?"

"I don't know how well I can manage the 'keep still' part, but all right. Why don't we meet at Shop Mart, the south corner of the parking lot? My mother won't stop asking questions if she sees you pick me up."

"Fine. I'll see you at a quarter to ten. That'll give me time to brief you on the way to the bank." He turned to go. "Wish me luck."

*You'll need more than luck.* Ellie kept the thought to herself as Jubal walked back to his pickup and climbed inside. She'd never met Clive Huish, but if the banker was unscrupulous enough to take advantage of a grieving Seth McFarland, he couldn't be expected to play fair.

If Jubal's ploy didn't work tomorrow, his hopes would be crushed before her eyes. It would kill her to see it, but she would be there for him.

What a time to realize—without a shred of doubt—how much she still loved him.

Ellie pulled the car into the driveway, parked, and switched off the engine. She needed time to compose herself before she went into the house to face her curious mother.

Clara meant well—she always did. But if Ellie burst through the door flushed and breathless, her mother would want to know why. And for now, Jubal would want to keep anything between them private.

At least she could talk about her ideas for helping Merle market her wares online. She also needed to break the news that she wouldn't be going to the Cowboy Christmas Ball. Even with Jubal and Gracie there, she didn't feel up to it. She could just imagine people eyeing her middle and taking bets on how soon she was going to pop.

As luck would have it, when Ellie went into the living room to put her gift under the tree, she found her mother asleep on the couch. She was lying with her hands folded and her ankles neatly crossed. A dainty snore escaped her lips.

Ellie slipped the package under the tree and stood for a moment, gazing down at her. In sleep this woman, who'd been a tower of strength all her life, looked like a frail child—too thin, with lines of weariness creasing her face. Clara had always made sure her daughter had everything she needed—the nicest clothes, dancing and music lessons, even a car of her own when she was old enough to drive. It couldn't have been easy for her, but no sacrifice had been too great for her children.

Ben had been worth it. He'd always been the perfect son. But Ellie had been a self-centered, willful little drama queen.

If only she could go back in time. She would have been kinder and more appreciative. She would have gone out of her way to make her mother's life happier. But it was too late to change the past. She could only touch the future.

Weeks, maybe days, from now, Ellie would have a daughter of her own—a daughter who would be her own little person from her first breath of air. What would their relationship be like?

Clara stirred, opened her eyes, and smiled. "So you're home. How did the doctor visit go?"

"Everything's fine. Can I make you some tea?" Over tea at the kitchen table, she could tell her mother about her ideas for Merle's shop and broach the news that she'd be skipping the Christmas Ball.

"The tea can wait, dear. Right now, I have a surprise to show you." Clara pushed herself up, took a moment to right herself, and hurried off down the hall.

Ellie took off her coat and hung it in the closet. She was about to go in the kitchen and start some tea when her mother came back with something hanging over her arm.

"What do you think, dear? Isn't it pretty?" She held up a dress of blue and burgundy flowered chintz with puffed sleeves and a high waist with sashes to tie in back. The lower part of the dress was full enough to accommodate a small circus . . . or a full-term pregnancy. It was for her, Ellie realized with a sinking heart. How could she stay home now?

"It's, uh, roomy," Ellie hedged. "You must've been saving that much cloth for some big project. There's enough fabric in that dress to re-upholster the couch."

"I was actually saving it for new curtains in my bedroom," Clara said. "But yesterday I looked at it and thought, why not? Now you'll have something to wear to the Christmas Ball!"

Ellie stifled a groan. Her mother was trying so hard to make her happy. She hugged her fragile shoulders. "Thanks, Mom. I guess if Scarlett O'Hara can wear her mother's curtains, so can I."

"It's not my best work, mind you. But I realize you'll only be wearing it one time. After that, maybe I can make some pillow covers or a bed ruffle out of that skirt."

"Then I'll try not to spill on it." Ellie took the

dress and laid it over her arm. "I'll put this away upstairs. Then I'll make us some tea. While we drink it, I'll tell you about the great new idea I had at Merle's today. If you have any suggestions, I'd love to hear them."

The next morning, when Ellie drove into the Shop Mart parking lot, Jubal was standing outside his truck, waiting for her. Even from a distance, she could see the tension in his rigid posture. His future, and his daughter's, could hang on whatever happened today.

With a murmured greeting, he helped her into the high passenger seat. He'd mentioned earlier that she'd be briefed on the way to the bank, but she knew better than to distract him with chatter. Jubal would talk when he was ready—and he did.

Hearing his plan didn't make her feel any more confident. So many things could go wrong. But she had to agree it was worth a try. And since it didn't involve money or the law, Jubal had nothing to lose.

They parked at the bank, and Jubal helped Ellie climb to the ground. She'd dressed up a little—if makeup, earrings, and a clean sweater counted as dressing up. She didn't plan on saying much, but for Jubal's sake, she wanted to make a decent impression.

He gave her his arm as they crossed the slippery parking lot. In his free hand he carried the manila envelope with the contract and other documents in it, which he planned to show to Clive Huish. As they passed through the double doors, she was tempted to squeeze his hand. But that, she feared, would only distract him.

The receptionist showed them back to Huish's office, which was smaller than the bank president's but furnished with a vast mahogany desk and a kingly red leather chair. The walls were decorated with photos of Huish with prominent Texas people—the current governor and his wife, a senator, even a former president of the United States. The man made no secret of his political ambitions. Ellie remembered her mother saying that he'd run for mayor in the last election. Evidently, he'd lost.

He rose from behind his desk, a big man, putting on weight and losing hair in middle age. His brown suit looked expensive.

"We haven't met, but I'd know Ben Marsden's sister anywhere. My wife mentioned meeting you at the baby shower." He extended a hand to Ellie, all smiles and charm. "Please take a seat."

Ellie accepted the handshake. "Thank you, Mr. Huish, but your business is with Jubal, not with me. I'm just here to listen."

A startled look flashed across his face but he made a swift recovery. "So what can I do for you, Jubal?" he asked, sitting again. "If it's a small loan, I'm sure we can work something out."

His condescending manner made Ellie want to punch him, but she moved back to a chair against the wall and sat down.

"This isn't about a loan." Jubal was still on his

feet. His voice showed no emotion. "It's about the ranch that was stolen from my father."

"Stolen? What makes you say that?" Huish's expression betrayed nothing.

"I found the contract he signed—when he borrowed five thousand dollars from your wife's elderly grandfather." Jubal drew the papers out of the envelope. "It was a scam, Huish. A scam to take the ranch for the oil rights. And you knew about it all the time. I can't prove it, but I'd bet money you were the one who set it up."

"Let me see that!" He snatched the contract out of Jubal's hand. His eyes scanned the pages, as if he already knew what was written on them. "This document is perfectly legal," he said. "Your father signed a note and put up the ranch as collateral. He received his money and evidently never paid back a cent of it." His gaze narrowed. Both men seemed to have forgotten Ellie, who sat with her hands gripping the arms of her chair and her heart in her throat.

"My father wasn't in his right mind," Jubal said. "If he had been, he would never have signed this contract."

Huish rose. Standing, he was tall enough to look Jubal in the eye. "Exactly what is it you want?" he demanded.

"I want my ranch," Jubal said. "Transfer the deed back to me, and everything I know about what you did, and how you lied to me, stays right here in this room."

There was a beat of silence. Then Clive Huish laughed—a harsh, almost evil sound. "Who do you think you're talking to, Jubal? So what if my wife's grandfather made your dad a loan with terms that only a fool would accept? Do you see my name anywhere on this document?"

"No." Jubal's voice was flat and cold. "But I know that your wife's grandfather was a recluse. My father could never have gained access to him without a family member to act as a go-between. I also know that you and your wife moved to Branding Iron six years ago to look after the old man. He wasn't competent to draw up a legal document. Somebody had to do it for him and get him to sign it."

A bead of sweat had formed on Huish's temple. "That's pure conjecture!" he snapped. "All your so-called evidence proves is that J. D. gave your father a loan on terms he agreed to. So if it's legal action you're planning, I'd advise against it. You'd be laughed out of court."

"Maybe so." A bitter smile twitched at a corner of Jubal's mouth. "But that doesn't mean I can't tell folks what I know you did. An old classmate of mine works the local news in Cottonwood Springs—does one of those features where they root out cheaters and scammers and exposes them on TV. He's always on the lookout for a good story. Then there's social media—the Internet's great for spreading news. I could also put in a word to your boss about how you flatout lied to me when I tried to get a loan here. Even if you don't lose your job, I can't imagine you'll have much of a future in politics."

Huish glared up at him. "I could rip up this

contract and swear that you're lying and that this conversation never happened."

"Go ahead. It's a copy. The one with the real signatures is in my safe. And my friend Ellie, here, has a great memory. She can back up everything we said." Jubal paused to let his words sink in. "You don't need that ranch, Huish. You're not cut out to work it. There's not a damned drop of oil under the land. And if you try to sell it, your dirty trick will go public. I don't want to ruin you. I just want my family's property back. This is your one chance to set the record straight and keep your reputation out of the mud."

Clive Huish had gone white around the mouth. Little by little, Ellie saw him crumble. His shoulders sagged. He took a handkerchief out of his pocket and dabbed his sweating face.

"It wasn't me who did this," he said. "It was Donetta, my wife. She was the one who came up with the scheme and got the old geezer to sign. As his heir, the property belongs to her." He glared up at Jubal. "She's a stubborn woman. Give me till the end of the week. If I can convince her to sign the deed back to you, we have a deal. If not, there's nothing I can do—and Lord help us both."

"You have my number. Either way, I'll expect your call. And you can keep that copy of the contract." Still stone-faced, Jubal turned away from the desk and extended his hand to help Ellie out of the chair. Together they walked out of the bank and into the clear morning air.

Only after they'd reached the parking lot did Jubal break into a grin. The war wasn't over but at least he'd won the battle. He squeezed Ellie's arm. "Thanks. It isn't a done deal yet, but I owe you," he said.

Ellie laughed, happy for him. "You don't owe me a thing. The entertainment was worth my time."

"This calls for a celebration," he said. "What do you say we go pick up Gracie for double cheeseburgers and shakes at Buckaroo's?"

"That sounds like just the thing!"

They had reached the truck. Jubal opened the door and offered his hand to help her in. Suddenly he paused.

*"Oh, what the hell, girl!"* he muttered, taking her in his arms. With that, he kissed her, deep and long and hard, by the open door where anybody could look.

Ellie kissed him back, the joyous tingle surging all the way to her toes. The colored lights on Main Street swirled in her head. Carols sang in her ears. For the first time since coming home to Branding Iron, she felt like Christmas.

# Chapter 14

Dressed in baggy blue sweats, with her hair caught back in a scrunchy, Ellie sat at the kitchen table, sipping her coffee and studying the screen on her laptop. She'd spent much of the week working out the plan to put Merle's business online. The idea that had begun as a spark had turned into a major project, one that would involve setting up a secure Internet account, photographing the items and writing descriptions, creating a Web page, and inserting links on sites like Facebook, Pinterest, Google, and Amazon.

Getting ready for the launch would take weeks, if not a couple of months. No way would she be able to get more than a start on it before the baby was due. But Merle had been patient and understanding. The sharp old woman also had plenty of business savvy. Her ideas, and her excitement about the new venture, made the work a pleasure.

Ellie was grateful for the distraction. She'd needed it to take her mind off Jubal and the ranch. Every day he'd called her with the same update—no word from Clive Huish. Feeling the worry Jubal was trying so hard to hide had almost undone her.

Now it was Friday morning, the last workday of a week that would end with the annual Christmas parade and the Cowboy Christmas Ball. If the banker hadn't yet talked his wife into returning Jubal's ranch, it wasn't likely to happen. Whatever went down, she would be there for Jubal. But failing to save the ranch would crush him. Ellie had done all she could to help. All she could do now was hope.

She was still gazing at the computer, trying to focus, when her cell phone rang. Her pulse skipped as she reached for it. But the caller wasn't Jubal. It was Jess.

"Hi, Ellie." Her sister-in-law was upbeat as usual. "Are you good for a girls' lunch today? My friend Kylie will be in town for some shopping. Since her husband and kids will be home with the baby, she wanted to get together and catch up. She says she could use a break. Something tells me you could, too. So what do you say?"

Ellie hesitated, thinking of the work she had to do. But she did need a break, and the company would cheer her. "Sure," she said. "Can I meet you somewhere?"

"I'll pick you up around noon," Jess said. "Glad you can make it."

Ending the call, Ellie glanced at the time. It was almost eleven. She'd get cleaned up now, then work until Jess arrived. Her mother was watching TV and surely wouldn't mind keeping an eye on Beau.

Half an hour later she was showered, dressed, and ready to go. She was back at the computer when she heard voices from the living room. Jess had come inside to greet her mother-in-law. They were visiting when Ellie came in with her coat. For an instant she felt a flicker of envy. Ben's wife was glowing with the joy of her pregnancy. Why shouldn't she be? She had a husband who adored her, a town and family waiting to celebrate her little one. Ellie faced nothing but an uncertain future here. Could she really build a life in a place where she'd never wanted to be, with a man who still had every reason to turn his back on her?

Jubal seemed to want her, but he hadn't said he loved her or asked her to marry him. Had he thought about the challenge of raising another man's child? When faced with that reality, would he get cold feet? How could she blame him if he did? She'd be a fool not to expect it.

"You girls have a nice time." Clara smiled from her rocker, where her hands were busy crocheting a baby sweater with soft, variegated pink and blue yarn from Merle's shop.

"You're welcome to come with us." Jess had her keys out and was starting for the door.

244

Janet Dailey

The crochet hook paused. "Thanks, but I'll be better off here, where it's warm and cozy. There's supposed to be a storm blowing in later today."

"Thanks for watching Beau." Ellie glanced at her dog, sprawled in his favorite spot under the Christmas tree.

"No trouble at all. He's good company. My, but he does love that tree." Clara returned to the sweater and her TV talk show.

Kylie was holding a booth at Buckaroo's when Ellie and Jess arrived. The place was busy at this hour with people stopping by for lunch.

"I hope you don't mind," she said. "I ordered an extra large Hawaiian pizza and Diet Cokes for us when I got here. Otherwise, we'd have to wait, and I don't have much time."

"You told me you had all afternoon." Jess took a seat, making room for Ellie to slide in next to her. Their drinks were already on the table.

"I know." Kylie laughed. "But Shane phoned me just as I got here. The baby threw up on the couch, Hunter and Amy are in time-out for fighting, and he got a call from the neighbor that a section of the east fence is down and needs to be put up before any cows wander out. Poor man. I've got time to eat, but then I really need to get home and free him from kid duty."

"You've got to hand it to him." Ellie had been told how Kylie, a military widow with two children, had come to Branding Iron two years ago and married the handsome, single rancher. "Being a stepfather to two teenagers can't be easy."

"Oh, I know," Kylie said. "But he's come through like a champ. Hunter and Amy adore him. Their father was hardly ever home. They love having a full-time dad. Shane's even petitioned to adopt them."

"Wow, that's great!" Jess glanced at Ellie. "But you've had some adjustments, too, Kylie. Going from army wife to ranch wife must've been a challenge."

"You mean all that ropin' and ridin' and brandin'?" Kylie's blue eyes twinkled with laughter. "Who's got time for that? I'm raising a family with the man I love. That's a full-time job. I wipe those big muddy boot prints off the kitchen floor and count my blessings."

The pizza had arrived. Ellie helped herself to a slice. Here she was, sharing lunch with two city women who'd come to town, married Branding Iron men—with children in the mix—and made it work. And now they were talking to her about it. This couldn't be a coincidence. Maybe it was time she called them on it.

"Why do I get the feeling I've been set up?" she demanded.

"Set up? By *us*?" Jess was all big-eyed innocence.

Kylie laughed. "All right, but give us a break, Ellie. We want the best for you. Anybody with eyes in their head can see how things are between you and Jubal. Now don't deny it. You've been seen together all over town."

"We understand that you have your doubts about staying," Jess said. "We just wanted you to see that it's possible to be happy here, even on a ranch."

Ellie forced a chuckle she didn't feel. "You might be able to convince me. But since Jubal's gun-shy, it won't make any difference. I hurt him when I walked away ten years ago. Now I'm back here, and about to have my ex's baby. Any man would have cold feet."

"I saw the way he looked at you that night we trimmed the tree at your mother's," Jess said. "Believe me, nothing about that man was cold."

"And don't sell Jubal short," Kylie said. "If Shane can take on two snarky teenage stepkids, Jubal shouldn't have trouble accepting a sweet little baby, especially with that little girl of his needing a mother."

"Enough!" Ellie drained her Diet Coke and set the glass down a little too hard. "I wish I could believe you two schemers, but nothing's going to happen. There are too many . . . complications. The subject is closed."

"We'll see about that." Jess gave her a knowing wink. "This story isn't over yet."

They finished the pizza and pooled their cash to leave on the table. After Kylie had rushed off, Jess and Ellie walked across the parking lot and climbed into Jess's SUV.

"I'm sorry if we crossed the line, Ellie," Jess

said. "It's just that we all want you to stay. Ben and I—we love the idea of our little ones growing up together. Clara needs family around her. And you're going to need us. What kind of support system will you have if you take your baby and go off to some big city? Even Kylie—she really likes you and wants to be your friend."

"None of this has anything to do with Jubal," Ellie said.

"It doesn't and it does." Jess turned at the corner and headed up the street toward home. "We want you to be happy and loved. We want you to have a family of your own. That's the way it should be."

"That's what I thought I was getting when I married Brent."

"Brent was a jerk. But sometimes life gives you a chance at something better. It happened to me. It can happen to you."

Ellie sighed. "Let's put this discussion on hold for now, okay? With the baby almost due, I won't be leaving for a while. In fact, I've even taken on what might work into a job." She gave Jess a quick rundown of her plans for Merle's business.

"What a great idea." Jess pulled into the driveway and stopped to let Ellie out. "Merle's a sweetheart. There's another reason for you to stay in Branding Iron."

"No promises, okay? And thanks for the break." Ellie climbed out of the SUV. With a farewell wave to her sister-in-law, she trudged up the sidewalk to the porch steps.

She was about to open the front door when her cell phone jingled. Fumbling in her purse, she caught it on the third ring. The caller was Jubal.

"You heard?" Ellie asked, her pulse slamming.

"I did." He sounded all right, but not jubilant. "It's a yes, but with conditions."

"Conditions?" She gripped the phone, barely aware of the chilling wind and the snowflakes swirling down beyond the porch roof.

"Two conditions. The first is that I sign a release, promising to treat this whole mess as if it never happened. As a witness, you'll need to sign it, too."

"That's no problem, as long as you get your ranch back," Ellie said. "What's the other condition?"

"Since my father never repaid the loan, they want their five thousand dollars plus interest— not on the original terms, thank heaven, but at the usual bank rate, compounded. Since it's been four years, I'll be paying them back about seven thousand."

Ellie stifled a gasp. She knew that Jubal had spent almost everything he had paying off his father's debts. She could spare the money, but she knew better than to offer. Jubal would never take it.

"Can you come up with that much?" she asked.

"I haven't got it, but I can get it. Huish actually offered me a bank loan—he just wants this thing cleared up. But that would leave a bad taste in my mouth. I never want to do business with that bank again."

"Can you hold out for less?"

"And give Huish's wife time to come up with more demands? It's not worth taking a chance." Jubal cleared his throat, betraying his emotion. "There's another way. One of my neighbors wants to buy that buckskin quarter horse of mine—he's registered and worth a good price. I've offered him a discount for cash up front. We've agreed on fourteen thousand—a bargain for such a well-trained, young cattle horse. I'll miss him, but the money will be enough to pay off the ranch, give Gracie a good Christmas, and buy myself a cheaper horse in the spring."

"So it's done?" Ellie sank onto the seat of the porch swing, her legs too unsteady to support her.

"Almost," Jubal said. "I'll be selling the buckskin this weekend. Monday we'll sign the paperwork and transfer the deed. When it's done, I'll be able to breathe again—and I hope you'll be ready to celebrate with me."

"Of course I will." Ellie felt a flood of warmth. He wanted to be with her and share this happy time.

"Will you be at the Christmas Ball tomorrow night?"

"I'm afraid so. I was going to stay home, but my mother made me a dress. What can I say?"

She sensed his smile as he spoke. "I promised to take Gracie. But I hope you'll save me a dance or two."

"Good grief, Jubal, I'd look like a hippo on the dance floor. I hope you'll settle for some friendly conversation."

"As long as it's friendly."

"And promise me you won't laugh at my dress. It makes me look like a big, flowered, overstuffed chair."

"You'll look beautiful—and I'm guessing I won't have any trouble finding you. See you at the dance."

After the call ended, Ellie lingered on the porch swing, watching the snowflakes. Everything was going to be all right, she told herself. Silas would have her car done soon. Jubal would get his ranch back. She would have a beautiful baby girl after the holidays. And somehow, the relationship between her and Jubal would work out as it was meant to. That was the way things happened in romance novels. Why not in real life for a change?

She was long overdue for a happy ending.

By Saturday morning the snow was four inches deep and still falling. Jubal dressed at dawn and trudged out to the barn. Nugget, his beautiful buckskin gelding, was in his stall. After feeding and watering all three horses, Jubal took a brush and groomed Nugget's smooth buff coat until it gleamed.

Prentiss Hansen, his neighbor on the far side of the highway, would be here at 8:00 with his trailer to take the horse away. Jubal knew that

Nugget would have a good home with a caring owner, but it was still hard to let him go. He'd never had a better cattle horse than the tall buckskin. But the cash from his sale would save the ranch, with enough left over to last until spring and maybe buy another horse—not as fine as Nugget, but good enough for working cows.

Gracie had cried when he'd told her that Nugget was being sold. To cheer her, he'd promised to take her to breakfast at the B and B, and then to the Christmas parade in town. They would leave as soon as Nugget was loaded, the bill of sale signed, and the payment locked in the old iron safe that had belonged to Jubal's great-grandfather.

Tonight they'd be going to the Cowboy Christmas Ball in the high school gym. Gracie, who hadn't gone to the ball since the loss of her mother, was beside herself with excitement. She could hardly wait to show up in her new dress and take part in the Old West games and dances that had been planned for the children.

Jubal was looking forward to the party, too, since Ellie would be there. Now that he wouldn't be losing his ranch, he couldn't put it off any longer—it was time to lay his love on the line. He needed to let her know that he wanted her— baby and all—in his life. He would do it tonight. If she made a fool of him again, so be it. He had everything to gain and nothing to lose but his pride.

Leaving Nugget in the stall, he walked out

into the falling snow. The cold flakes melted like tears on his skin. Life had its hard times—so hard that they broke your heart. All you could do was take the good things—good times, good people—and hold on tight for as long as you could.

From the direction of the highway he heard the sound of a truck engine. A moment later, Prentiss Hansen's heavy-duty pickup rolled up the lane, towing a horse trailer.

It was time to say one more good-bye.


Jess had offered to pick up Ellie and Clara for the Christmas Ball. Ben, as usual, had volunteered for patrol duty. With so many families at the ball, and so many empty houses with presents under the tree, it was prime picking for anybody with burglary on their mind. So Jess, who'd been put in charge of ticket sales and had to be there early, would be going without him.

The snow had been drifting down all day. By now it was more than six inches deep. But not even a snowstorm could stop the Cowboy Christmas Ball. As Jess drove her SUV to the gym, Ellie thought of Jubal driving in from the ranch with Gracie. The roads would be snow-packed and slick. But the old truck had good winter tires and four-wheel drive. *Stop worrying,* she scolded herself. *Next thing you know, you'll be turning into your mother.* But maybe that was natural.

They entered the high school and hung their

coats in the hall. Jess, with her red hair and still-tiny waist, looked stunning in the forest green velvet gown that had once been Ellie's. Clara wore the same lace-trimmed blue dress she'd worn to the ball for years. And Ellie . . .

"Goodness, Ellie, those colors are lovely on you." Jess's compliment fell a little flat. "Those big pink flowers are—"

"I believe they're cabbage roses," Ellie said, fingering one of the pink and fuchsia blooms that decorated the crisp, ivory chintz fabric. "At least they're as big as cabbages. And at least there are enough of them to cover me. That's saying a lot."

Clara had gone into the gym ahead of them, so Jess felt free to laugh. "Come on," she said, linking her arm through Ellie's. "You're always so elegant. Whatever you're wearing, people will think it's the latest Paris fashion."

Walking into the decorated gym was like stepping back in time. The same old strings of lights and tinsel hung between the basketball hoops. The tree in the center of the floor wore the familiar decorations. The Badger Hollow Boys—the Nashville band that had been coming to this celebration for years—was warming up to play all the old-time country songs that people loved and expected to hear.

Only Ellie had changed. The carefree girl who'd had boys scrambling for a dance with her was a woman now, about to become a mother. As for the boys, there was only one man for her—

and when he walked through the door with his little daughter, he was the only man she would see.

It was early yet, with people just beginning to arrive. Many of them brought donated food for the buffet table at the far end of the gym—cheesy potatoes, hams and barbecued ribs, fried chicken, mac and cheese, salads, biscuits, pies, and cakes.

Ellie sat next to Jess at the ticket table. They'd be handling the first shift, when the most people would be coming in. Jess would be collecting cash and making change for people paying at the door. Ellie would be taking prepaid tickets and rubber-stamping hands. When the rush thinned out, someone else would take over, freeing them to eat and relax.

By the time the band struck up the opening tune, a steady crowd was pouring in. The Cowboy Christmas Ball was a family affair, and even babies were welcome. Kylie was there with her handsome husband and their lively brood. Silas, Connie, and Katy were already filling their plates at the buffet table. Jess's mother, Francine, dressed as a saloon girl in red satin, was on the arm of her steady beau, the man who owned Hank's Hardware. Ellie greeted several of the women who'd been at her baby shower. But there was no sign of Donetta Huish or her husband.

With crowds streaming in, Ellie had become too busy to watch the door. She was collecting tickets when a deep baritone chuckle caused her to look up.

"So they've put you to work." Jubal stood there, grinning down at her. Freshly shaved, combed, and dressed in a Western shirt with a leather vest, he looked like a movie hero. Gracie stood next to him, her grin matching his. In her new blue dress, with her hair French braided, she looked so adorable that Jess wanted to reach out and hug her.

"I'll catch you two later," Ellie said.

"We'll hold you to that." Jubal was counting out cash to give to Jess, who gave Ellie a playful nudge under the table as she stamped his hand.

"See, didn't I tell you?" she whispered as he and Gracie headed for the buffet table.

"No comment." Ellie laughed, grateful that Clara had talked her into coming. She had high hopes for the rest of the evening.

After the rush of the first half hour, only a few people were trickling in. Clara came over to sit at the ticket table and take care of the latecomers. By then the dancing had started.

"I'll keep an eye on your mother and see that she gets some food," Jess said. "You go enjoy yourself. That's an order." With a playful wink, Ellie sashayed across the floor toward the buffet.

Jubal had risen from the table where he and Gracie were sitting. Walking toward Ellie, he held out his hand. "I was afraid you were going to be busy all night. Come have some dinner with me. Gracie's eaten, but I wanted to wait for you."

"Thank you." Ellie took his hand with a smile, feeling like Cinderella at the ball. She might look like an overinflated balloon, but Jubal was the handsomest man in the room, and the proud way he walked made it clear—he wanted everyone to know she was with him.

He pulled out her chair. As she took a seat, Gracie grinned at her from across the table. "Hi, Ellie. I like your dress. Did you bring Beau?"

"Not tonight. With so many people here, he could get lost or scared." She'd left the little poodle snoozing under the tree. Hopefully, by now, he was familiar with the house and wouldn't mind being alone. Otherwise, she'd be coming home to ripped pillows and scattered newspapers.

"I want to square dance with the other kids," Gracie said. "They're doing it across the hall. Is that all right?"

"Sure," Jubal said. "I didn't know you could square dance."

"All the kids can. We learned in school." She darted off toward the hall.

"Remind me to thank your mother," Jubal said. "That pretty new dress has given Gracie the confidence to have fun tonight."

"She's a great kid, Jubal," Ellie said. "You have every reason to be proud of her."

His jaw tightened, as if holding back emotion. "You must be hungry," he said. "I'll fill our plates. Anything special you'd like?"

"It's all good. Just not too much. I have to go back to the doctor next week and get on that scale. You don't want to know how much I weigh."

"Stop worrying about it, Ellie. You're the most

beautiful woman here tonight." He turned away, walked to the buffet table, and came back with two plates—his loaded with a working man's portions, hers lighter but still more than she could eat. She nibbled at the fried chicken, salad, and cheese potatoes, too keyed-up to be hungry.

"Did you sell your horse?" she asked, knowing he'd planned to.

"He went this morning. Damned good horse. Wish I could've kept him. But at least I can pay off the ranch now." The glow of Christmas lights cast his eyes in shadow. "I've learned that about life. Even when you want to hold on, the good things tend to go—you, Laura, the animals I've loved, even Gracie. God willing, she'll grow up and go off to make something of herself."

"Or maybe she'll stay here in Branding Iron and start a family of her own."

"I'd like that. But only if it would make her happy." He laid his fork down. His hand captured hers on the tablecloth. "Dance with me, Ellie."

"Jubal, I don't think—"

"I know you said you didn't want to. But it's been a long time. If this is our one chance to do it again, I don't want to miss it."

How could any woman say no to that? Rising with effort, Ellie accepted his arm. Maybe it wouldn't be so bad. The lights were low over the dance floor, and the band was playing an easy Texas two-step. She could do this, she told herself as Jubal's sure hand found the small of her back. He had to hold her at arm's length. Still,

after the first few steps, there was a sweet famil-
iarity in the way their bodies moved together.
The years fell away as they blended into the swirl
of dancing couples. She looked up, met his dark
blue eyes, and gave him a smile. His hand tightened on her back.

"See, it's not so bad, is it?"

"No, but it's not quite like high school." Ellie
remembered how they used to dance close, her
head resting against his cheek. That would be
awkward tonight.

"We can't go back, Ellie," he said. "But that
doesn't mean we can't go forward. That's why
I'm asking you to stay—at least long enough to
give you and me another chance."

Ellie's throat tightened. She'd been wanting
to hear those words from him. But there were so
many unanswered questions, so many fears that
something would go wrong. "We're different
people now," she said.

"We were a couple of crazy kids back then.
But we've both faced tough times and grown up.
There's nothing wrong with that."

"What about the baby?"

"Little babies are easy to love. If things worked
out, I'd welcome a bigger family. So would Gracie. I'd even take in that fool dog of yours. But
this isn't a proposal. I don't need a yes or no. All
I'm asking for is time."

Ellie's pulse quickened as his words sank in.
This was exactly what she'd hoped to hear—no
pressure, no promises, just the chance to enjoy
each other and work things out. It was what they

both needed. And this time it felt very, very right.

She was about to reply when she felt an odd tightening sensation, low in her body.

"What is it?" he asked. "Did I say something wrong?"

She'd stopped dancing. "No. I'm feeling a little strange, that's all. Maybe we'd better—"

Her words ended in a gasp as a warm, wet cascade gushed down her legs.

"Ellie?"

She clutched his arm, her fingers digging into his sleeve. "My water just broke. I need to get to the hospital."

# Chapter 15

*T*ake it easy, this isn't your first rodeo, Jubal reminded himself as he put a supportive arm around Ellie's shoulders and walked her to the nearest chair. He'd managed fine eight years ago, getting Laura to the hospital for Gracie's birth. So why was his heart pounding like a runaway steam locomotive now? This wasn't even his baby.

Ellie huddled in the chair shaking. Her hand clung to his sleeve. "Stay right here," he said. "As soon as I tell your mother and make sure Gracie will be all right, we'll be out of here. Are you hurting?"

She shook her head. Her grip on his sleeve tightened. "Jubal, I'm scared," she whispered. "What if something's wrong?"

"Don't be scared." He kissed her damp forehead and gently loosened her grip on his sleeve.

"Sit tight while I tell somebody and get the truck. You'll be fine."

*Was that the right thing to say? Ellie wouldn't be afraid for herself. She'd be afraid for her baby. He had to get a grip on himself.*

Before he could leave her, he saw Jess hurrying toward them. Her worried expression told Jubal there was no need to explain what was happening.

"I'm driving her to the hospital in Cottonwood Springs," he said. "Let Clara and Gracie know. One of you will need to take Gracie for the night."

"No problem," Jess said. "Gracie would probably love staying with Clara and the dog. But I can drive Ellie to the hospital if that's easier."

"My truck will be safer in the snow." That was only part of the reason Jubal wanted to drive. Right now, nothing mattered more than just being there for Ellie.

Jess crouched by Ellie's side and took her hands. "Can I get you anything? Some water?"

Ellie gave her a nervous smile. "No water. I'm soaked under this dress."

"Any pain?"

"Just a twinge now and then. I'll be fine."

"I've heard that first babies can take a while. You may be in for a long night."

"As long as the baby's all right, I'll be fine." Ellie's voice shook. She was trying to be brave, but Jubal sensed that she was terrified.

"I'm going to pull the truck around front," he

told Jess. "Get Ellie's coat and have her at the door in about five minutes."

"I'll call the hospital and let them know you're on your way," Jess said. "And I'll write down my cell number so you can let us know how she's doing."

"Good idea. Thanks." Jubal strode out of the gym, sprinted down the hall, and raced out into the parking lot. Snow was falling in thick, velvety flakes. By the time he reached the truck, his clothes and hair were coated with white. He'd left his sheepskin coat in the truck—a lucky oversight. Until the heater kicked in, Ellie would be shivering in her damp clothes. The heavy coat would help keep her warm.

He climbed into the truck, started the engine, and backed out of the parking place. The snow was deep and getting deeper. The forty-mile drive to Cottonwood Springs usually took less than an hour. Tonight, in the storm, it might take twice as long. But Ellie's labor had barely started. Laura's contractions had lasted nine hours before Gracie was born. There should be plenty of time to get Ellie to the hospital.

He thought briefly of Gracie. Too bad there'd been no time to find her and tell her he was going. But she'd be all right. Staying overnight at Clara's would be a treat for her. He would give her a call after he got Ellie to the hospital.

Ellie, wrapped in her quilted coat, was waiting with Jess under the overhang of the school entrance. Jubal left the engine running to warm up while he helped her down the steps and into the truck. With the doors closed and the heater on high, they headed out of the parking lot.

The truck's oversized tires gripped the snow-slicked road as they swung onto the highway that led out of town. The windshield wipers and the defroster barely kept the windshield clear. The headlights glared off a white wall of falling snow. If the clinic hadn't been closed for the weekend, Jubal might have taken her there. But tonight the hospital was the only option.

He glanced over at Ellie. She was huddled under his sheepskin coat. The truck was warming up but she was still shaking. Her eyes reminded him of a cornered doe's. Reaching past the console, he squeezed her hand. "We're all right," he said. "The truck's got good tires. We'll make it okay."

"It's not that, Jubal." Her voice was a taut whisper. "It's the baby. She's been kicking up a storm for a couple of months. Now I can't feel her moving. I can't feel her at all."

Ellie stared through the windshield. The motion of the wipers was hypnotic, the night outside a blur of flying snowflakes. She could hear the tires crunching their way over the snow that coated the road. The truck seemed to move at the pace of the minute hand on a clock. Going faster would be dangerous, she knew. But her baby could be in trouble. She needed to get to the hospital.

"How are you doing?" Jubal kept both hands

on the wheel and his eyes on the road. There wasn't much traffic, but they'd already passed one wreck, an SUV that had slid off the road and landed on its side in the barrow pit. Two police cars were already there, lights flashing a garish red and blue against the snow. There'd been no ambulance to take her on board—and tonight, not even a police escort could have gotten Jubal's truck up the road any faster. All they could do was drive on.

"I'm doing fine . . . considering." Ellie's effort at a joke fell flat. She was anything but fine, and they both knew it.

"Any pain?"

"Some. Not too bad yet." The contractions were happening, but so far she could stand them. She thought about timing them on the dashboard clock, but what good would that do? And the pains were nothing compared to the fear that something might be wrong with her baby.

"Have you thought of a name?" Jubal asked, making conversation.

"Not really," Ellie said. "I'm thinking something simple and old-fashioned like Emma or Hannah, or Margaret. But I won't know for sure until I see her." *If I see her. Please, God, let her be all right.*

"And her last name?"

"Not her father's name if that's what you're wondering. I'll be taking my maiden name back as soon as I can wade through the paperwork. It'll be her name, too."

"And you're still not going to tell him?"

"Brent doesn't deserve to know. He doesn't deserve to be her . . . father." She gasped. The sudden pain was like being squeezed by a giant vise. Her teeth clenched. Her hands doubled into fists.

"Bad?" he asked as the contraction ebbed.

"Bad. How much longer before we're there?"

"We're more than halfway. Twenty or thirty minutes, I'd say. Can you hang on?"

"I'll have to, won't I?"

He released his grip on the wheel long enough to reach over and squeeze her hand. "That's my girl. Don't worry, we'll make it. You're going to be fine."

"That's easy for you to say, mister. You're not the one having this baby."

"I love you, Ellie."

The words were the last thing Ellie had expected. She stared at him, wondering if she'd heard wrong.

Jubal kept his eyes on the road. "I meant to say it earlier, at the dance. But we never did have great timing, did we? So I'm saying it now. I love you, Ellie. I guess, deep down, I never stopped."

Ellie could feel another contraction building, but she didn't want him to stop talking. She needed to hear what he was telling her. She needed to know it was true.

"If we can make this work—Lord, girl, I know this isn't the best time. But when you get this baby into the world, know that I'll be there for you. I'm not going any—"

"*Jubal!*" The cry tore from her throat as the

pain ripped through her. Low in her body, she felt something move and shift. No—this couldn't be happening. But every instinct told her it was. *"The baby!"* she gasped. *"I think it's coming now!"*

"Hang on!" Punching the hazard light button, Jubal swung the truck onto the shoulder of the road and yanked the parking brake. With the vehicle at a stop and Ellie writhing on her seat, he raced around to the passenger side and carefully opened the door. Ellie felt the icy breath of wind on her face. The brightness of the dome light made her squint.

"Help me . . ." She forced the words through the pain.

"Don't worry, I've got this." He levered the seat as far back as it would go and lowered it into a reclining position.

"You're sure about that?" The contraction had eased some, but Ellie could still feel the pressure, as if she was being pushed apart.

"You bet I'm sure." His confidence sounded like pure fakery. "I've delivered more than a few calves. This can't be much different."

"Oh, thanks a lot! Remind me to moo!" Ellie's unsteady smile became a grimace as a new contraction seized her—a hard, clenching pain that went on and on. She could feel Jubal's hands bunching up her long skirt.

"There's the head," he muttered. "She's on her way. Push now, as hard as you can . . . that's it . . . harder."

Ellie pushed until her eyes bulged. Her teeth clenched with effort. Then there was a wet, sliding sensation as her baby slipped out into the world.

Silence.

*Please* . . . Her lips moved in prayer. *Please let my baby be all right.*

She heard a slap and a tiny gasp, followed by the most beautiful sound in the world—a lusty, full-blown baby wail. Tears stung her eyes. She was a mother.

For a reason she couldn't fathom, Jubal seemed to be laughing. Ellie could feel him moving the baby but she couldn't see beyond her skirt-covered knees.

"Let me see her!" she pleaded. "Is she all right?"

He chuckled. "Your baby's fine. But I think you'd better brace yourself for a shock."

Her heart lurched. "What is it? Is something wrong?"

"Nope. Take a look." Blocking the cold wind with his body, Jubal held up her baby, revealing what the murky sonogram had failed to show.

"Congratulations, Ellie," he said. "You have a beautiful, healthy baby boy."


As the truck roared toward Cottonwood Springs, Ellie held her newborn son close. Jubal had tied and cut the cord, wrapped the baby in his warm cotton flannel shirt, and covered them both with his sheepskin coat. It was the best that could be done until they reached the hospital and the medical team took over.

She fingered her baby's damp hair—thick and dark like her own. She loved the feel of him, the smell of him, the small, warm weight of him in her arms. When she thought of all the fluffy pink girly outfits she'd bought, she wanted to laugh. This tiny boy seemed so right, so perfect, as he was meant to be all along. Maybe Jess would be able to use the girl clothes.

Outside, the snow was still falling. Wind buffeted the sides of the truck. Jubal, wearing his thermal undershirt, glanced at Ellie. "Are you all right?" he asked.

"Never better." It was true. Her body felt as if it had been cranked through an old-fashioned clothes wringer, but she couldn't remember a time when she'd been happier. "Turn on the radio," she said. "I want to hear Christmas music."

Jubal punched the button. Tonight the station, which played Christmas pop songs during the day, had switched to more traditional music. The sounds of a choir, singing a selection from Handel's *Messiah*, drifted out of the speakers.

*"Unto us a child is born . . . unto us a son is given."*

It was perfect.

Twenty minutes later, the ER attendants were wheeling Ellie and the baby down the hall on a gurney. As the swinging doors closed behind them, Jubal settled onto a waiting room chair. It was still sinking in that he'd just delivered a baby.

His cell phone was in his vest, which he'd

grabbed from the truck. Finding the paper Jess had given him, he punched in her number and gave her the news. Her response was a happy squeal. "A boy? And you delivered him in the truck? Oh my gosh, wait till I tell Ben!"

"Would you let Clara know? I don't want to risk waking her."

"Something tells me she won't be sleeping until she knows Ellie's all right. Gracie's at her house. Do you want me to tell her, too?"

"I'll call her myself. I need to make sure she's okay with my leaving her the way I did."

"Fine. When you talk to Ellie, tell her we'll come by and see her tomorrow."

"Will do. Thanks." Jubal ended the call and dialed Gracie's cell phone. She answered on the first ring.

"Hi, Dad." She sounded happy. "Guess where I am."

"I give up. Where?"

"I'm in Ellie's bed with Beau and all her stuffed animals. We're having a slumber party. How's Ellie?"

"She's fine. She's got a brand-new baby boy."

"A boy? But she was supposed to have a girl!"

"I know. We're all surprised."

"What's she going to name him?"

"I don't know. Maybe you can think of some good boy names to help her. I'm going to stay here for a while. I'll pick you up in the morning after chores."

"Can I go see Ellie and her baby?"

"Maybe in a day or two. We'll see. Sleep tight."

Jubal ended the call and settled back in the chair. He knew there was no need for him to stay. It would take an hour or so to get Ellie and the baby checked over, cleaned up, and settled in a room. And after that she'd just want to rest. But he didn't want to leave without seeing her one more time, and seeing the little boy he'd helped bring into the world.

Getting up, he walked to the hospital canteen, found the coffee machine, and filled a disposable cup. Someone had put up a bushy Christmas tree in the hospital's front lobby. Lights twinkled and glittered, reflecting their glow in tinsel and shiny glass balls. The air smelled faintly of pine.

He sat on a handy couch and sipped the hot, dark liquid. The caffeine sharpened his senses, but the fatigue he felt was more emotional than physical. Holding Ellie's baby boy had brought tears to his eyes. Only now did he realize how deeply the loss of his own unborn son, and Laura's, had affected him.

Despite the coffee, he was drifting off. He didn't realize he'd fallen asleep until an attendant in scrubs gave his shoulder a gentle shake.

"Mr. McFarland?"

Blinking himself awake, Jubal nodded.

"Ms. Marsden's in her room with the baby," the young man said. "She asked me to find you."

"Can I go back and see her?"

"Follow me. I'll show you the way."

Minutes later, Jubal walked into Ellie's room. She was sitting up in bed, exhausted but radiantly beautiful.

"Motherhood becomes you." He walked to her bedside and bent to kiss her lightly on the forehead. "How are you doing?"

"Sore. Tired. Happy. The doctor says my blood pressure's a little high. Nothing serious, but they want to keep me an extra day or two to monitor it. The baby was almost two weeks early, but they say he's fine. Seven pounds, three ounces." She lifted a fold of the flannel blanket that wrapped the baby. "Would you like to get acquainted with my son?"

Heart pounding, Jubal lifted the precious bundle in his arms. A knit hat covered the baby's hair, but he had Ellie's dark eyes and generous mouth. He brushed the perfect little hand with his fingertip. His heart turned over when the tiny fingers closed around his. If Ellie married him, Jubal thought, he could be the one raising this boy. He imagined teaching him to ride and fish and shoot, to care for animals, to value honest work . . .

But he was getting ahead of himself. Ellie hadn't said yes. She hadn't even said she loved him. He'd be a fool to start building dreams.

"No name yet?" he asked.

She laughed and shook her head. "I'm still in shock. Ask me in a few days."

"Gracie wants to come and see the baby."

"That's fine. But let's not rush it. Jess called. Ben's bringing her and my mother for a visit tomorrow. Why not bring Gracie the next day? I'll be better company when I've had some time to rest."

"The day after tomorrow is Monday. I'll be meeting with Clive Huish and his wife in the morning. If we can sign the paperwork and transfer the deed without any trouble, I should be okay to bring Gracie in the afternoon."

"That would be great. I'll be thinking about you and crossing my fingers that all goes well. Will it be a problem if I'm not there to sign the confidentiality agreement?"

"Given your situation, I'm sure they'll let you sign it later, or I can bring you a copy to sign here." He lowered the baby into her arms. "I'll go now. You need to get some sleep."

"So do you." She paused, then reached out to squeeze his arm. "Thank you, Jubal. If you hadn't been there to drive me and deliver my baby, anything could've happened. I owe you."

"You don't owe me anything." He bent down and gave her a light kiss. "The two of you are all right. That's all that matters. Rest. I'll see you on Monday."

Jubal walked outside to a diamond-clear sky. The storm had passed, cloaking the world below in pure, glistening white. He glanced at his watch. It was almost midnight. He would drive home, catch a few hours of sleep, do the morning chores, and pick up Gracie in time to have her ready for church.

It would be hard tomorrow, not seeing Ellie or the baby, who'd already nestled into his heart. But Ellie needed to rest and see her own family. He had no claim on her, he reminded himself. True, he'd laid his heart on the line, told her he loved her, and asked for a second chance. But she'd gone into labor before she could respond. Until—and unless—her answer was a yes, she wasn't his. Neither was the tiny boy he'd helped bring into the world. Easy as it might be to pretend otherwise, that was his reality.

He scraped the snow off his truck and hauled his weary body into the cab. The radio came on when he started the engine. *Silent night . . . Holy night . . .* The old song crept around him, sweet and lonely, as he pulled out of the parking lot and headed for home.

"You should sleep." The nurse held out her hands. "Let me put your baby in the bassinet. Don't worry, he'll be right here next to your bed."

Ellie shook her head. "Not yet. I don't want to let him go."

"He's the little guy who was born in a truck tonight, isn't he? I hear your husband delivered him like a pro."

"He's not my husband," Ellie said. *But he should be,* she thought. Jubal would make a wonderful father. She'd seen him with Gracie, and she could tell he already loved her baby. No man she'd ever known would be better suited to raising a boy.

But what about *her?*

Pretty, practical Laura, a farm girl, with her hand-me-down clothes and calloused palms, had been the perfect wife for Jubal. Ellie was everything Laura hadn't been—pampered, self-indulgent, and ambitious beyond the role of wife and mother. Kylie Taggart had married a rancher and made it work. But Ellie knew she was different. She wasn't ready to spend her days wiping up muddy footprints and counting her blessings.

She had never loved anyone the way she loved Jubal. But he'd have to be crazy to take on a woman like her. Even if he proposed—and he seemed on the verge of it—she wouldn't be doing him any favors by saying yes.

From the cradle of her arms, her son gazed up at her with wise, innocent eyes. Looking down at him, Ellie felt her heart swell, break, and overflow. "What do you think, little one?" she whispered. "If you could give your foolish mother advice, what would you tell her?"

On Monday morning, Jubal took the money from Nugget's sale out of the safe, drove into town, and dropped Gracie off for an activity at the library. Pulse racing, he drove to the pretentious-looking brick home where Clive and Donetta Huish lived.

He'd been braced for something to go wrong. But Clive, who welcomed him with cold politeness, had everything ready. The process of reading the documents, signing them, and turning over the cash took less than thirty minutes.

Donetta Huish, who had signed earlier, did not appear.

Ellie's absence was excused. Jubal took a copy of the agreement for her to sign and drop in the mail.

"I hope we can put this little misunderstanding behind us." Clive offered his hand at the door.

"I'm getting my ranch back. That's all I care about." Jubal forced himself to accept the handshake. The Huishes were cheats and liars. He was glad to be done with them.

From the house, he went straight to the county recorder's office and filed the deed. At last the ranch was truly his. Now he could move ahead with his plans—and hopefully with Ellie.

Before picking up Gracie at the library, he made a call to the phone in Ellie's room. She answered on the second ring.

"It's done," he said. "The ranch is mine."

Her happy little squeal was the way he remembered it from the old days. He could tell she was feeling better. "So when are you and Gracie coming to see us?" she asked.

"I'm about to pick her up. If she's hungry, I'll get her something to eat. Then we'll be on our way."

"Could you do me a favor?" she asked.

"Name it."

"I don't have my purse. I left it in my room when I went to the Christmas Ball. Could you pick it up and bring it with you?"

"Sure. No problem."

"Thanks. I need my insurance card, and I feel lost without my cell phone, lipstick, and all that good stuff. Oh—my mother said something about her book club luncheon today. If nobody's home, the back door should be unlocked. You can go on in. Just be careful not to let Beau out."

"We'll be careful. See you in an hour or so."

He drove down Main Street to the library. The sky was bright and clear, the sidewalks lined with drifts of shoveled snow. Lights twinkled in shop windows. Holiday music filled the air. Jubal found himself humming along. He had never felt more like celebrating Christmas. Maybe later today he would ask Gracie what she really wanted to find under the tree. After paying off the ranch, he had money to spare for a really nice gift—maybe a bicycle or even some new furniture for her bedroom.

Gracie was waiting for him at the library. He bought her a kid-sized burger and a soda at Buckaroo's. Then they drove to the Marsden house to get Ellie's purse.

"I know right where it is," Gracie said. "She left it hanging on the closet doorknob."

"Since you know where it is, why don't you just run inside and get it," Jubal said, pulling into the driveway. "I'll wait here. Remember, don't let Beau out."

"Don't worry. I'll be right back." Gracie jumped down from the truck and climbed the steps to the front door. When it proved to be locked, she hurried off the porch and disappeared around the house.

A few minutes later she was back, clutching Ellie's generously sized black leather purse. Holding the bag tightly with one hand, she climbed back into the truck and fastened her seat belt.

"How about some Christmas music?" Without waiting for an answer, she switched on the radio and turned up the volume.

"That's pretty loud," Jubal said.

"I like it that way. Sing with me."

Jubal sang along as they drove up the highway toward Cottonwood Springs. They were about halfway and had made it through "Frosty the Snowman," "Rudolph the Red-Nosed Reindeer," "Here Comes Santa Claus," and a half dozen other songs when Jubal noticed that another voice had joined in. Barks and whines were coming from Ellie's purse.

"What the—" He found a plowed spot and pulled off onto the shoulder of the road. A fluffy white head was poking out of the purse's top.

"Blast it, Gracie—"

"Please don't be mad." Her eyes would have melted granite. "Beau really misses Ellie. And I bet she misses him, too. I wanted to bring him along and surprise her."

"You can't bring a dog into the hospital. It isn't allowed."

"Yes, it is. I saw it on TV. This kid was sick and they let his dog come in."

Jubal sighed. Gracie was usually an obedient

child, but when she thought she was doing the right thing, she could be even more stubborn than he was.

"We can't leave Beau in the truck," Gracie argued. "He'd get cold. Or somebody might break in and steal him. And"—she added as if knowing she'd won—"it would take too long to drive him back to the house."

"All right." Jubal knew when he was beaten. "But he stays in the purse. When it's time to leave, I'll put him under my jacket."

"Thanks, Dad." Gracie grinned as she lifted the little poodle out of Ellie's purse and cuddled him in her arms.

Ellie freshened her face with a damp washcloth and fluffed her hair with the comb that had come in the hospital bag. Jubal and Gracie wouldn't be expecting movie star glamour. All the same, she wanted to look nice when they walked in.

She glanced at the clock. More than an hour had passed since she'd spoken to Jubal. Even with feeding Gracie and stopping by the house to pick up her purse, he ought to be here soon.

Leaning to one side, she looked down at her son, asleep in his bassinet. The love that flowed through her was almost dizzying in its power. She would do anything for this tiny bit of wonder—anything to protect him, anything to provide for his needs.

At last she understood what it was like to be her mother.

She heard a rap on the closed door. That would be Jubal and Gracie. She'd missed them yesterday. Being with them felt almost like family.

"Come in," she called.

The door opened. The tall, blond man who strode into the room was dressed in a tan Burberry coat with a dark blue cashmere sweater. He smiled, showing perfect veneers, as he walked toward her bed.

"Hello, Ellie," said Brent.

# Chapter 16

Ellie stared at the man she'd never wanted to see again. Seconds passed before she found her voice. "How did you—?"

"How did I know? And how did I find you?" His Hollywood smile was as dazzling as it was cold. "It wasn't that hard. You never filed a change of address with the health insurance company. When the statements came to me, I knew you must be pregnant. Since you'd already registered at the hospital, all I had to do was pull a few strings and ask to be notified when you checked in. I caught a flight as soon as I heard."

Cornered in her bed, Ellie glared at him. "What makes you think the baby's yours?"

He laughed. "I can count. And I know you, Ellie. You're too much of a Goody Two-shoes to have cheated while you were still married. He's mine, all right." He glanced toward the bassinet on the far side of the bed. "Now, how about introducing me to my son?"

"He's sleeping. And as far as I'm concerned, you gave up all rights to him when you went off and married Valerie."

His smile fell away like a mask, revealing a face that was as arrogant as it was handsome. "That's not what the law says. As for Valerie, that didn't work out. She's filed for divorce."

"How much is she giving you?" Ellie used sarcasm to keep him at bay. Inside, she felt gut-wrenching fear. Brent was a lawyer. He would use every trick in the book to manipulate her. And now he had a weapon—his legal right to her baby.

"We had a prenuptial. I got what I was entitled to. But that's not why I'm here." He cleared his throat. Ellie reached for the call button on the remote, prepared to ring for the nurse if he made a move toward her baby.

"So why *are* you here?" she demanded.

He moved closer to the bed. "This is hard to say, Ellie. I made the biggest mistake of my life, cheating on you and forcing you out of our marriage. I want you back, darling. I want you and I and our son to be a real family."


Jubal parked, climbed out, and walked around the truck to hold Ellie's purse while Gracie jumped to the ground. He wanted to make sure the fool dog didn't wriggle out of the purse and escape into the parking lot.

"Watch him. You know how he likes to get loose and explore." Jubal handed the purse back to his daughter, freeing his hands to lock the truck. "I hope you know you're in big trouble for bringing him."

"I know." Gracie skipped ahead of him, clutching the purse. At least she hadn't said she was sorry. She knew better than to lie to her father.

Jubal lengthened his stride to keep up with her. He barely glanced at the shiny black Lincoln Town Car with rental plates that was parked next to the curb in a handicapped spot. His mind was on what he wanted to say to Ellie, and on the little velvet box he'd taken out of the safe that morning and slipped into his pocket.

Gracie rushed through the automatic double doors and into the hospital lobby. "Hold on." Jubal caught up with her as she passed the glittering Christmas tree. "You don't even know where you're going."

"Sorry, I just want to see Ellie and the baby."

"They're right down that hallway—past the arrow sign that says MATERNITY. But you'll have to stay with me and be quiet. People are resting."

The Cottonwood Springs hospital wasn't large. It was constructed on a single floor, with the lobby front and center and the rooms going out in wings. Jubal kept Gracie next to him as they walked down the corridor toward Ellie's room.

"Dad"—Gracie nudged him—"I have to go to the bathroom."

"Okay. Let's find you one before we go in." Jubal glanced up and down the long hallway. Across the hall from Ellie's room was a closet-sized door with a unisex symbol on it. "That should do. Let me make sure it's empty." Jubal tested the door and looked inside. "All clear. I'll wait out here for you. Want me to take the dog?"

"Beau will be fine with me. Don't go in the room till I come out, okay? I want to surprise Ellie." She carried the purse into the restroom and closed the door.

Jubal moved against the wall to wait. Ellie's room was a few feet down the hall. The door stood ajar. From inside he could hear the sound of a man's voice. Maybe the doctor had stopped by, or one of the male staff was seeing to her needs.

As the voice grew more strident, he could make out words. Only then, as he caught their meaning and their arrogant tone, did he remember the luxury rental car parked outside. His heart dropped as he realized who was in the room with Ellie.

*Walk away,* a voice in his head shrilled. *You don't want to hear this.* But how could he go and leave Gracie? He had little choice except to stay and listen.

"This is the plan, Ellie," Brent was saying. "We get remarried, our son gets two parents, and you get it all back—the condo, the clothes, the lifestyle, the whole package. We can hire a live-in nanny, so you'll be free to travel with me, or anything else you want to do. When the boy's old enough, he'll go to the best schools and make the kind of friends who can help him succeed later on. He'll never want for anything."

Ellie's murmured reply was too low for Jubal to hear. Was she arguing with the bastard, or was she liking the idea? She'd left Branding Iron for the kind of life Brent was describing. Now she had a chance to get it back. All she had to do was remarry the father of her child. She might not do it for herself, but she could be capable of doing it for her son.

Jubal felt as if a knot had jerked tight in his stomach. Brent could provide all the comfort and security Ellie needed, and a world of advantages for her boy.

What could a poor man like him offer except the hard work and challenges of ranch life? And love, of course. No man could love Ellie as much as he did. But love hadn't been enough ten years ago. And it wouldn't be enough now.

Right now, all Jubal wanted to do was take Gracie and leave.

Brent was talking again. "Hell, it wasn't that bad, was it? We did manage to make a baby together. Think about that baby now. Doesn't he deserve to grow up with his real father and mother?"

Again, Ellie's reply was muffled.

"I don't have to play nice, you know," he said. "I could sue for joint custody. No judge in the world would deny me that. But you'll be spared that if we're man and wife . . ."

From the restroom, Jubal heard the sound of

water running. An instant later Gracie came out into the hall. Ellie's purse dangled from one hand. The other hand cradled Beau against her shoulder. Jubal made a move to stop her, but he wasn't fast enough. Thrusting the purse at him, she headed through the door into Ellie's room.

No way was Jubal letting her go in there alone. Still holding Ellie's purse, he followed her.

"Hi, Ellie . . ." Gracie's voice trailed into silence as she saw the tall, blond stranger standing next to the bed. He turned toward her with a look that was almost chilling. Uncertain, Gracie set Beau on the blanket next to Ellie.

Suddenly the little dog went crazy.

Snarling like a miniature hellhound, he lunged at Brent. His teeth clamped onto the man's hand, catching the web of skin between his thumb and forefinger. Cursing and waving his arm, Brent shook the dog loose. Beau yelped as he flew through the air and landed, stunned, on the tile floor.

"I'll kill that damned dog!" Brent swung a foot. Jubal moved to block the blow, shouldering him off balance. Brent stumbled against a bedside table, sending a water glass crashing to the floor.

Gracie was crying. Before she could reach Beau and pick him up, the little poodle scrambled to his feet, darted out the door, and rocketed down the hall.

"*No!*" Gracie pushed past her father, and raced after him.

Ellie had pressed the emergency button. The gray-haired nurse who walked into the room looked tough enough to stare down a charging grizzly. "Stay with her," Jubal said. "Don't leave her or the baby alone with this man until I get back."

"Don't worry, I've got this," she said.

Reassured, Jubal charged after his daughter and the dog.

The bite on Brent's hand was oozing pinheads of blood. Muttering, he dabbed at the wound with a damp paper towel.

"Don't worry, Beau's had all his shots," Ellie said.

He glared at her. This was the real Brent, the man she'd left and divorced. "That damned dog hates me," he said.

"He has every reason to."

He turned to the nurse, who stood next to Ellie's bed. "Don't you have a Band-Aid or something?"

"The emergency room's in the other wing. You'll see the sign outside."

"Never mind," he growled. "This isn't over, Ellie. We'll talk later."

"We'll talk now, and then you'll go," Ellie said. "First of all, I wouldn't remarry you for all the money in the world. I gave you a second chance, and you showed me you hadn't changed. You never will.

"Second, if you try to get custody of my baby, I'll fight you with everything I've got. I'll use everything I know about you."

His eyes narrowed. "Yeah? Like what?"

"That you cheated."

He shrugged. "And?"

"That you were an abusive husband who would probably be an abusive father. Something tells me that would carry some weight with the judge."

"Abusive? Hell, I slapped you around a little, mostly because you deserved it. But I never hurt you. I never broke any bones or put you in the hospital."

"Did you slap Valerie around, too? Is that why she's divorcing you? Maybe I should call her. We could have a very productive conversation. She'd probably even back me in court if I asked her to."

His lip curled. "You wouldn't dare."

"I'd do anything to keep you away from my son—even make sure your clients and partners found out what a poor excuse for a human being you are. Don't mess with me, Brent. Try it and you'll be sorry. That's all. You can leave now."

His gaze swept the small room, coming to rest on the bassinet. "Will you at least let me see him?"

"Don't even think about it."

He made a move to go around the bed. The nurse blocked his way. "One more step, buster, and I'm calling security."

Brent deflated with a hiss of breath. "You haven't heard the end of this, Ellie," he muttered.

"Fine," Ellie said. "Do your worst. Now go. I have nothing more to say to you."

With a last, venomous look, he turned and stalked out the door.

The nurse touched her shoulder. "Hang on, honey. I want to make sure that jackass really leaves. For what it's worth, if you need me in court, I heard every word."

As the woman walked out of the room, Ellie pressed her hands to her face. She was shaking, scarcely able to believe what she'd just done. In the years of her marriage, Brent had stripped away her self-confidence. She'd taken his cheating and abuse, blaming herself and knowing that to stand up to him would only make things worse. Now, with her baby to protect, she'd become a tigress.

But something else had lent her courage. Her beloved little dog, all four fighting pounds of him, had remembered what Brent had done in the past and sprung to protect her—and Brent had almost killed him. Tears flooded her eyes at the thought of Beau's devotion.

Was he hurt? Was he hiding somewhere in the hospital, scared and in pain? All she could do was wait and pray he was safe, and that Gracie and Jubal would find him.

\* \* \*

After twenty minutes of searching, there was still no sign of Beau. Jubal and Gracie had searched the length of the maternity wing, peeking in the rooms, apologetically, to check the floors and closets. They'd checked the supply rooms, the restrooms, even the laundry collection bins. Nothing. If they didn't find Beau soon, they would have to search the other wings. Maybe the hospital would send out an alert on the P.A. system.

"He's got to be hiding somewhere," Gracie said. "He was really scared, maybe hurt, too. Why do you think he attacked that awful man?"

"He was protecting Ellie," Jubal said. That was the only explanation. Dogs had long memories. If Brent had hurt Ellie in the past, Beau would remember and see him as a threat. Strange, Ellie had mentioned that Brent cheated on her, but she'd never told him she'd been physically abused. Maybe she'd been in denial, or too ashamed to be open about it.

Jubal's own protective instincts flared. So help him, if Brent ever came near Ellie or her baby again, he would beat the man within an inch of his life.

"Dad." Gracie tugged at his sleeve. "I've got an idea. I know where Beau might go to feel safe."

"Okay. Where?"

"What's Beau's favorite thing—besides Ellie?"

"I don't know . . . maybe trees?"

"I bet that's where he'd hide if he was scared—under the tree! Come on!" Gracie took off ahead of him, racing down the corridor toward the lobby. Jubal had warned her against running in the hospital, but he couldn't fault her now.

When he caught up with his daughter, she was belly-down on the polished floor, sliding under the Christmas tree. With the prickly branches almost touching the floor, it had to be tough going, but Gracie was a small package of determination. He heard her voice, gently coaxing, heard an answering whimper.

"I've got him, Dad," she said. "Pull us out."

Bystanders passing through the lobby stopped to watch as he seized her boots and pulled her gently backward. Pine needles clung to Gracie's hair and clothes as she slid out from under the tree with Beau clutched in her hands. As Jubal helped his daughter to her feet, the watchers cheered and moved on.

The tiny dog was wide-eyed and shaking. Dry needles and bits of pine gum clung to his coat. But he appeared to be more scared than hurt. Gracie cuddled him close, murmuring little comforts and kissing his head.

From where he stood, Jubal could see through the glass doors to the curb. He hadn't seen Brent leave, but the black Town Car was gone. Dare he hope it was gone for good?

As he and Gracie walked back down the long hallway, Jubal recalled the things he'd wanted to say to Ellie. He'd already waited too long. Today he would say all of them, and more, with Gracie as his witness.

*I love you, Ellie.* His thoughts formed the words. *I want to be there always for you and your son. I want to make a family with you, Gracie, the baby— and yes, even your fool dog. I want to be your husband and your son's father. And if Brent tries to interfere, I want to be there to fight him for you.*

*If you'll have me, I can't promise that our lives will be easy. But I promise to give you all the time and space you need. I'll never try to change you or force you into someone else's idea of what a wife should be, because I respect and love who you are, as you are.*

*We'll have plenty of things to talk over—but I'm offering you a start. Which way we go from here is up to you.*

It was a lot to say. She'd probably get tired of listening before he was through. But he meant every word, and she needed to hear it.

He could only hope that, after she'd heard everything, Ellie would say yes.

In an agony of waiting, Ellie watched the second hand creep around the face of the clock. Almost twenty minutes had passed since Jubal had gone after Gracie and Beau. What if her precious dog had gotten lost, or been picked up and taken by some passerby? Or what if something else had gone wrong—an accident, or an ugly altercation with Brent?

The baby was awake and fussing—not hungry, just wanting to be held. Ellie could already tell the difference. Shifting to the side of the bed, she lifted him out of the bassinet. As she gathered him close, he stopped fussing and lay in her arms, warm and contented. Holding him, watching the expressions come and go on his tiny rosebud face, Ellie was filled with wonder. As she imagined watching him grow, learning to walk and talk, becoming a boy, then a man, one thing became sure.

She wanted to raise him with Jubal, in a loving home with Gracie as his big sister, and more little ones, fathered by the man she loved.

But did Jubal want her? What if he'd grown tired of the ongoing drama that swirled around her? What if he'd taken Beau back to the house and decided not to return?

But no, she had to believe he'd come back. When he did, she wouldn't let him leave until she'd told him all the things she'd waited far too long to say.

*I love you, Jubal. I've always loved you. And if you'll have me, I want us to be a family—you, me, Gracie, and our son. You're the only father I want for him, the only man I want to share my life with. . . .*

She heard the sound of footsteps in the hall. Gracie burst into the room with Beau in her arms. Ellie's heart soared as Jubal walked in behind her and she saw the smile on his face.

At the sight of Ellie, Beau broke into joyous yips and wiggles, struggling to get free and go to her. His fluffy white coat was smudged with dust, pine needles, and bits of pine gum, but no matter. Laughing, Ellie passed the baby to Jubal and held out her hands for her brave little dog. He leaped into her arms, wagging, whimpering, and smothering her face with doggy kisses.

When he'd calmed down, Ellie handed her dog back to Gracie and cleaned up with a moist wipe before she took her son back. Cuddling her baby close, she smiled up at Jubal. "I have something to say to you," she said, "something I should have said a long time ago."

"And I have something to say to you," Jubal said. "So who wants to go first?"

"Me!" Gracie grinned, bouncing in her boots. "I want to go first!"

"All right." Jubal gave her a puzzled smile. "Go ahead, Gracie. What do you want to say?"

"Just this." She took a deep breath. "I know what I want for Christmas. I want you two to get married."

There was a moment of silence. Then Ellie burst out laughing. "That says it for me," she said.

"And me," Jubal added.

They all hugged. Then Jubal took the little velvet box out of his pocket, took out the ring he'd offered Ellie ten years ago, and slipped it on her finger. "I'll get you a bigger diamond later, I promise," he said.

Ellie shook her head. "No, this one is perfect. I'll wear it forever."

He bent and kissed her.

Christmas had come a few days early this year.

# Epilogue

*Christmas, one year later*

One-year-old Matthew, named for Ellie's father, was toddling toward the Christmas tree again. "Grab him, Jubal!" Ellie called from the kitchen, where she was helping Gracie make salad. "We're busy in here."

Jubal rose from the couch, scooped up the mischievous little boy, and lifted him onto his shoulders. "I can't believe the kid's only been walking a couple of weeks. He's turned into a two-legged tornado!"

Matthew shrieked with laughter as Jubal jogged him around the room. Ellie blinked away a sentimental tear. Jubal was the best father her little boy could have—and soon Jubal would be his father for real. After much legal pressure, Brent had finally signed away parental rights, giving permission for Matthew to be adopted. The process would take place over the next few months.

The past year had flown by, bringing a world of changes. Jubal had secured a business loan from a bank in Cottonwood Springs. The money had allowed him to update the ranch equipment, buy a prize-winning bull and a dozen good heifers, and replant some of the pastures. Come spring, the first phase of his new organic, grass-fed beef operation would be under way.

Meanwhile, Ellie's commission on Merle's booming Internet business was helping bridge the financial gaps. Merle was doing so well that she'd hired two assistants to help manage the orders. Ellie worked mostly from home, keeping the site updated and taking care of her family.

Money had been tight at times. But Ellie had managed to make some improvements in the house—new living room furniture, fresh paint in most of the rooms, and Gracie's framed artwork on the walls. Laura's photo remained on the mantel, and her cherished decorations hung on the Christmas tree—out of Matthew's reach. She was Gracie's mother, and her memory was an honored part of the family.

Today they'd be going to Ben and Jess's house for Christmas dinner. Violet, their tiny daughter, had made good use of the girly outfits Ellie had bought. Gracie loved holding the baby almost as much as she loved playing with Beau.

"Where is Beau?" Ellie glanced around for her dog.

"He's asleep behind the tree, where Matthew can't get to him," Jubal said. "I think all the Christmas commotion wore the little guy out."

"We'll leave him to enjoy the peace and quiet while we're at dinner," Ellie said. "Is everybody ready to go?"

They boxed up the salad and homemade pies they were taking, put on their coats, and headed outside to the late-model sport wagon they'd purchased. Krystle Martin Remington had bought Ellie's BMW and was proudly driving it all over town.

There were times when Ellie missed her beautiful car. But the wagon was more practical for their growing family—a family that would have one more by next fall. Ellie was still keeping her secret, but she planned to tell Jubal tonight. He would be over the moon.

With everybody buckled in, they pulled out of the yard and headed down the lane to the highway. "Turn on the radio, Dad," Gracie said. "I want Christmas music. And I want to sing."

They sang all the way into town.

Read on for an excerpt from Janet Dailey's New Americana series, coming soon!

## REFUGE COVE

**Refuge Cove, Alaska, stays true to its name when a woman who has lost hope and a man in need of healing come to each other's rescue . . .**

She'd come to Alaska on the promise of marriage, only to find herself on the run from her would-be husband. Lost and alone in the wilderness, Emily Hunter nearly weeps with relief at the sight of a small plane in the distance—until the rugged bush pilot makes his way through the brush to help her. Can she trust this stranger any more than the menacing predator on her trail? But there's something in John Wolf's dark eyes that wills her to believe in him, something about his gentle nature that allows her to accept his offer of protection . . .

He'd let her into his life because he knew she was in trouble. The last thing John Wolf expects is to feel so much so quickly for the vulnerable woman in his care. For sharing his lonely wilderness home with Emily means allowing her to see his sorrow—the son he longs to reconnect with, the loss of the family he once dreamed possible. Sharing his heart with Emily means being willing to risk everything to keep her safe . . .

*Southeast Alaska*
*Early autumn*

Along the Tongass Narrows, the cruise ships that plied Alaska's Inside Passage and spilled tourists onto the docks at Ketchikan were gone with the season. The harbor was quiet, the fishing boats at rest. The souvenir shops on the boardwalk were closing their doors.

Dead salmon carpeted the shallow streams, their bodies spent in the grueling race to reach home and spawn. White flocks of seagulls gorged on the remains.

Behind the town, and the highway leading up the coast, evergreen-cloaked mountains towered against the sky. On the narrow lowland that skirted the water, clumps of cottonwood and willow blazed with autumn gold. Alder, dogwood, and mountain ash lent rich hues of bronze and crimson.

Fall in Alaska was a time of fleeting beauty. But that beauty was lost on Emma Hunter. As she fled in terror through the deep-shadowed forest, only one thing mattered—staying alive.

*Run!* The word shrilled in Emma's mind as she fought her way through the maze of thorny undergrowth, rotting stumps and fallen trees. Low-hanging limbs whipped her face. Tangled roots snagged her feet.

*Run!*

Again and again, she'd tripped and fallen. Her hands were scratched and bleeding, her jeans ripped, her thin sneakers soaked. Her breath came in gasps. But she mustn't stop, not even to catch her breath or to ease the ripping pain in her side.

If Boone caught her, he would kill her—or make her wish he had.

When Boone Swenson had proposed, two weeks after meeting her at a church dance in Salt Lake City, Emma had felt like the heroine of a romantic novel. The prospect of a life in wild Alaska with the rugged man of her dreams had swept away a lifetime of caution. By the time she'd discovered the truth, it was too late. She was trapped in a nightmare of her own making.

Through the trees behind her, she could hear the hellish baying of Boone's dogs as they followed her scent. The two surly wolf hybrids were probably on leashes. Otherwise, by now, they would've raced ahead of their master and caught her.

If—or *when*—they found her, would Boone turn them loose on his bride, or would he call them off and drag her back to the trailer for his version of a honeymoon?

Boone was unpredictable. She'd already learned that. But one thing was certain. Given what she knew about him, he would never let her go free.

Her ankle twisted on a root. A hot pain flashed up her leg. Teeth clenched, she ran on, dodging through the shadowy undergrowth. Giant spruces and hemlocks towered above her. A squirrel scolded from a high branch. A jay screeched an alarm, startling a flock of small birds to flight—all signs of her presence that Boone would recognize.

*Why go on, you fool?* The voice in her head seemed to mock her. *You're miles from the coast, with no place to go—no road, no neighbors, no food, water, or shelter. You haven't got a chance.*

Refusing to listen, Emma struggled on. Her lungs were burning. Her legs quivered with every step.

The sinking sun cast fingers of light through the treetops. Somewhere to the west lay the highway, her best hope of finding help. But something told Emma she'd never make it that far. Between the coming darkness, her waning strength, and the dogs, there was only one way this chase could end.

*It's over,* the silent voice argued. *Boone doesn't want you dead. He wants a wife. Give up and go back with him. You can always escape later.*

But giving up was not an option, Emma resolved. Whatever happened, she would keep going. She would run until she dropped. And when she could run no more, she would fight.

The trees were thinning now, giving way to brambles and stands of devil's club, a leggy weed with sharp-edged leaves and spines that burned like fire at a touch. Beyond the trees, she could see an open bog, dotted with pools of dark water. *Muskeg*—that was what Alaskans called places like this, where layers of rotted vegetation, laid down over decades and centuries, clogged the growth of everything but sickly looking moss, yellowed marsh grass, and a few twisted trees that would never grow tall.

The bog was about half the size of a football field. Going around it, or veering off in another direction, might be safer. But if there was any chance of reaching the road, a straight westward dash across the muskeg would be the shortest way.

She could hear the dogs, getting closer. Fueled by terror, Emma gathered the last of her strength and burst into a headlong sprint.

The outer edge of the muskeg was firm enough to support her. But within a few yards, murky water began welling around her sneakers. With every step, the muck grew deeper. Soon it was closing over her ankles, making a sucking sound as she freed each foot. By now, she'd gone too far to turn around. As her feet sank deeper, the effort drained her strength, slowing her progress to a crawl.

When her bare foot came up without the shoe, Emma knew she'd made a fatal mistake. Unfamiliar with muskeg, she hadn't realized how unstable the ground could be. Now she was stuck halfway to her knees, and too exhausted to go on.

She was trapped.

John Wolf slowed the vintage de Havilland Beaver to 75 mph and lowered the flaps for the descent into Refuge Cove. The mail run to the scattered villages up the coast had taken most of the day. Tonight he looked forward to a solitary meal in his cabin, a hot shower, and a good book by the fire.

Through the windscreen of the sixty-year-old single engine prop plane, he checked the landscape below. Like a yellow stain against the dark green forest, a familiar patch of muskeg lay directly under the flight path. Using it as a marker, he knew he could make a turn there and line up his bearings for a perfect landing in the cove.

He was banking for the turn when he glimpsed something out of place. In the middle of the muskeg, a living creature was struggling to get free. A young deer or bear cub—that was John's first impression. But as he corrected the turn and leveled out to a full view of the muskeg, he realized that it was a woman, caught in the treacherous muck.

What would a lone woman be doing out here? Whatever her story, she was in one hell of a bad spot.

John put the plane into a shallow dive and zoomed in low. There was no place to land here, but he wanted the woman to know she'd been seen and that help would be coming. She waved frantically as he passed overhead. He glimpsed long chestnut hair and a plaid shirt before he climbed again and circled back.

Now what? He could—and would—radio for rescue. But it would soon be dark, and the night would be cold. Even with a helicopter, a rescue team might not be able to reach her before hypothermia set in. And there was another danger. Trapped as she was, the woman would be easy prey for the black bears that roamed the forest and had little fear of humans.

A hardcore loner, John made it a habit to keep to himself. Other people's problems were none of his damned business. The last thing he wanted was to be somebody's hero. But even he couldn't leave a helpless fool woman out here alone.

The Beaver's floats would only allow the small plane to land on water. The soupy surface of a muskeg might do in an emergency, but this open patch, surrounded by dense forest, was way too small. His best bet, a quarter mile from the muskeg, was a place where a creek had eroded its banks to form a shallow lake. From the air, the lake hadn't looked much bigger than a puddle. But he remembered estimating its length to be a little over a thousand feet—barely enough distance to land and take off again. The width was maybe a third that distance. The landing would be hairy as hell, the takeoff even riskier. But it was his best chance of reaching the woman. Maybe the only chance.

He took a moment to radio his position and pass on what was happening. Then he banked, made one more low pass over the woman, then headed for the lake.

Emma's flash of hope faded as the plane vanished over the trees. She was sure the pilot had seen her. But now he'd gone.

Was he looking for a place to land, or had he simply radioed her position and left her to wait for rescue?

But what difference would it make? She'd already run out of time.

The drone of the plane faded with distance. Then, abruptly, it stopped, leaving an eerie silence in its wake. It took a moment for Emma to realize that she could no longer hear the dogs.

Her mind scrambled to piece together what was happening. Boone would've been aware of the plane—and it made sense that he wouldn't want the pilot, or any other witness, to see him. He must've silenced the dogs and pulled back into the forest to wait until the coast was clear.

Boone wouldn't wait long. As soon as he could be sure the pilot wasn't coming back, the chase would be over. She would be at his mercy.

But the plane's arrival had bought her time and given her hope. She couldn't give up now.

Dropping forward and sprawling belly down to even out her weight, she dragged herself ahead. One foot pulled free of the muck, then the other. Both shoes were gone now. Even if she made it onto solid ground, her tender feet wouldn't get her very far. But she couldn't stop—not as long as there was any chance of rescue.

As she crawled toward the far side of the muskeg, she focused her thoughts on the plane and the unseen pilot.

*Come back . . .* she pleaded silently. *Please, come back . . .*

The landing had been tight, leaving only a few feet of water between the floats and the bank. John took a long breath, then reached back for the coiled rope he kept in the plane. His Smith & Wesson .44 magnum revolver, which he carried as a precaution against bears, was tucked under the seat. He took it out and buckled on the shoulder holster before climbing out the door, stepping onto the float and wading through shallow water to reach the bank.

By his reckoning, the muskeg would be about ten minutes due south. There was no trail, but he'd flown over this stretch of forest countless times going in and out of Refuge Cove. The map was fixed in his mind.

With the rope slung over his shoulder, he set off at a ground-eating stride. The lady wasn't going anywhere fast, but his danger instincts were prickling. There was only one reason a woman would get herself stranded in the middle of a muskeg. Something—or more likely some-one—was after her.

Whoever that someone might be, it wouldn't hurt to let them know he was on his way, and that he was armed. He paused long enough to draw the .44 and fire two shots in the air. As the echo died away, he broke into a run.

Emma heard the shots. But with her head down, there was no way to tell which direction they were coming from or who was firing. All she could do was stay low and keep moving.

She was nearing the edge of the muskeg. The going was easier here, the ground firmer beneath her weight. But she was wet and shivering with exhaustion. Beyond the ring of scraggly brush and devil's club, the evergreen forest lay deep in twilight shadows. She might be able to hide among the trees, but with the dogs on her trail, how far could she run without shoes?

There was no sign of Boone, but that didn't mean he'd given up and left. Emma knew he'd be just out of sight, waiting for the best chance to rush her. As for the pilot—

She gasped as a man stepped out from among

the trees. He was tall and dark, dressed in khakis and a heavy shirt. A rope was coiled over one shoulder. The opposite hand gripped a heavy revolver.

"You're the pilot." Her teeth were chattering.

"Let's get you out of here."

He slid the gun into its holster, then paused as if deciding on a course of action. He'd brought a rope, but by now she was only a few feet from firm ground. Stepping past the edge of the bog, he planted his work boots for balance, reached down, and caught her bleeding hands. There was no gentleness in his clasp. If anything, his manner suggested that having to rescue her was nothing but a bother.

Emma bit back a whimper as he dragged her off the muskeg. He had just pulled her to her feet when a shot rang out from the forest on the far side of the bog. Missing by inches, the bullet slammed into a tree behind them.

"Get down!" He shoved her to the ground as another bullet whined past. "Sounds like a damned bear rifle," he muttered. "And the bastard's a good shot. I'm guessing it's somebody you know."

"Yes." Emma forced the words through chattering teeth. "My husband."

His stony expression didn't even flicker. "So why would your husband want you dead?"

"It's a long story."

"Come on. And keep low." Crouching, he yanked her along with him into the safety of the trees. Dry pine needles jabbed her feet. She willed herself not to cry out.

"He's got dogs," she said.

"Stay here." Leaving Emma huddled at the base of a stump, he drew his pistol and moved like a shadow to the edge of the clearing. The sound of the pistol, as he fired across the distance, made her ears ring.

Seconds later he was back, offering an impersonal hand to pull her to her feet.

"Why did you shoot?" she asked him. "You couldn't have hit anything in the dark."

"You said he had dogs. Now that he knows I could shoot them, he'll be less likely to send them after us." He gripped her arm above the elbow. "Let's go. The plane isn't far."

She took a step. A sharp pine cone jabbed her foot. Emma yelped,

"What now?" He scowled down at her.

"My shoes. I lost them."

"Hang on." He shoved the pistol into its holster and adjusted the coil of rope. Scooping her up, he slung her over his shoulder like a fireman carrying an unconscious victim out of a burning house. Her hair dangled down his back. Her hips rode his shoulder. The hand that balanced her rested on the backs of her thighs, just below her rump.

"Comfortable?"

"Don't even ask."

"It won't be for long," he said, striding out. "Let me know if you hear anybody behind us."

"What if it's a bear? Will you drop me and run?"

"Don't tempt me, lady."

"My name is Emma."

"Pleased to meet you, Emma," he muttered. "Now let's get the hell out of here."

# More from Bestselling Author
## JANET DAILEY

## Available Wherever Books Are Sold!

# Books by Bestselling Author
# Fern Michaels

# More by Bestselling Author
# Hannah Howell

| | | |
|---|---|---|
| __Highland Angel | 978-1-4201-0864-4 | $6.99US/$8.99CAN |
| __If He's Sinful | 978-1-4201-0461-5 | $6.99US/$8.99CAN |
| __Wild Conquest | 978-1-4201-0464-6 | $6.99US/$8.99CAN |
| __If He's Wicked | 978-1-4201-0460-8 | $6.99US/$8.49CAN |
| __My Lady Captor | 978-0-8217-7430-4 | $6.99US/$8.49CAN |
| __Highland Sinner | 978-0-8217-8001-5 | $6.99US/$8.49CAN |
| __Highland Captive | 978-0-8217-8003-9 | $6.99US/$8.49CAN |
| __Nature of the Beast | 978-1-4201-0435-6 | $6.99US/$8.49CAN |
| __Highland Fire | 978-0-8217-7429-8 | $6.99US/$8.49CAN |
| __Silver Flame | 978-1-4201-0107-2 | $6.99US/$8.49CAN |
| __Highland Wolf | 978-0-8217-8000-8 | $6.99US/$9.99CAN |
| __Highland Wedding | 978-0-8217-8002-2 | $4.99US/$6.99CAN |
| __Highland Destiny | 978-1-4201-0259-8 | $4.99US/$6.99CAN |
| __Only for You | 978-0-8217-8151-7 | $6.99US/$8.99CAN |
| __Highland Promise | 978-1-4201-0261-1 | $4.99US/$6.99CAN |
| __Highland Vow | 978-1-4201-0260-4 | $4.99US/$6.99CAN |
| __Highland Savage | 978-0-8217-7999-6 | $6.99US/$9.99CAN |
| __Beauty and the Beast | 978-0-8217-8004-6 | $4.99US/$6.99CAN |
| __Unconquered | 978-0-8217-8088-6 | $4.99US/$6.99CAN |
| __Highland Barbarian | 978-0-8217-7998-9 | $6.99US/$9.99CAN |
| __Highland Conqueror | 978-0-8217-8148-7 | $6.99US/$9.99CAN |
| __Conqueror's Kiss | 978-0-8217-8005-3 | $4.99US/$6.99CAN |
| __A Stockingful of Joy | 978-1-4201-0018-1 | $4.99US/$6.99CAN |
| __Highland Bride | 978-0-8217-7995-8 | $4.99US/$6.99CAN |
| __Highland Lover | 978-0-8217-7759-6 | $6.99US/$9.99CAN |

## *Available Wherever Books Are Sold!*

Check out our website at
**http://www.kensingtonbooks.com**